A TASTE FOR BLOOD

Jimmy was about to reach for the card when he felt a presence in the office with him . . .

"I'll be right with you," he said.

. . . a cold presence.

He turned to look behind him and felt a cold, cold hand on his head, holding it firm as another hand grabbed his wrist and pulled his arm away from his body.

And then cold lips and a point of hot, searing pain on his arm where he'd scratched himself.

"What are you doing?" he said, struggling against the hand on his head, unable to move.

"Let me go!" he screamed, but already the strength was ebbing from his body. He could feel something being pulled out of his arm, sucked out, as if by great force.

It hurt like hell, but slowly the pain subsided.

He felt light-headed.

Dizzy.

Eventually the hand came away from his head and the guy's mouth—his mouth—came away from his arm.

The bruise was huge and what had once been a scratch was now a long open rent in his flesh. But there was no blood coming out of it. He should have been bleeding profusely, but instead there was nothing. . . .

Books by Edo van Belkom

SCREAM QUEEN

BLOOD ROAD

Published by Kensington Publishing Corporation

More Books From Your Favorite Thriller Authors

BOOK YOUR PLACE ON OUR WEBSITE AND MAKE THE READING CONNECTION!

We've created a customized website just for our very special readers, where you can get the inside scoop on everything that's going on with Zebra, Pinnacle and Kensington books.

When you come online, you'll have the exciting opportunity to:

- View covers of upcoming books
- Read sample chapters
- Learn about our future publishing schedule (listed by publication month *and author*)
- Find out when your favorite authors will be visiting a city near you
- Search for and order backlist books from our online catalog
- Check out author bios and background information
- Send e-mail to your favorite authors
- Meet the Kensington staff online
- Join us in weekly chats with authors, readers and other guests
- Get writing guidelines
- AND MUCH MORE!

**Visit our website at
http://www.kensingtonbooks.com**

BLOOD ROAD

EDO VAN BELKOM

PINNACLE BOOKS
Kensington Publishing Corp.
http://www.kensingtonbooks.com

ACKNOWLEDGMENTS

Several people made significant contributions toward the completion of this book and I'm happy to have the chance to thank them here. So, thanks to: Ontario Provincial Police Sergeant Joe D'Alessandro; our family physician, Dr. Sheldon Katz; Beverly Adams of Gamma DynaCare Laboratories; John C. Smith, former editor of the magazines *Truck News* and *Truck West* (who also got me started writing trucking fiction); and good friend and fellow writer Robert J. Sawyer. Finally, thanks to my wife, Roberta, whose love and support over the years has made this book, and all my other books, possible.

Prologue

In the distance, the drone of an engine and the relentless moan of rubber against asphalt joined together to create a sound like the buzzing of some giant insect.

In the darkness, a pair of white dots appeared atop a crest in the highway, like eyes. The eyes grew—in size and brightness—illuminating the highway in front of them and a small patch of forest on either side of the road, all of it returning to darkness the moment after the eyes passed.

As the highway flattened out, the buzzing lowered in pitch, and the eyes seemed to flicker and jump as the truck behind them slowed to pull off the road.

The giant machine eased to the right and when its passenger-side wheels touched the gravel shoulder, the insectlike whine of the tires transformed into the roar of a tiny hurricane. Stones and dust rose up in a plume, overtaking the truck when it finally came to a stop on the soft shoulder by the side of the road.

And then all was silent . . .

Except for the constant rattle of the Peterbilt 379's Caterpillar diesel engine. At idle it sounded as if the engine was nothing more than a steel box full of nuts and bolts, yet there was a throaty rumble beneath it all that suggested a powerful monster slept under the hood.

The truck sat on the shoulder of the empty stretch of

highway for several minutes, its headlights the only ones to be seen for many kilometers in either direction.

A valve let out a blast of air beneath the truck, sounding like the snort of a racehorse after a long, hard run. The engine seemed to skip a beat when the valve let go, then settled comfortably back into its monotonous metallic thrum.

Moments later the passenger-side door of the truck popped open, its highly polished black finish glinting under the light of the pale full moon.

The door remained open for several seconds . . .

And then a body fell out of the truck, making it only part of the way down to the gravel shoulder before a leg caught on something inside the truck and the body became stuck, half in and half out of the cab.

Somebody inside the truck cursed; then the driver's-side door slowly opened as well.

A moment later a man climbed down from behind the wheel. At first he was little more than a silhouette shrouded in darkness, but as he made his way around the front of the truck, he was caught within the beams of the Peterbilt's headlights.

He was a short, squat man whose worn boots flopped on his feet like slippers as he walked. He wore a stained pair of pale blue sweatpants that were held up around his expansive midsection by a pair of reddish purple suspenders. At one time his shirt had been white, but it had been stained long ago and was now a dingy yellow brown. The bottom of the shirt barely met with the top of his pants and a crescent of flesh smiled grotesquely from the gap between the two. Even though he wore a slick leather jacket, it was obvious that his arms were large and powerful, ending with a pair of stubby hands that appeared to be filthy. And even at a distance it was obvious the man was in need of a manicure.

After crossing the front of the truck, he turned the corner at the right front fender, stepped around the open door, and stopped next to the body hanging halfway out of the cab.

It was the body of a young girl, one leg snagged by the seat belt, the other jutting out at a harsh angle, its foot caught between the seat and the open door. Her head was less than two feet above the ground, but the tips of her long brown hair brushed over the gravel stones with the gentle shifting of the breeze. Her skin was a pale, pale white, and her half-open eyes revealed a pair of upturned eyes that were oblivious of her predicament. Her thin arms hung down loosely from her shoulders, the backs of her hands resting against the ground. Her right arm was a clean, ghostly shade of white that made it hard to discern where her T-shirt ended and where her arm began. But her left arm . . .

The inside of her left arm was discolored by clouds of purple and gray and spotted by a line of tiny black holes. A few of the holes had been leaking and black streaks had raced down her arm toward the ground, only to stop halfway as each of the holes ran dry.

The short, heavy man grabbed the body by the hair and gave it a hard yank. The body jerked and rose up, but didn't come free of the truck. He tried again, this time grabbing one of the arms and punching at the leg caught between the seat and the door frame.

The body dropped six inches, then stopped.

The man wrapped his arms around the body's waist and pulled with all his might.

The body came loose, slid out of the truck, and landed heavily on the highway shoulder in a crumpled mass of flesh and bone.

The man took a step back and the body slowly rolled onto its side, its right hand falling onto one of his boots as if the girl were trying to grab at him, trying to make one last attempt to fight back.

But of course, she couldn't fight back.

She was dead, had been for a good half hour.

He'd been waiting for a clear length of highway to let her off and had settled for the stretch of Highway 69 near Nobel. The highway was quiet at the best of times, but in the middle of a weeknight in November the roadway was absolutely desolate.

He reached down and grabbed hold of her lifeless body, one hand on her arm at the right shoulder, the other on her right leg at the knee. Then he picked her up as if she were little more than a rag doll and stepped away from the truck.

The gravel shoulder was no more than eight feet wide. After that there were scattered areas of knee-high grass and scraggly bushes, all scrambling to survive as the days grew colder and the nights grew longer. When he reached the edge of the grass, he looked up and down the highway for any signs of oncoming traffic.

There were none.

He took several steps onto the grass, turned his body sideways, and then swung the girl's body back and forth several times in an attempt to gain some momentum.

One . . .

Two . . .

Three swings, and he released the body.

It flew through the air, turning several times, heels over head, before landing in the deep grass between a thick bush and a maple sapling some twenty-five feet from the highway shoulder.

After the body hit the ground there was a frantic series of scurrying and chittering sounds in the grass as if the sudden appearance of the dead human had turned the world of a few roadside animals upside down.

And then all was quiet again.

Except for the continuous rattle of the Peterbilt still idling on the side of the highway behind him.

He turned and headed back to his truck.

When he reached it he examined the shoulder for any telling signs of what had just happened.

There were none, except . . .

Except for a tiny smudge on the side of the truck behind the door. It was a dark stain, almost invisible on the truck's black finish, but he spotted it immediately.

He reached up and wiped the stain away with the tips of his fingers, then sucked on each one of his fingers until they were clean.

When he was done, he closed the door, then headed back around to the driver's side of the truck. When he got there, he made one last check of the highway, then climbed up into the truck and slid behind the wheel.

A hiss of air called back as he disengaged the parking brake. Then the engine roared into life and the giant black beast lurched forward in the first of its eighteen gears, slowly at first but then faster with each passing second.

Moments later he was back on the highway, methodically climbing his way up through the gears and heading farther north into the cold dark night.

Chapter 1

— 1 —

Harry Thomas thrust his hands into the pockets of his work pants and hunched his shoulders in a futile effort to stave off the cold. The days had been unseasonably warm the past couple of weeks, allowing his corn to linger a little while longer on the stalk. But all of a sudden the weather had turned cold as if it were making up for lost time, catching a lot of people off guard, Harry included. He'd left his house to walk his fields wearing just a shirt and pants. It had been enough clothing when he was within sight of the farmhouse, but now that he was walking the western border of his farm and the farmhouse was little more than a speck on the horizon, he felt almost naked. The wind easily found its way through his clothes and was now working on his skin, seeping through the flesh and settling in on his joints and bones. A shot of Canadian Club to warm his insides and a steaming hot bath to warm his outsides sounded like a nice way to end the day.

Just the thought of it made him feel a little bit warmer.

As he walked north with his cornfield on his right and Highway 69 on his left, someone gave him a toot on their horn. Harry looked over at the road and saw a gray Dodge Neon speeding past. He wasn't sure who the driver might be, but he waved just the same. After forty-seven years farming the same patch of land, there were all sorts of people who knew him well enough to honk as they passed him by. He'd be damned if he knew *half* of who they were, but as long as they were being friendly there was no reason why he shouldn't return the favor. Besides, it wouldn't be too many more years that he'd be able to say hello.

At seventy-five, Harry was getting a bit old for farming, old for just about anything for that matter. Sure, he'd had three sons and had hoped at least *one* of them would follow him into farming and tend to the farm for him, but no matter how sweet he made the deal, none of them would take him up on it. The oldest went to law school, the middle one was a teacher, and the youngest, well . . . he was still trying to figure out what he wanted to do, although he'd pretty much ruled out farming a long time ago. And so, year after year, he kept planting corn, doing what work he could himself and hiring other people to do the jobs he couldn't. At first he didn't mind it so much because the farm had kept his body busy and his mind off the death of Lorraine. They'd been married forty years and it had been hard to even imagine running the farm without her. But he'd managed, struggling badly in those first few years, and then taking some pride in having been able to operate the farm all by himself. But now he was seventy-five years old, for crying out loud! He was supposed to be soaking up the sun in a deck chair of some retirement home in Vero Beach, not worrying about whether he'd produce enough bushels per acre this year to cover his costs.

Another season, maybe two, and that would be it. Sure, he'd said it plenty of times before, but this time he damn well meant it. Enough was enough!

He turned to check the ears of the corn row on his

right, rubbing the husks between his fingers to figure out whether the cobs were dry enough to harvest. They could probably do with another day, but Harry's instincts told him that with the weather turning colder, his crop was about as good as it was going to get.

Just then Harry's attention was caught by movement in the grass between his field and the highway. He could see the grass moving back and forth, moved by something other than the wind.

And the sound . . .

It sounded as if a couple of dogs were having a fight, their jaws locked on the throat of the other and refusing to let go.

Harry fisted his hands and regretted not having his shotgun with him. Of course, he'd never needed one before, and if he were spotted out walking by the side of the highway with a gun over his shoulder, well . . . the provincial police would be on him before he could touch the pavement. This was Ontario, after all. Still, there was trouble in the grass, and he didn't even have a damn walking stick with him.

He approached the ruckus slowly, trying to see through the grass, but unable to make out anything other than a dark shape in the general area ahead of him. A few more steps and he was sure that whatever was in the grass was down in between a patch of scrub brush and a small maple. When he was even with the maple tree he put a hand up against the wire fence that edged his field, leaned forward, and saw—

"Christ on the cross!" he exclaimed.

A pair of wild dogs—maybe they might even be wolves—were tearing gobbets of flesh from something dead on the ground between them.

A dead human body . . .

The arms and legs of it had been shredded and flaps of skin hung off the bones like strips of wet paper.

"Get away!" Harry shouted. "Shoo! Scat!"

The wolves stopped feeding for a moment, lifting their heads and looking in Harry's direction to see who had dared interrupt them.

"Away!" he screamed again. "Get away!"

The wolves resumed their meal.

Harry lifted his right leg and climbed over the wire fence.

The wolves noticed he was now on their side of the barrier, but they did nothing about it.

"Shoo!" he said, moving toward the wolves.

It occurred to Harry that the animals might turn on him since there were two of them and only one of him, but he wasn't too worried. If this was his time, then so be it. If not, there was a body lying there in the grass that deserved better.

"Get out of here!" he said, raising his arms above his head. "Go away!"

One of the wolves started to move, then stopped and set its body in a partial crouch, as if it might just stick around and fight.

Harry picked up a few stones off the ground.

"Shoo! Scat!" he cried, throwing stones at the animals. It had been close to five decades since he'd thrown a baseball, but he managed to get the first couple of stones in the general vicinity of one of the wolves.

The wolf took a few steps away.

Harry threw a few more stones. . . .

One of the stones caught the wolf in the haunches. It bounded away, then stopped, still not willing to give up its meal so easily.

Harry ran forward then, throwing the rest of his rocks all at once.

At last, both wolves must have come to the conclusion that the man was either crazy or dangerous, because they turned away from him and started heading north, their bodies partially hidden in the tall, tall grass.

Harry came up to where the dead body lay, or at least what was left of the body.

He could make out several major organs, and a lot of the bone structure, which was a brilliant, shiny white.

Might have been a woman, Harry thought. *Young one, maybe. Maybe good-looking, too. God, I hope she was dead before the wolves got to her.*

And then Harry fell to his knees and vomited up the coffee and scones he'd had just before heading out of the house.

When he looked up there was a car pulling to a stop on the side of the highway. *Must have seen me keel over,* he thought, *figured I was in trouble.* He hoped whoever it was had a cell phone.

First, he needed to call for help.

Then he needed to call a couple of real estate agents. One in town, another in Vero Beach.

"Hey, mister . . . are you all right?" the man asked as he approached.

"No," answered Harry.

— 2 —

By the time Ontario Provincial Police Constable Larry Sharpe arrived on the scene, an ambulance was already parked on the side of the highway with its lights flashing. In front of the ambulance was the big black station wagon belonging to the coroner's office in Parry Sound. Sharpe wondered how the coroner had gotten here so quickly when rescue vehicles and other OPP officers were just beginning to appear in his rearview mirror.

It was well after six and what little traffic there was on the highway was slowing down in an attempt to figure out what was going on. Constable Sharpe sighed as he pulled his cruiser onto the highway shoulder and shifted it into park. If what dispatch told him over the radio was true, the people passing by on the highway wouldn't have a clue about the situation no matter how wild an imagination they might have.

Sharpe didn't quite believe it himself.

Not so soon after the last one, anyway.

They'd told him that Harry Thomas had been walking his field and had come across a body lying in the grass. The body had been torn apart by wolves . . . if you could believe that. There couldn't be more than a dozen wolves in the hundred square miles surrounding Nobel, but somehow they'd found this body while it was still fresh and had made a feast out of it.

Just like they'd done to the other ones along the highway.

Sure, the other bodies had been discovered farther up Highway 69, but Sharpe had kept himself abreast of the details even though it had meant he had to access the information through the force's Police Records Management System, the RMS, or the Computer, as he liked to call it.

Constable Sharpe was what they called a "Road Warrior." He had joined the OPP thirty-five years ago when a case file meant a stack of papers in a brown file folder, not a bunch of pixels on a computer screen. Back in the day, he'd enjoyed spending hours out on the road catching bad guys, or putting in time in the office poring over files looking for something out of the ordinary, something that didn't quite fit. But now . . . now after an hour or so in front of a computer screen his eyes became fatigued and his wrist got numb from sliding the mouse around. Carpel tunnel syndrome, they called it. Used to be carpel tunnel syndrome was a manly man's kind of illness. Machinists and mechanics used to get it wrenching steel. Now all kinds of people got it, from computer programmers and secretaries to damn graphic artists. And cops . . . now cops got it, too.

Sharpe smoothed the brim of his dark blue Stetson and pulled it tight onto his closely shaved head. He kept his hair short and got a trim every couple of weeks no matter where he was in the province. He liked the fact that he could walk into any barbershop in the country, North America even, and ask for a number two all-around, and the barber would know exactly what to do for him.

He got out of the cruiser, immediately felt the cold against his face, and got his jacket out of the car. He had a feeling he was going to be out in that field for a while and the day sure wasn't getting any warmer.

As Sharpe headed toward the crime scene, he instructed a young constable just arriving to protect the scene and to make sure traffic kept flowing smoothly past the site.

They'd added a lot of young people to the Parry Sound detachment in the past few months and Sharpe was having a hell of a time keeping them all straight in his mind. This one's name was Muscat, MacKay, or McCarthy . . . something beginning with an M. Sharpe smiled and nodded at the young man, but didn't say a word. The officer returned the nod and immediately began point duty trying to keep people moving.

Sharpe stepped off the shoulder onto the path, noting how flat and level the side of the highway was here. About ten yards from the highway, the paramedics and several civilians stood holding white sheets between their outstretched arms. It was a temporary measure meant to dissuade rubberneckers from slowing down out on the highway, but it also served more like a flag to passing motorists that something terrible had just happened here.

"You have dinner yet?" asked August Bonomo, one of the paramedics out of Parry Sound who was on his way back toward the highway.

"That bad?"

Bonomo had been a paramedic almost as long as Sharpe had been a police officer, and the look on the man's face didn't bode well for what he might find on the other side of those sheets.

"Yeah," Bonomo nodded. "That bad."

Sharpe stepped past Bonomo, doing his best to stay on the faint path that had already been trampled by the people on the scene. When he reached the site, he moved around the people holding the sheets and saw the medical examiner bent over what looked like, well . . . more like a piece of roadkill than the remains of a human body.

He felt the bile rise up in his throat, but swallowed hard and managed to keep it down.

Then he moved in closer.

"Ah, Constable Sharpe," the coroner, Dr. Sharon Casey, said.

"How'd you get here so fast?" he asked.

"I was on the highway when the call came over the radio. Practically had to slam on my brakes before I drove right past it."

Dr. Casey was an old woman in her sixties who'd been the coroner in Parry Sound almost since she graduated from medical school. At first, working for the coroner's office had been a way to supplement the young doctor's income, but she'd stayed with it even after her family practice took off. Now, she'd retired as a GP but continued on as the region's coroner partly because she was fascinated by the work and partly because northern Ontario was woefully short of doctors and their time was better spent looking after the living.

"You'll be investigating?" she said without looking up from the body.

"The Criminal Investigation Bureau will likely be taking over the case, but I've worked with CIB in the past, so I'll likely be assigned to assist them with their investigation." Sharpe took a quick look around. "*And* I'm first officer on the scene."

"Well, I don't envy you."

"Why's that?"

"You're not going to have much to go on."

"How much is 'not much'?"

"There's the condition of the body for a start," she said. "It's been ravaged pretty bad. The man who found the body, Harry Thomas, said it had been torn apart by a pair of wolves."

Sharpe found that hard to believe. Harry Thomas was getting on in years and probably mistook a couple of dogs for wolves. He'd question Harry about what he saw later, but for now he was more interested in what else the doctor had to say.

"The face is pretty much gone, so an ID is going to have to be made through dental records. About all I can tell you right now is that it's a woman. Approximate height, weight, and the rest of it will have to wait until I make a full examination at the hospital."

"That's it?"

The doctor looked at Sharpe with a cynical eye. "What do you want me to tell you . . . that I found a strand of the killer's hair under her fingernails . . . that there was a note in the girl's back pocket explaining what happened?"

Sharpe felt a little embarrassed by the doctor's response. Perhaps he had been expecting a little too much from a preliminary on-site examination, but he wasn't about to let on to the woman that she was in the right. "Those things would be nice if you have them."

The doctor's expression softened, and for a moment he could see the deep lines the stresses of this job had etched into her old woman's face. She'd seen plenty of terrible things during her time and each one of them had left its mark.

"There's got to be *something* else you can tell me now," he said, guessing that the doctor knew more than she was letting on.

"Technically, I'm only supposed to declare the person dead on the scene." She paused a moment, then said, "But there are a couple of things that don't make sense to me that I can tell you about, as long as you don't treat them as fact just yet."

Sharpe nodded.

"For one, there's very little blood in the body."

"She must have bled to death."

The doctor shook her head. "If she did, the bloodletting was almost surgical. And even if she did bleed to death, there would still be some blood left in the muscles, but there's hardly any."

Sharpe felt his stomach turn as he tried to imagine how the body ended up at the side of the highway without any blood inside it. "Maybe the wolves lapped up the blood. . . ."

"Maybe, but animals, especially wolves, aren't too particular about how they eat." She waved her finger over the area around the body. "There are no spatters on the ground, no stains, nothing. . . ."

"Okay."

"Which brings me to the other interesting point." She pointed at the skull where it sat on the ground. "See how deeply it's embedded in the earth?"

Sharpe nodded. "It's been here a couple of days?"

The doctor shook her head. "More likely less than a day. There were maggots feeding on the flesh, but the beetles and spiders hadn't shown up yet."

Sharpe nodded. The life cycle of insects was so fixed and precise they served as natural clocks for dead bodies. "Then what does the impression in the earth mean?"

The doctor spread out her hands. "She landed here in this spot from a great height."

"Okay . . . the killer carried her on his shoulder, then dumped her here between the bush and the tree."

"No, see how the indentation starts over here?" She pointed to a spot three inches from the head where the gouge in the ground was just beginning. "The killer didn't drop her straight to the ground, but probably threw her from somewhere over in that direction . . ."

Sharpe looked toward the highway some twenty feet away.

". . . meaning your killer is a bloodthirsty monster with the strength of ten men."

Constable Sharpe adjusted his Stetson and wiped a hand over his suddenly sweat-soaked face.

"Sorry," the doctor said, "but you did ask."

— 3 —

There were dozens of rest stations like it dotting the highway from Toronto to Thunder Bay. They thinned out a bit the farther north you got, but they were all basically the same.

It all started with a gas station. They used to be called "service stations" but they hardly even served gas anymore. The gas was all *self-serve* now, and if your car broke down along the way, you'd be lucky to find a place that had a couple of repair bays and a mechanic who knew what the problem was. If you were really lucky, your car might break down while the mechanic was actually on duty, but more than likely your breakdown would happen while he was off duty and you'd have to wait around a-few-or-twelve hours for his workday to begin. Mostly, all gas stations did these days was sell gas, oil, and windshield washer fluid. Attached to the gas station, there might be a "convenience store" that sold soda pop, chips, and cigarettes for a lot more than you were used to paying. *Convenience,* after all, comes at a price.

After that it was sort of hit-and-miss.

There might be a restaurant or three across the parking lot from the gas station, but you could never count on the food being any good. Closer to Toronto and some of the bigger towns, you might come across a Wendy's or a Harvey's, maybe even a McDonald's, but the farther away from the cities you got, the slimmer your chances were of finding a franchise operating by the side of the road. More than likely it was some no-name greasy spoon, or mom-and-pop joint that didn't have a single combo on its menu. The coffee was black and hot and decent enough to tide you over until you reached a Tim Hortons, Country Style, or Coffee Time nearer to civilization.

This particular rest station was situated just north of Espanola, seventy-five kilometers west of Sudbury on the Trans-Canada Highway. Like most of the rest stations along this stretch of highway, it had an independent gas station, a greasy spoon, and a coffee shop. But while this rest station was interchangeable with dozens of others, there was still something different about it, something that set it apart not only from all of the other rest stations in the province, but from all the other rest stations in the country.

While truckers and travelers filed in and out of the

restaurant looking for a burger and a hot coffee to sate their hunger, a sleek black Peterbilt 379 sat at the far end of the parking lot—as far away from the other vehicles as the lot allowed. The bright midday sun seemed to fade against the truck's gloss-black finish, and the chrome of its twin exhaust pipes redirected sunlight away from the truck like a pair of highly polished mirrors. Even the truck's windows were blacked out with dense, dark fabric that prevented even a sliver of light from shining through.

And as the world rolled past . . .

The truck sat still and silent.

Its doors locked, its windows closed tight.

The interior absolutely black and desolate.

And behind the curtain of darkness a short stout man with blood on his lips slept like a dead child, his arms crossed over his chest and his glassy eyes open wide and waiting for the night to call him back onto the road.

Chapter 2

It was just after six and the supper crowd had all been served and were now sitting around sipping their coffee, putting off the drive home for as long as they could.

"Hey, sweetie," said a man named Cookie. He was a regular at the Big Wheel Restaurant and Motel and never left the place before he'd had three cups of coffee. "How about heating this up?" He pushed his cup forward on the counter.

Amanda Peck showed Cookie a smile. "Sure thing, hon."

At the sound of the word *hon* Cookie grinned, exposing rows of teeth that looked a lot like a picket fence well past its prime. There couldn't have been more than eight of them in his whole head, each one spaced far enough apart to drive a Toyota through.

Amanda dutifully topped up his cup. "There you go, hon."

Cookie wasn't one of Amanda's favorites, but he was a regular and he did leave her a tip now and then. She knew his name was Cookie, knew the names of more than a dozen of the diner's regulars, but she preferred to refer to all of them as *hon*. At least that way she didn't have to remember their names. And besides, it made her seem more friendly, and a few of the old-timers really seemed to get a charge out of it.

Like Cookie.

"If I was only twenty years younger . . ." he said, giving Amanda an exaggerated wink.

She stopped wiping off the counter and looked at him with an arched eyebrow and one eye half closed. "If you were twenty years younger, I'd still be in diapers."

The few men in the diner within earshot of Cookie laughed.

Even Cookie managed a chuckle. "Yeah, maybe," he said, "but I'd still be twenty years younger."

The laughter got louder.

Amanda continued wiping down the counter, glancing at her watch as she worked. Just fifteen more minutes and she'd be out of here and on her way home.

Too bad she wasn't looking forward to it.

Home for Amanda had become a lot like work—a dead end. She went through the motions, put on a brave face, and tolerated her situation, but she knew that that part of her life was going nowhere, pretty much like her job at the diner. She could easily picture herself in the exact same situation in both places twenty years from now and that scared the hell out of her. By then Cookie would be gone of course, dead some ten years, but there would surely be some other plow-jockey taking his place. Someone not named after a snack food, but after a garden tool like "Rake" or "Hammer" who'd wink at her every time she called him *hon*.

She felt old just thinking about it.

And to think, back in high school she'd imagined she would be a famous actress or singer by now, or at the very least a suburban mom with a couple of kids and a big SUV to take them all to soccer games and swim practice.

Instead she was here at the Big Wheel serving the all-day breakfast to a man named Cookie. She wondered if things might be different for her somewhere else . . . anywhere else.

"See you, darling," Cookie said, getting up from his stool.

"Bye, hon."

She cleared the counter and saw that Cookie had left her a fifty-cent tip. *Better than nothing,* she thought, dropping the two quarters into her apron.

The saddest thing about it all was that there were girls in town who thought Amanda had it made.

— 2 —

The walk home from the Big Wheel wasn't too bad when the weather was good, but in the snow or rain it was a hike that seemed to take forever. Plenty of customers had offered her rides before, but she'd convinced them all that she preferred walking. She actually hated having to walk, but if she accepted rides from the regulars they might expect her to return the favor somehow. She could handle doling out an extra slice of pie or cup of coffee every so often, but what if they wanted something more from her? The thought of an old-timer like Cookie, or any of the others puckering up and asking her for a "favor" made her skin crawl. Better not to put herself in that position.

Besides, accepting rides, even in exchange for a slice of pie, would help entrench her in her present situation. She'd become more comfortable at work, people would consider her one of them, and she'd eventually become a fixture at the diner. The waitress with a heart of gold.

That's not what she wanted.

What she wanted was out.

Not in.

As she walked west along Bowes Road into town, nothing on either side of her but forest-covered rolling hills, Amanda discreetly began counting the day's tips. She usually waited to tally them up on the walk home since it was something to look forward to and it made the trip pass more quickly. It had been awkward the first few days, counting bills and coins in her pockets while she walked, but she'd worked out a system whereby she could almost do it all with just a single hand. She began with the bills, which she had to look at, but they were always easy to count since there usually weren't more than two or three of them. Today there were six, including a few large bills, given to her by customers who'd come in to square away their monthly tabs. Then it was on to the dollar and two-dollars coins—loonies and toonies, they were called—which were different enough in size and texture to distinguish by touch. After that the quarters, dimes, and nickels were easy enough to separate since she exchanged most of them for larger coins and bills throughout the course of the day.

At the end of it all, Amanda was surprised to find that she'd earned over a hundred dollars in tips, double her previous best. It meant that she'd be able to pay off a few bills and have a bit of breathing room before the start of the next month.

Maybe things aren't so bad around here after all, she thought, quickening her step and looking forward to getting home to share the news.

Home was a trailer. That's the way she thought of it and that's the way everyone in town referred to it even though it was technically a "mobile home." A mobile home was bigger than a trailer but was a lot less mobile. Trailers got to move around some, ride the roads, and see the country. Mobile homes were towed to some trailer park, set up on a patch of ground, and left there to die a slow ugly death or be scooped up and scattered to the four winds by some trailer-killing tornado. Since the Town of Parry Sound wasn't prone to tornadoes or funnel clouds, Amanda's trailer was slowly dying by degrees.

When the roof started leaking in the spring, the trailer's owner pumped a line of white rubber caulk into every crack, hole, and seam in the thing's white aluminum body. The job had looked good for about a week until the white caulk started to turn a dirty, speckled gray. It was quite an effect, making the trailer look as if it were a creation of Dr. Frankenstein, assembled from pieces that were stitched together with strands of dirty gray thread.

There were other problems too, like window screens that had been shredded by the previous occupant's cats, a toilet that needed to be flushed twice or it would back up when someone used the shower, and the broken hinge that left the front door hanging on an angle as if it were tired of being a door.

But it was home . . .

And really, what could you expect for four-fifty a month? Still, Amanda had managed to save a bit of money and in another year or two, she might have enough for a down payment on a trailer of her own.

If she stayed around that long.

A short walk south on Forest Street, a left on Parry Sound Road, and then another short walk south on Emily Street and Amanda had reached the Small Pine Trailer Park located halfway between Emily and McCurry Lake. When she got to the end of the drive that led to her trailer, she saw that there was a light on in the front room. She hurried up the drive and turned the handle on the front door. It was locked. She fished her keys out of her purse and opened it.

As the door swung out, it dropped off its top hinge and hung at an angle.

"Hey, Ronnie!" she called out, struggling to close the door behind her.

Ronnie was her live-in boyfriend, Ron Stinson. They'd been together for six months and her future with him was just as uncertain as every other part of her future.

"Ronnie!" she cried, louder this time. It wasn't necessary to shout since the trailer was so small, but she thought she'd give it a try just in case he was in the bedroom listening to a CD with his headphones on.

There was no response.

She thought about shouting again, but her neighbors had already heard her calling for him twice, and a third time would summon one of them to tell her, "Haven't seen him all day."

"Son of a bitch!" she cursed under her breath, making sure her voice was low enough to remain unheard. "The least he could do is be home for me at the end of the day."

That was the least he could do. Even better would be to pick her up after work and drive her home. Better still would be to be out looking for a job so they could get out of this hole they seemed to be stuck at the bottom of.

In the six months they'd been together, Ron had worked three different jobs. He had no trouble finding work in town since he'd been a junior hockey star with what had seemed like an inside track on a professional career. But in his draft year, playing with the Major Junior Brampton Battalion, he was caught with his head down and broke his right leg in three places. Two of the breaks required pins to set his legs right and he missed the rest of the season. Then, wanting to make some kind of impact before the National Hockey League's entry draft, he came back early to make an appearance in the playoffs and broke the leg again. On the big day, he went undrafted and took comfort in six-packs of beer all summer long. But his skill as a player was such that he was eventually picked up as a free agent the following October by a team in the East Coast Hockey League. He'd been okay for the first five games or so, but after a summer spent boozing and with no rehabilitation work on his leg, his level of play trailed off and he began seeing less and less ice-time. Not surprisingly, he got depressed, handled the problem with alcohol, and was eventually sent home.

People in town would shake their head, say, "Too bad about the leg," and then offer him a drink. He lived out the year like that, drinking and telling stories about what might have been until the money he'd received as a payout was all but gone. That's when he wound up at the Big Wheel asking for water to go with his day-old donuts. Amanda didn't charge him for the donuts and he came back the next day like a stray cat looking for a meal. When he asked her out, she told him only if he got sober. That seemed to work since he showed up a few days later scrubbed and pressed. They went out a few more times and he wound up moving in with her. After a couple of days he got a job at the Northland Market stocking shelves and things seemed to be going great. But six weeks later he went to a party hosted by the Parry Sound Shamrocks Junior A hockey team and didn't come back for two days.

After that he drifted from job to job, getting sober for a week before finding the bottle again. Lately he'd taken up gambling. But while he'd always played the lotteries—Lottario, 6/49, Super 7, and *all* the scratch cards—now he liked to play poker, winning or losing hundreds in a single evening. He'd come home ahead just once, and was a loser every other time . . . whether he had the money to lose or not.

Amanda went to the fridge and looked for a note that might let her know where he'd gone to. There was none. She opened the fridge door and put in a plastic container with a hamburger and French fries in it that she'd carried home for him in her bag. Ron ate just about everything she brought home for him. She was grateful for that since she didn't have to spend much money to feed him, but that hardly made up for the rest of it.

She was paying for their relationship in a bunch of different ways: financial, emotional, and psychological.

Sometimes she wondered why on earth she let him stay.

Because . . . because sometimes he was a wonderful man. Proud and thoughtful. Strong and protective. Sometimes in his arms she would feel as if the world couldn't lay a finger on her. She was safe there. And he would say such wonderful things about his plans and the things he was going to do. She never wanted to believe him, but she couldn't help herself. He was so good at saying the words, he could convince her that the sky was green if he put his mind to it.

But then he'd have a drink and the cycle would start all over again.

Just then the door to the trailer opened and Ron Stinson was standing there looking hungover, or maybe he was drunk. He was either one so often that it was hard to know the difference between the two.

"Where have you been?"

"How was your day?"

"Where have you been?" Amanda said again, determined not to give in to Ron's charms.

"Petzoldt's got a game going," he said, stepping into the trailer. "We broke for dinner, but we're starting up again at eight."

Amanda was curious to know if he'd won anything, but

knew if she asked the question it would seem as if she approved of what he was doing.

So instead she just looked at him.

Ron kept his eyes on the floor, unable to raise them to meet hers.

They stood that way, like fighters squaring off inside the ring, just waiting for the other to flinch.

Ron flinched first.

"Can you spare me a few bucks?" he said.

Amanda felt her heart drop into the pit of her stomach. Of course he was losing. If he'd won *anything* he would be over at the After Dark buying drinks. Well, he wasn't going to get any money from her for anything, not for a drink and not for a chair at the poker table.

"Did you look for a job today?"

"I went around this morning," he said. "No one's hiring."

"Who's not hiring?"

"Nobody is."

"Who? Who did you ask for a job? Where did you apply?"

Ron stood there in the middle of the trailer saying nothing.

"You didn't go looking for a job today at all, did you?"

Again, he said nothing.

"Well, they need a pot washer at the diner . . . and Julie told me they're hiring at the packinghouse tomorrow."

Ron just shook his head. "I'm not washing any pots for minimum wage, especially not at the place where you work, and there's no way I'm sexing chickens, not for all the money in the world."

Amanda let out a sigh. "Then what are you going to do? What *can* you do?"

"I can do lots of things," he said, sounding like a

schoolboy trying desperately to avoid being labeled the school yard spaz.

Having been down this path before, Amanda fell back onto the couch, making herself comfortable and not even bothering to take off her coat. "Like what?"

"I can play hockey."

"Yeah, years ago, maybe."

That hurt Ron, and Amanda hated herself for saying it, because Ron really could play hockey. He'd been a great player and should have been a star. But it had been a while ago, and scoring six goals in pickup games on Sunday morning didn't quite put food on the table.

"Maybe I can coach. Work with kids, maybe."

"When? No one's going to come here looking for you. And they sure as hell aren't going to pull you out of the After Dark to drag you down to the arena."

"I can work with my hands." Ron was obviously running out of ideas. It was a sad thing to watch, like someone drowning in a couple of feet of water.

"Fine, then why don't you do that?"

Ron was about to say something, then hesitated. "Okay, I will, then."

Amanda didn't believe him. He'd said as much far too many times to have any credibility left.

"First thing tomorrow morning, I'll go to Double-B Landscaping and put in an application. The owner there coached me in peewee and said I could call him if I needed work."

"Uh-huh," Amanda said. He sounded so convincing. In fact, this one was even a little better than the last few times he'd promised to find work.

There was a long silence between them. Amanda was about to tell him there was a burger and fries in the fridge, but Ron was the one who spoke first.

"So how about it?"

"How about *what?*"

"Can you spare me a few bucks?"

What? she thought. *Can he really be that dense?*

"No," she said. "I can't."

Ron's face seemed to change somehow. It got darker. Turned ugly. She could see his teeth, even though he wasn't smiling. And the smell of beer on his breath was fetid, as if he'd been drinking all afternoon.

"Then I'll take it from you!" he said.

And that's when he lunged at her.

Amanda tried to turn aside to keep the pocket with her tip money away from him, but he was too strong for that.

He grabbed her roughly by the shoulders, turned her around, and shook her. "Give it to me!"

There was a glint of desperation in his eyes, and more than a hint of shame. He didn't want to be doing this to her, but something inside, some desperate need was compelling him to do it.

A hand dug into one of her outside coat pockets.

"No, don't," she protested. "I need that money."

He tore at the pocket, ripping it open.

The pocket was empty so he tried the other.

It was full of cash.

Amanda twisted away from him. "It's for paying bills."

But Ron wasn't listening. He knew there was money there and he had to have it.

He lifted her up off the couch and threw her down on her side so the pocket with the money was turned up and facing him. He swiped at the pocket, tearing it open like the other.

Bills fluttered in the air.

Coins burst from the pocket like water from a pipe, then landed on the floor like metallic rain.

Amanda wasn't fighting him anymore.

She was covering her face and sobbing into her hands.

Ron picked up the paper money and left the change where it lay.

"Petzoldt's bringing over a couple of patsies," he said, slightly winded from the altercation. "These guys are filming something in town and word is they've got lots of money. . . . I'll pay you back tomorrow from my winnings."

Amanda didn't answer him.

Didn't look up.

She just stayed where she was on the couch, crying into a pillow until she heard the door open and close, and his car drive away.

Then, when she was sure he was gone, she slowly picked herself up off the couch . . .

And started packing.

— 3 —

Constable Sharpe slipped on his reading glasses, checked the number in his directory, and dialed up the coroner, Dr. Sharon Casey. One good thing about having a coroner who's retired from her medical practice is that autopsies were usually performed the same day a body was discovered, usually within a few hours of discovery.

The phone rang five . . . six times.

Sharpe waited for the doctor's voice mail to kick in but the phone just kept on ringing. He let out a long sigh. Even though he had an answering machine of his own at home and could be paged any time of day or night, Sharpe hated the fact that all these things had somehow replaced human contact. When he called people when he'd first started with the OPP, even if they weren't in, someone else would answer their phone. That person would tell him where the one he was looking for could be reached, take a message, or call the person he was looking for to the phone. Nowadays voice mail took care of all that *and* allowed the person at the other end of the line the luxury of either not returning the call, or returning it days later when it was convenient for them to do so.

The doctor was usually pretty good about returning calls, but every once in a while she would leave him hanging and—

"Coroner's office."

"Ah, you're there," said Sharpe, trying hard to keep the surprise from his voice but failing badly.

"Of course I'm here," the doctor said, obviously irritated by his tone. "And if you must know, I was busy cleaning guts off my hands so I could answer the phone."

Sharpe thought it best not to say anything more at that moment, and waited patiently for the doctor to carry on the conversation.

"I suppose you'd like a report?"

"Yes."

"You could always get one from the Ident officers who were here while I did the postmortem."

"Sharon, you know it's always best to get it straight from the horse's mouth."

There was a moment of silence and Sharpe knew the doctor was smiling on the other end of the phone. "Well, I haven't written anything up yet, but I have finished examining the body."

The phone went silent again and Sharpe could hear the doctor lighting up a cigarette.

"I wasn't able to identify the body past its being a young female in her early twenties, about five foot two, one hundred and twenty-five pounds. She had brown shoulder-length hair, four piercings in her left ear, and at least two in her right—"

"At least two?"

"The rest of the ear was eaten by a wolf."

"Oh."

"Most of her face was gone too, so you can forget a photo. And all of her fingers were chewed up pretty bad so I suspect you'll only be able to lift partial prints from the ring and pinky finger of the right hand. But . . ." A pause as she inhaled. ". . . all her teeth are intact so you'll be able to ID her with those eventually."

The doctor sounded somewhat apologetic about not being able to provide him with more information about the girl's identity, and Sharpe wondered if she had a daughter or granddaughter the same age as the victim, which would account for the woman's sentiment. But whatever the reason for the doctor's regret, Sharpe wasn't disappointed by the lack of any solid leads. For some reason—call it instinct, call it experience—Sharpe had a strong feeling that whoever the girl was had little to do with the reason she was murdered. It could have been any girl, any*body* lying out there on the side of the highway. To find this killer, Sharpe knew he would have to concern himself more with the *why* than with the *who*.

"Okay, so our victim is Jane Doe."

"Basically, but there are a few things about her that were unique."

"Such as?"

"Well, on the flesh that remained on her left arm I found a series of bruises and needle marks."

"She was an addict?"

"Maybe, but there were no other signs of drug abuse. Of course, the full toxicology tests will take another week or so."

"But there *were* needle marks?"

"Six that I counted. There might have been four or five

more in the flesh that wasn't there, but that's just guess-work."

Sharpe sighed. "Anything else?"

"Yes. As I told you at the site, there seemed to be very little blood in her system."

"So she bled to death somewhere else and was dumped on the side of the road?" It was a statement, but somehow Sharpe had managed to turn it into a question.

"No, not just bled to death. Even in bodies that have lost a lot of blood there's usually some pooling in parts of the body like the lower extremities, but in this case she was pretty much drained dry."

"Why would someone remove all her blood?"

He could almost hear the woman shrug at the other end of the line. "Maybe somebody needed it."

"You mean like a doctor?"

"Or someone making a sacrifice."

At mention of the word *sacrifice,* Sharpe felt his stomach churn. "Well, which one is it?"

"I don't know, Constable. It's your job to find out."

"What does your gut tell you?"

"That it's well past my supper time . . ." the doctor quipped.

Sharpe let the comment slide, wondering how she could even think about eating after just completing an autopsy.

". . . but if I had to take a wild stab at it, I'd say your killer is a vampire."

"Oh, come on, Doctor."

"You asked me what my instincts told me and I answered you."

"So will I be able to find the word *vampire* anywhere in your official report, then?"

"No. In the report the cause of death will be attributed

to hypotension and multiple organ failure due to acute blood loss."

"And that spells *vampire* to you."

The doctor was silent for several moments, then she said, "Did you see any of those police profiling shows on the Discovery Channel?"

"Sorry, I must have missed them."

"Well, let me just ask you this. What sort of killer would *you* say fits the facts?"

Sharpe didn't have an answer.

— 4 —

Amanda managed to pack just about everything of value she owned into her burgundy Roots backpack. It was a promotional item for the 2002 Winter Olympics and it had served her well the past couple of years. Now it was going to carry her belongings into the next stage in her life.

Away from Ron.

Away from the Big Wheel.

And as far away from Parry Sound as she could manage.

Her plan was simple. She'd travel a few days until she found some city or town she was comfortable in. Then she'd get a job waitressing and try to get her life on track all over again. It would be like starting new, from scratch. But even though she'd be back waitressing, she'd still be ahead of the game since she'd be without Ron Stinson dragging her down. Maybe she'd even meet somebody new. Someone with a job, and a sense of responsibility who didn't have a drinking problem and who would never think of laying a hand on her.

Pie in the sky.

Maybe.

But at least the sky would be clear for a while, and if the clouds rolled in, well, then she'd have no one to blame but herself.

She left the trailer without locking the door behind her. There wasn't anything worth stealing inside it, but you just never knew what people in the trailer park thought was valuable. She once had a barbecue brush stolen off the picnic table out in front of the trailer, and the damn things cost a dollar at the Loonie Shack in town.

In a way she almost hoped someone wandered into the trailer and stole something . . . something of Ron's. One of his stupid hockey trophies, maybe, or a six-pack of Molson Canadian in the fridge. *Wouldn't that send him for a loop?* Maybe, if there was any beer in the fridge.

She turned at the end of the drive and headed up the road toward Highway 69, enjoying the slight breeze blowing against her face. At the first bend in the road, she turned around to take one last look at the trailer. She'd left the lights on, and in the autumn twilight the illuminated windows at the front end of the trailer looked like a pair of eyes. She usually thought they were a sad pair of eyes, but seeing them now they looked evil as if the trailer were alive and keen on making her suffer.

Well, no more.

It was Ron's turn to suffer, or at the very least to grow up.

What will he do, she wondered, *when the food's all gone from the kitchen, or the electric bill is due, or the rent?* The realization that she didn't really care was a revelation. Maybe it really was time to get out.

It was a short walk to Bowes Road and it would take her a few minutes to reach Highway 69 against a pretty stiff wind, but she was determined to do it. After all, she would be doing a lot of walking in the next few days so there was no point in worrying about a few kilometers now.

Still, it wouldn't hurt to try and hitch a ride.

Amanda turned around, began walking backward, and hung her thumb out for oncoming traffic.

Cars and trucks passed her without even slowing.

One minivan almost hit her as it veered onto the shoulder as it roared past. Amanda's first thought was of Stephen King, who'd nearly been killed by just such a driver while walking on the highway near his home in Maine. She gave the driver the finger—*from me and Steve*—but kept her hand close to her body, just in case the driver caught sight of it and turned out to be a road-rager with a short fuse. The last thing she needed was to have her escape cut short by some rural redneck with a hair-trigger temper.

After several more minutes Amanda was ready to give up trying to hitch a ride. No one had even slowed down and it was starting to get dark. The sun would soon be gone from the western sky and she'd wanted to be on the main highway before dark. Once she was on Highway 69 there would be more traffic and plenty of chances to catch a ride that would put some distance behind her.

She turned around and quickened her pace.

Behind her, the roar of an oncoming big rig seemed to lessen and the engine's back pressure blasted out a staccato rhythm through its exhaust.

Amanda turned around to see a large dark tractor pulling over onto the side of the road.

She stepped to one side and watched the truck come to a stop in front of her.

The passenger door opened up . . . as if by magic.

"Howdy," said the driver. The man had dark features, with a long black beard that looked as if it hadn't been combed in days, and long black hair that fell down over his shoulders like oil-soaked rags.

"Hi there," Amanda answered, managing just the weakest of smiles.

"Where you headed?"

Amanda looked up the road. "To the highway."

"I can take you there."

She hesitated a moment, looking back up the highway and then back down in the direction she'd come. She wanted a ride, but this man looked so . . . *dirty* that she didn't think she'd be able to sit beside him for more than ten minutes before her skin started to crawl.

"Maybe I'll walk."

"It's getting cold out."

She nodded, as if she'd just made up her mind. "That's okay, I'll walk."

The man smiled at her, showing her two rows of bent and dark-stained teeth. "Don't worry, sweetheart. I don't bite."

Amanda wasn't sure what it was, but something about the way the man said the words and smiled at her told her that she'd be fine.

She took a step toward the truck.

This was an adventure after all, and what kind of adventure would it be if it didn't include a few risks?

"That's a good girl," he said, reaching out with his right hand to help her into the truck.

She grabbed his hand and marveled at how hard the surfaces of his palm and fingers were. And the tattoos! Chinese snakes and dragons curled and twisted all the way up his arm, disappearing under the dirty yellow sleeve of his T-shirt.

He must have noticed her staring at his arm, because he said, "They go all over my chest and back, too."

"Wow!"

"My name's Bill, Bill Droine."

"I'm Amanda."

"Close the door, Amanda."

She reached over and pulled the door closed, realizing that the adventure was about to begin and she was embarking on what was probably going to be the ride of her life.

"Don't forget your seat belt," he reminded her.

Amanda reached over her shoulder and strapped herself in.

The driver shifted into gear.

The air from the brake system let out a hiss.

A moment later the truck lurched forward . . .

And she was on her way.

Chapter 3

After two hours, Ron had managed to put himself up forty dollars. He wanted to gather up his winnings, push himself away from the table, and say adios, but he'd already agreed to just one more hand. And now that things were looking kind of iffy, he was cursing himself for not doing what he knew was for the best.

He was supposed to be on his way home to Amanda right now, with some flowers in one hand and the money he'd taken from her—with interest—in the other. He'd tell her he was sorry, even that he'd been stupid, he'd promise to do better in the future, and then they'd spend the night making love.

That would have been sweet.

Instead he was still at the table, a fresh beer to his right and almost everything he had in the middle of the table riding on this one hand.

And this one hand had potential.

He'd begun with the three, four, five, and six of hearts and that had started him off betting large. He discarded a single card for the first draw, hoping for either the two or seven of hearts, any heart, or any two or seven. That meant that any one of seventeen cards would have resulted in a straight flush, a flush, or a straight.

"Raise you a hundred," said one of the men from the television production named Hammond, whom everyone called Hamm. They were actually filming a television commercial at one of the cottages on the Sound and these guys had plenty of money to throw around. Hamm was supposedly the steady-cam operator and judging by the size of his arms and shoulders, he'd been carrying a camera around for years.

"That puts me out," Petzoldt said, folding his cards onto the table.

"Me too," said the other out-of-towner, a grip (whatever the hell that was) on the production.

Which left just Ron.

He had a decent chance of drawing one of the seventeen cards he needed for a decent hand. Of course, there was a good chance that several of the cards he needed had already been dealt to the other players, but even so he guessed there had to be at least ten cards in the deck that would give him the win.

He tossed in the last of his money. "I'm in."

"Gimme two," said Hamm.

Petzoldt dealt him two cards.

Ron asked for a single card.

Hamm slipped his new cards into his hand, putting them in different spots, as if sliding them into their proper sequence.

Ron drew the card in toward himself and turned up the corner . . .

King of spades.

. . . but let none of his disappointment show.

"Raise you another fifty."

Ron could feel the sweat starting to dampen the back of his shirt. He had nothing. He was going to lose this hand and go home empty-handed. And when he arrived it wouldn't be with flowers and cash, it would be with nothing but a story about how he just had a streak of bad luck. How in the world was he going to make up for the way he'd left if he didn't come home with *something* to show for it?

He had only one chance.

"See you fifty and raise you another."

Hamm looked over his cards and across the table at Ron. "You don't have any money left."

"I'm good for it."

Hamm glanced over at his friend, the grip. The grip shrugged.

"You gotta let me play out the hand," Ron said, trying to keep his voice even and steady.

"Not with money you don't have."

Ron raised his right hand. On the ring finger was a large gold ring. "Then I'll raise you *this*."

"What the hell is that?"

"It's my Memorial Cup ring. We got if for winning the national junior hockey championship—"

"I know what the Memorial Cup is, ass-wipe."

"Ron, don't do it," Petzoldt said.

He didn't want to bet his ring . . . it was the only tangible thing he had left to remind him that he'd once been a star hockey player. But he didn't have any money left to bet and if he was going to bluff this guy into folding, what better way to do it than with a gold ring with priceless sentimental value?

"Well?" Ron asked.

"Sure," Hamm said, pulling out two hundred dollars from his shirt pocket to cover the ring.

Ron felt his heart sink into the pit of his stomach.

"What do you got?"

"You first."

Hamm laid down his cards. He had three sevens.

Ron took a deep breath, let out a long sigh, and showed his cards.

"Shit!" said Petzoldt.

"He's got nothin'," said the grip.

Hamm just let out a laugh. "Ha!"

Ron pressed his lips together in a tight line and put his hands on the table to keep himself from falling out of the chair.

Hamm raked in the pot and tried to put the ring on his finger. "Doesn't fit, but I can probably melt it down and make something useful out of it." He held his finger up to the light to examine the ring more closely.

Ron rubbed the spot on his finger where the ring had been for the past four years. He couldn't imagine it not being there anymore. It was his. One of the few things he'd worked hard for in his life.

He'd *earned* that ring.

Without warning, Ron jumped up from the table and snatched the ring from Hamm's finger. Then he turned for the door, fumbling with the handle.

The grip grabbed him, swinging his fists at Ron's head and body while trying to pull him away from the door. A couple of the punches connected and Ron was surprised by how strong the guy was for his size.

Another punch caught Ron square in the mouth.

He swung back with his right fist, catching the grip just below the left ear and knocking him to the floor, where he rolled around in a slight daze.

Hamm was up on his feet now, striding across the room toward him.

Ron feigned a punch at the big man, then without the slightest hesitation, kicked him in the balls. He could feel something soft being crushed under the toe of his shoe.

Hamm grabbed at his crotch, toppled over, and puked on the floor.

"Jesus!" cried Petzoldt, probably realizing he would have to clean up the mess.

"Sorry, man," said Ron, opening the door to leave. "But I couldn't let them take my ring."

— **2** —

Constable Sharpe drained the last of his coffee and tossed the brown paper cup into the garbage can next to the desk he'd been working at. The taste of the thick creamy coffee lingered in his mouth. The daughter of a friend who worked at the Tim Hortons on Bowes Street in Parry Sound said that it wasn't the coffee that made their product taste so good, but rather the cream they used. Apparently, it was a few percentages thicker than regular coffee cream and that was the thing that kept customers coming back for more.

It sure was good coffee. If only they could figure out a way to keep it from going right through you. It wasn't so much of a problem working in the office, but when you were out on patrol there wasn't always a bathroom nearby . . . especially once you got outside of Parry Sound.

Sharpe straightened up the top of the desk and moved the keyboard into position in front of him. He wasn't a fan of the RMS computer but there wasn't any other way to access the information he needed short of asking someone else to access the list and print up a hard copy for him.

He'd done that only once before and the ribbing about it had gone on for months. Little bottles of liquid paper by his computer screen, a copy of *Computers for Dummies* at Christmas. Stuff like that.

No, thanks.

From then on, he'd struggled with the Records Management System on his own and asked for help only when he really needed it—and even then, he did so reluctantly . . . and discreetly.

Sharpe clenched and unclenched his fists to loosen up his fingers, then accessed the system.

There was a list of missing persons from around the province in the OPP database and there was a chance he'd be able to match one of them up with the body. He was hopeful when the list first came up on his screen, but as he went down the list of fourteen people, it became increasingly obvious that none of them were an easy match.

First off, four people on the list were boys, and two others were Alzheimer's patients. Another six of them had been missing for several years. While it was possible that the dead woman had been missing for that long, Sharpe doubted it very much. He guessed she hadn't been gone more than a few days, maybe a month at the most. That left just two possible matches, but neither of their descriptions were even close to the one the coroner had given him earlier in the day. Beverly Fallis was nearly six feet tall and blond, while Gwendolyn Spaulding was a young girl not yet twelve years old.

Of course it was possible that the woman still hadn't been reported missing, which meant she still might turn up in the system in the coming days. Then again, the fact that she'd been dumped on the side of the highway suggested she'd been traveling, or at least hitchhiking. And if that was the case she could have been reported missing from just about anywhere in the country.

Sharpe realized he'd have to cast a wider net, accessing the Canadian Police Information Computer—CPIC for short—for a list of missing persons across Canada, and the American NCIC system for a similar list of missing persons in the States. Knowing who the victim was probably wouldn't help move his investigation forward all that much, but at least it would allow some grief-stricken family to know what had happened to their daughter.

But that would come later.

For now the woman's identity would remain unknown.

He checked the force's Criminal Investigation Bureau's file for the number of bodies that had been discovered by the side of the Trans-Canada Highway in the past few months and wound up naming the dead girl . . .

Jane Doe 5.

Sharpe couldn't believe the number, it couldn't possibly be that high.

Five.

This was the first body that had turned up in Sharpe's part of the province. The others had been found several hundred kilometers farther north, and so far CIB investigators in that part of the province had been able to identify two of them, but this one . . . this young girl was the *fifth* body.

Jane Doe 5.

Constable Sharpe felt sick at the thought of that number.

He hoped to God there wouldn't be a sixth.

— 3 —

"You know," said Bill, "I've got a daughter your age."

Amanda looked at him curiously. He was sitting behind the wheel of a Freightliner, but he looked as if he were riding a Harley-Davidson. His hands were big and beefy and there were as many scars on his arms as tattoos. Funny thing was he didn't look old enough to be Amanda's father.

And so she said so.

"You're not old enough."

He smiled, showing her those yellowed teeth of his. Strange they didn't look as menacing now as they did when she'd first gotten into the truck.

"I was a father at seventeen, and a grandfather at forty-one."

Amanda did the math and realized it was possible.

"I'll admit I wasn't much of a father in those early years, but I grew up pretty fast."

"What about now?"

"Now, I think they're the best thing that ever happened to me. . . ." He gave a little laugh under his breath. "Only thing I did that ever turned out right."

They came to a stoplight.

"What does she do? The daughter who's my age, I mean."

His smile widened with obvious pride. "She's at university right now. Wants to become a lawyer. Can you imagine that?"

Looking at the girl's father, a truck-driver biker with bad teeth and an arm full of tattoos, Amanda had to admit that she couldn't imagine it, but she knew enough to know that all kinds of strange things happened in the world.

People could be full of surprises.

"You must be proud."

"Damn straight. That's why I'm drivin' so much. You have any idea how much a university costs these days?"

Amanda had no idea, even though she'd had thoughts of getting an education plenty of times. "I bet it's a lot."

The light turned green and they started off again.

"I kid her all the time about paying me back by defending me in court . . . like I'll be her number-one client." His laugh was hardy, and edged by a wheeze obtained from years of cigarette smoke.

Even though Bill looked like one of America's Most Wanted, she somehow couldn't picture him on the wrong side of the law. Maybe sometime in the past, but not anymore. He just seemed too proud of his daughter to ruin her chances of making something of her life.

"I doubt she'll ever have to do that."

He let out another laugh. "Probably not, but I do know a lot of people who are always in need of a good lawyer."

Amanda nodded, gave him a smile. That she believed.

After a few moments of silence, he said, "What about you?"

"What about me?"

"Where are you headed?"

Amanda had been so intent on *leaving* she hadn't given much thought as to *where* she would go. She was tempted to say, "Anywhere but here," but knew that would raise more questions than she was willing to answer at this point. So instead she simply said, "West."

"It's a big country," he said. "Any particular spot out West, or just west?"

"I have a sister in Winnipeg," she lied. "She said I could visit her any time I wanted." The only family Amanda had was an aunt in Toronto, but she didn't know where the woman lived in the city.

"So you're hitching a ride out of town at night because you're going to visit your sister?"

She nodded. "That's right."

"You wouldn't be running *away* from something, would you?"

Amanda said nothing, even though she had a feeling that remaining silent would solicit a lecture from the former bad apple who managed to turn his life around. But instead of giving her a speech, the man was understanding.

"It takes courage to leave a bad situation," he said.

"Sometimes you don't have any other choice. And a lot of times things work out for the best in the end and it turns out to be the best decision you ever made in your life."

Amanda said nothing, but looked at the man for a long time as headlights passed them by, and streetlights passed overhead. Here was a man whose circumstances couldn't have been any worse than Amanda's at the same age. Sure, he was still a little rough around the edges, but she sensed he was basically a good man. If he'd been able to turn his life around, then there was a good chance that she could do the very same thing with hers.

Hell, maybe even a lost cause like Ron could be saved.

The truck slowed.

Bill pulled over onto the side of the road just before the on-ramp for the northbound Highway 69. The crunch of gravel slowly subsided under the truck's tires and the rig eventually came to a stop.

"You sure you want to get out here?" he asked.

Amanda hesitated a moment, wondering if this was what she really wanted. Actually, it wasn't even close. What she wanted was stability in her life, a home of her own, and the love and respect of a good man. Riding in a truck with a stranger wasn't anywhere near that, but it could very well be the first step on the path toward it.

"Yeah, I'm sure."

Bill nodded. "Then be careful, and good luck."

"Thanks," she said, gathering up her backpack.

"And remember . . ."

She turned to look at him.

"Just because somebody looks like a psychopathic killer, doesn't mean he is one, okay?" He smiled and gave her a wink.

"Thanks, I'll remember that."

She stepped down onto the shoulder and closed the

door behind her. The Freightliner pulled away with a single sharp blast of the air horn, and slowly faded into the night.

Amanda was alone.

Below her traffic flowed by on Highway 69, like fish in a river, with electric eyes to guide them through the murky darkness.

As she walked down the on-ramp, the certainty she felt about this little adventure being the right thing to do took a bit of a knock.

It was dark out, the night was beginning to turn cold, and she was at the mercy of the kindness of some stranger who might stop by the side of the highway and give her a ride. She was supposed to be taking charge of her life, but the power over where she went and when was beyond her control. Still, she had to do it. If she turned back now, she'd be a failure at even just *trying* to turn her life around.

She deserved better than that.

And so she continued on, cutting across the grass in the middle of the circular ramp to get to the highway more quickly.

Minutes later her thumb was out and she was headed north.

Cars passed without slowing down.

Some even came dangerously close to hitting her, their drivers unaware that someone was on the side of the road. After the second close call, Amanda undid her coat so that her white T-shirt would be visible to oncoming traffic.

More people saw her, but none of them stopped . . .

Until a big dark truck slowed as it passed her, then pulled over onto the side of the highway.

Amanda ran toward the truck, reading the name

CROWTHER on the side of the trailer and PETERBILT on the side of the truck.

She climbed up the passenger side and opened the door.

"Hi there," said the driver.

He was an older man, gray and thinning on top and wearing a pair of wire-rimmed glasses. He was thin, looked weak, and was probably close to retirement. The name on the ID badge hanging from the visor read CROWTHER, just like on the trailer.

"Hey," said Amanda.

"Where you headed?"

"West." Then, realizing the highway headed north until it cleared the Great Lakes, then turned west toward Manitoba, she said, "Eventually, that is. North's fine for now."

"Your lucky night. I'm on my way to Calgary. You can ride as long as you want."

"Thanks," she said with a smile as she climbed inside the truck. "Thanks so much."

"Don't mention it," he said. "An old guy like me enjoys the company of a female every now and then. If you know what I mean."

Amanda had an idea or two about what he meant.

And her smile slowly began to fade.

Chapter 4

Ron spat onto the sidewalk in front of him.

Instead of the usual spit, there was a spot of blood at his feet bathed in the glow of an overhead streetlight. "Shit!" he said.

He slid his tongue over his bottom lip and realized it was split and bleeding.

No problem. He'd played hockey since he was a kid, and a season didn't go by when he didn't have some cut or bruise on his face. It would heal quick enough. Wouldn't make him any more handsome, but it would heal.

Ron dug his keys out of his pocket.

He drove a 1989 Buick LeSabre that his parents had bought for him when he played junior hockey in Brampton so he could drive home every once in a while between games. It had over 250,000 kilometers on it and still ran great. Of course, there were things on it that didn't work so well, like the passenger-side window that didn't go down anymore, or the blocked-up HVAC system that kept hot air from blowing into the car in winter, and cool air from coming in from outside in the summer. These things were only a problem in August and January, but for the rest of the year the car was problem-free.

Ron unlocked the door, opened it, and eased himself into the driver's seat.

And a bolt of pain shot up his side as if he'd been burned with a red-hot poker.

Obviously the grip had caught him with a couple of good shots in the ribs. It felt like one or two of them might be broken, or maybe just cracked. Or if he was lucky, maybe the damage was restricted to the cartilage between the bones. If that was the case, the pain would clear up in a few days, just like his lip.

He slid the key into the ignition and put his foot on the accelerator. That's when he realized he was also missing one of his shoes. Maybe it had come off when he kicked Hamm in the nuts. *Man, did that guy ever fall over like a sack of shit!* The thought of the big man grabbing his jewels and crumpling into a little ball brought a smile to Ron's face.

He let out a little laugh and the pain in his side cut him like a knife.

And his laugh suddenly turned into a scream.

He wrapped his left arm around his midsection and breathed slowly until the pain subsided. *You really did it this time, didn't you?* he thought.

In the space of just a few hours he'd pushed Amanda around (maybe even smacked her . . . he couldn't remember), stolen money from her, lost that money, *and* put himself deeper in debt; he'd bet his Memorial Cup ring and stolen it back, kicked a man named Hamm in the nuts, and was now sitting in his car waiting for the pain in his ribs to subside enough to allow him to go home and beg Amanda to let him back into their shitty little trailer. And if she didn't he'd have nowhere else to go and would likely have to spend the night sleeping in his car.

Wouldn't be the first time.

"I'm Ron Stinson," he said, as if it was supposed to mean something. "How the fuck did I get here?"

Ron knew the answer, had known it for years.

Even now, spitting blood and holding his ribs as if he were keeping his body from falling apart, he wanted a drink. If he could just get home and have a couple of beers he'd be all right. Maybe a shot of Canadian Club too, to deaden the pain.

But there wasn't any beer in the fridge.

And the last time he'd had any whisky of his own, it had been a Christmas gift from his father.

Maybe he could visit a couple of buddies. He knew all kinds of guys who were always good for a few drinks. Most of them even liked it when he came over, as if his being there—the former hockey star—made their lives just a little bit better.

Imagine, Ron's visit was an event.

He spat blood onto the floorboard between his feet.

"How the hell *did* I get here?" he said again, shaking his head. After a charmed life as a winner, he had suddenly turned his life around and was a loser of the first stripe. No money, no job, no future, and a girlfriend who was this close to saying, "So long!"

The thought of losing Amanda had a sobering effect on him.

Mandy was the absolute best thing in his life . . . the only thing he really had going for him right now, and to lose her would put him so deep into a hole that he knew he'd never be able to make it back out again.

"I gotta do something," he whispered. "I gotta do something today."

First, he'd beg Mandy to forgive him. She probably

wouldn't, but that'd be okay. He would have to prove himself to her and maybe that's just what he needed to do. Prove himself. Like trying out for a hockey team. He had to show that he belonged, that he could contribute, and when he'd done that, maybe they'd be a team.

Mandy and Ron.

It was a good thought.

Something worthwhile to shoot for.

The best thing about it was that he'd come to this conclusion all by himself. Usually he said these things just so Mandy would take him back, or have sex with him, or lend him some money. Right now, he didn't want any of those things. All he wanted her to do was give him another chance.

Next, he'd stay away from the booze. He knew plenty of people who didn't drink. He'd wondered how they could function without alcohol, but somehow they did and he'd have to find out how. That's all.

Maybe Mandy would help him.

As if she hadn't tried already.

But this time he'd work at it, not just *say* he would try and change. This time he'd do it. Really do it.

And a job. He'd have to get one.

That was going to be tough. People were used to seeing him in the spotlight, doing great things. For a few years there his picture had been in the paper more often than the mayor of Parry Sound. Great things had been expected of him, but none of them had panned out. Now he'd be asking around for some minimum wage job where people would see him and say, "Didn't you used to be Ron Stinson?"

And then he'd have to try and convince them that he still was. He wasn't looking forward to it, but he knew it couldn't be that bad. Hell, people were already saying stuff like that to his face as it was.

The pain in his side had eased up and he was able to raise his left hand up to the top of the steering wheel.

Then he reached for the ignition.

"Out of the car, asshole!"

Ron looked to his left and saw Hamm hanging on to the car, pulling on the door handle.

The grip was coming up behind him, opening up a penknife.

Ron had a good idea about what the man was planning on doing with that knife. If he didn't get out of here in the next couple of seconds, his tires would be shredded and he'd have to face the wrath of Hamm.

He turned the key in the ignition.

The Buick dutifully turned over, and started.

"I said, get out of the car!"

This time Hamm pounded his fist against the window. The glass buckled some, but did not break.

Ron put the car into *reverse* and stomped on the accelerator with his stockinged foot.

Hamm pounded on the window a second time, putting a spiderweb crack in the middle of it.

The Buick's front wheels spun, sending dirt and gravel flying forward as the car jumped back.

The grip rolled out of the way, coughing and spitting dirt out of his mouth.

Hamm hit the top of the hood with his fist, putting a dent in the middle of it.

Out on the road, Ron put the Buick into *drive*. It skidded to a halt and then shot forward, the front wheels shuddering to get hold of the pavement.

"I'll be looking for you, asshole," Hamm shouted, his right hand pointing at Ron as he drove away, his left hand still cradling his swollen balls.

"Thanks for the warning," Ron muttered as he hurried off into the night. "I'll add your name to the list."

— 2 —

"Sharpe," said one of the constables working the front desk at the Parry Sound OPP detachment on Bay Street overlooking Parry Sound Harbour.

"Yeah."

"Call for you from Paul Hrycyna."

"Thanks."

Paul Hrycyna was a psychologist, and the OPP's profiling expert, and had been working on the current string of murders since the first body had been discovered outside of Dryden three months ago. He'd also worked on dozens of similar cases, not only for the OPP but for just about every major police force in the province from Toronto to Windsor. He'd even consulted with the RCMP and had done work with the FBI and several big police forces in the States.

Constable Sharpe had a rough idea of the type of person he was looking for, but he imagined that Mr. Hrycyna would be able to provide a few insights into the killer's personality that wouldn't have occurred to him in a hundred years.

"Constable Sharpe," he said, after picking up the phone.

"Evening, Constable, this is Paul Hrycyna."

"Thanks for returning my call, Mr. Hr-r." He struggled to pronounce the name.

"It's Her-Xena."

"You mean like the warrior princess?"

"Exactly."

"Well, thanks for returning my call, Mr. Hrycyna."

"Please, call me Paul."

"All right, my name's Larry."

"You're working late tonight."

He'd been putting in plenty of extra hours, but he figured he could always take some time off when there wasn't a murder to solve. And while the bodies had turned up spaced several weeks apart, that didn't mean people wouldn't be in danger of their lives over the next few days. Besides, the trail of the killer was still warm, so he needed to do as much as he could *now* before everything cooled off.

"So are you," Sharpe said in response to his comment.

"It's a busy time for all of us. Anything new on your case?"

"Still waiting on DNA and full toxicology reports. There's been nothing new since the coroner's report."

"And thanks for sending that along so quickly."

"You're welcome. . . . Did it help any?"

"A bit," he said. "Mainly it confirmed a lot of the things I'd already concluded."

"Like what?"

"Okay, here's what I've got so far."

"Should I take notes?"

"If you like. I'll be sending you a copy anyway."

Sharpe was usually able to keep track of things in his head, and any notes he'd make would be cursory at best, relying more upon the official reports when they arrived. Still, it wouldn't hurt to write things down till then. He cracked open his notebook and waited. When the line was silent for a bit too long he said, "Go ahead."

"The similarities in the condition of the bodies suggest that all five women were killed by the same person."

Sharpe noted he didn't say *man*. He'd assumed he was

looking for a man, but obviously the force's profiler wasn't so quick to make such judgments.

"All of the bodies have been ravaged by wolves, which is somewhat baffling because wolves weren't known to inhabit a couple of areas where the bodies were discovered."

"Like the one we found here," Sharpe said.

"Yes, like the most recent one. The man I spoke with at the Ministry of Natural Resources had no explanation for them being there, especially so close to the highway."

Sharpe wrote the word *Wolves* in his notepad.

"And then there's the blood . . . or lack of it in the victims' bodies. Obviously the killer needs blood for something."

"Like what?"

"My first inclination is that it's for an occult ritual of some kind. You know, like a sacrifice, but that wouldn't explain why the killer would need so many victims. Rituals usually aren't celebrated on such a regular or frequent basis."

"So if it's not ritual killing, then what?"

"Could be anything. Maybe the killer's a painter and likes to mix blood in with his paints, or a macabre chef who makes real blood pudding . . ."

Sharpe closed his eyes and turned away from the phone for a moment in disgust. It was such a revolting thought, but the man's voice hadn't even wavered when he'd said it. Obviously he'd seen plenty of heinous crimes in the past and wasn't discounting anything at this point.

". . . or a woman who likes to bathe in the blood of her victims."

"Jesus!" Sharpe exclaimed.

"It's possible, Larry. Elizabeth Bathory, a sixteenth-century Hungarian countess, used to bathe in the blood of young girls brought to her castle, thinking it would help keep her young. And the only physical link between the victims is that they were all young and healthy, which suggests that their youth made their blood all the more desirable."

"All right," he said. "I'll keep an open mind." He wrote the word *Blood* in his notebook in big bold letters.

"Wide-open, Larry. This case has got a lot of strange aspects to it."

"Oh, really?" Sharpe was being sarcastic, but Hrycyna didn't seem to notice, or perhaps this one was just a tiny bit more strange than what he usually dealt with and the man thought they were both on the same wavelength.

"Yes. Usually a serial killer will work in one area, either a big city or a section of rural area, but the victims have been spread out across the province thousands of kilometers from each other. Most times when that happens the murders are in different jurisdictions and are never linked together until much later. But Ontario's so big, and the modus operandi has been so consistent that it's obviously the work of a single killer."

"So what does it mean?"

"Unless the killer is driving for days just to dump his victims, I'd say he's mobile and drives a route that can be mapped out by the location of the bodies, probably driving it quite regularly."

Sharpe wondered how he figured out that last bit, but realized that Hrycyna was the expert and would have his reasons even if they weren't apparent to him.

"That's about as much as I could deduce from the victims. There were needle marks found on a few of their arms, which would suggest they were drug addicts, but for the most part their systems were clean of any drugs. . . ."

Sharpe wrote down the words *Needle Marks*.

"That leaves us with the killer. A driver of some kind is most likely. Maybe a bus, but probably a truck driving a regular route along the Trans-Canada Highway. The distance the bodies were found from the side of the road suggests the killer is a male, simply because of the strength that's required to throw a body that far. If we assume the killer's male, there's a temptation to think he might be good-looking, or at least a friendly face, but that's pure speculation. It's more likely he's average-looking and able to blend into the crowd. That's his real talent because he's more than likely a loner, as you would expect someone who drained bodies of blood to be. So thousands of people along the route have seen him, but nobody knows him . . . and that's the way he likes it."

Sharpe's pen scratched out the words *Strong Male. Average looks. Loner.* He waited for the man to continue outlining the profile, but the line was silent.

"Is that it?" he said at last.

"Just about, except maybe for one thing. . . ."

"What?"

"The fact that he's so mobile bothers me. I think his mobility is an integral part of the way he kills."

"Meaning?"

"He probably drives because it makes him a better killer, or perhaps a killer that is that much harder to catch."

"So he's put a lot of thought into it."

"Exactly. He'll probably move on in a little while. In fact, I suspect there are similar patterns of killings elsewhere in Canada and the U.S. that have yet to be identified as such."

Sharpe could see that. After all, how many bodies were discovered on the sides of roads and highways every year?

"My guess is that you've probably got a few weeks to catch him; after that . . ."

"After that?"

"He'll be gone and killing somewhere else. . . ."

Sharpe nodded.

"Any type you think I should be looking out for more than another?"

"Yes," he said. "I'd be suspicious of any vampire truck drivers that come up in the course of your investigation."

He let out a sigh.

"That was a little joke," he said. "Profiler humor."

"I know," Sharpe answered. "And it's a good one."

"So why aren't you laughing?"

"You're not the first person to make that little pronouncement."

— 3 —

The driver hadn't said much for at least twenty minutes and he was starting to give Amanda the creeps. From what she knew about truck drivers, they all loved to talk. That was one of the reasons they picked up riders . . . to have someone to talk to. But while this one wasn't saying much, his eyes, well, they were doing double duty watching the road in front of them *and* her body all at the same time.

Well, not exactly *at the same time*.

He would watch the road for a while, then sort of glance over at her for a few seconds before turning his attention back onto the road.

"I'd feel a lot safer if you'd just stop the truck and allow yourself a good long look."

"What?" he said, blinking his eyes and looking at her as if he'd just been caught with his hand in the till.

"You've been stealing glances at me ever since I got in the truck." She sat up straight, leaned against the door, and crossed her arms over her chest so he couldn't look at her breasts anymore. "You either keep your eyes on the road, or you stop and take a good look, 'cause you sure as hell can't do both."

The old-timer laughed. "Caught me starin', huh?"

"You haven't even tried hiding it."

"No, I suppose I haven't at that."

"Well, would you please stop?"

He nodded. "All right."

She waited for him to apologize, but he didn't.

After a few minutes of silence between them, he said, "I suppose we got off on the wrong foot. My name's Brian."

"I'm Rachel," Amanda lied. She wasn't about to tell this man the truth about anything.

He extended his hand to shake. Amanda didn't want to touch him, but there was no way to avoid shaking his hand. Not in such a confined space, anyway. And so she shook his hand. He had a strong grip, especially for such an old man, and it seemed he didn't want to let go. When he eventually did, Amanda felt as if her hand was covered with slime . . . even though it was bone dry.

"Well, Rachel, you have to understand an old fella like me just doesn't get the chance to see pretty young things like you out on the road." He shook his head. "No, sir. You're a beautiful young woman and I doubt there isn't a man with a pulse and a heartbeat who wouldn't have been doing the very same thing I was a few minutes ago."

Amanda wondered if she was supposed to be flattered by what he was saying or not. If that had been his intention, he was way off the mark. She felt dirty . . . and the more he talked the dirtier she felt.

"And I'm probably gettin' a bit tired too," he said around a yawn. "I've been driving since the sun came up and I'm just about done for the day."

Amanda said nothing.

"You tired?"

"I'm fine."

" 'Cause I'm thinking of pulling over somewhere for the night. You can take the sleeper if you want . . . I'll just stretch out here in my chair."

"That's kind of you."

"Of course, we could get a room for the night." He was looking directly at her when he said that and Amanda saw there was a light in his eyes, as if he thought there was actually a chance that he'd be spending the night with her.

Together.

In the same bed.

The thought of it nearly made her sick.

The man was old enough to be her grandfather and had all the grace and wisdom of a fourteen-year-old. She looked over at his right hand riding the shift lever and couldn't imagine any scenario in which she'd enjoy those bony fingers roaming over her body.

And that's when it hit her.

The sheer ridiculousness of her plan.

Here she was in the middle of nowhere, in the middle of the night, hoping that some withered old man wouldn't try to rape her. She'd taken charge of her situation, only to put herself at the utter mercy of a total stranger.

It was crazy.

She was crazy to think that she could just run off in the night and have everything work out just as she'd wanted. Running away required a plan, a real plan. She'd have to give some thought as to *where* she wanted to go, *when* she wanted to go, and *how* she was going to get there. She needed money, a bus ticket, reservations, a backup plan.

I need to get out, she thought. *Now!*

She'd return home to Parry Sound, go through the motions for the next couple of weeks while she planned a proper escape, and then she'd be gone without warning, halfway to where she was going before anyone knew she was gone.

But before she could do any of that, she needed to get out of this truck. And even though the driver, Brian, was a withered old man, she had a feeling he wasn't about to just pull over and let her out.

"A room sounds nice," she said.

"What?"

"I said, a room sounds good. You know, hot shower, clean sheets."

"You want to stop for the night?" he said, the disbelief in his voice unmistakable.

She wondered how many riders had ever taken him up on an offer of a motel room. Amanda was probably the first. Ever.

"Sure, why not?" she said. "But I'm hungry. I'd sure like a bite to eat first."

"Of course, no problem," he said. There was a sickening sort of glee on the man's face, and incredible as it seemed, he was actually licking his lips. "There's a rest station coming up in twenty klicks. . . . Can you hold on till then?"

"I think so," she said, scrunching her nose up as if she were his little bunny.

"Hot dog!" he said, pressing a little harder on the accelerator.

They pulled into a rest station halfway between Estaire and Sudbury about ten minutes later.

He parked behind the restaurant between a tanker on the left and a car carrier on the right. He got out of the truck first, then went around to Amanda's side to help her get down out of the rig. Amanda laughed inwardly at that. *Even an asshole can act like a gentleman if he thinks he's going to get some.*

"What would you like to eat?" he asked.

She dropped her head slightly onto her right shoulder. "I have to go to the bathroom first, but you could order me a burger and fries. And a Diet Pepsi. Is that okay?"

"Sure, sure, anything you want."

"Great." She smiled at him. "I'll be right in."

"I'll be waiting for you," he said, entering the restaurant.

I bet you will, she thought, following him in, then walking past the door to the women's washroom and right on out the front door of the restaurant.

Outside, she crouched down low so she would remain hidden below the glass windows, and then once she was clear of the rest station, she ran down to the highway.

It wasn't easy crossing the highway, even during the day, but traffic was light and she managed to travel the four lanes before a single vehicle passed her by.

Minutes later, only slightly winded, she had her thumb out and was looking for a ride to take her south.

Back home again.

So she could plan her escape properly.

Because the next time she left home, she was going to do it right.

— 4 —

His lip had stopped bleeding, but his ribs still felt as if they were on fire.

Ron pulled up the drive in front of the trailer and killed the engine. Then he took a good long look around to check for anyone hiding in the bushes, or behind one of the neighbor's trailers.

Hamm and the grip didn't know where he lived, but it was possible that they'd gotten the information out of Petzoldt. Petzoldt was a tough son of a bitch—he'd been a bit of a goon in junior hockey, earning himself the nickname "Pounder Petzoldt"—but there was no way he was going to take a beating for Ron, especially after what Ron did at the card table. He'd broken one of the golden rules of gambling, which was not to bet any more than you could afford to lose.

Ron shook his head at the thought of betting his Memorial Cup ring in a card game. *How stupid was that?*

"What the hell was I thinking?" he said under his breath as he twisted the ring around his finger.

He reached over, grunting against the pain, and picked up the flowers on the passenger seat next to him. Most of the flowers were roses. He'd picked them up in front of the Rhinegolds' trailer on his way home. The Rhinegolds were a retired German couple who had family in Parry Sound and used their trailer as a second home on weekends and a couple of weeks each summer. Whenever they were up at the trailer they seemed to spend all of their time on their garden and flower beds . . . and it showed. They won prizes at the McKellar Fall Fair every year and they'd been written up a couple of times in the Parry Sound *North Star*. Ron felt bad picking their flowers, but he *needed* them. He had to have something to break the ice with Amanda and he was sure the Rhinegolds would be happy to know that their flowers had died, not in vain, but to bring a couple of young people closer together.

Ron made one last check to see if anyone was lurking out there in the dark, and then he got out of the car.

There were plenty of lights on in the trailer, and the outside light was on too. That was odd. Amanda usually turned off all the lights after eleven to make it harder for him to find his keys in the dark. And she usually waited for him to come home, mostly so she could give him a piece of her mind, but at least she was always there for him to come home to.

He singled the trailer key out from the rest on the ring in his hand, but when he tried the door he found he didn't need it. The door was unlocked and that was odd, too. Amanda always locked the door when he went out, even chained it shut a lot of the times so he couldn't sneak back in if she fell asleep waiting for him.

He opened the door slowly and stepped inside.

His eyes had a bit of trouble adjusting to the light, but even before he could open his eyes wide it was obvious that there was no sign of Amanda anywhere. *Maybe she's in bed already*. Ron would have loved to get undressed and crawl into bed beside her, but he knew enough to know that that would be a bad idea tonight. Besides, his ribs were too sore for any of that stuff.

Ron switched on a light in the kitchen and got a vase out of the small storage cupboard beneath the sink. He filled the vase with water, slid the flowers inside it, and put the vase on the table. *Amanda will appreciate them in the morning,* he thought. *Something bright and beautiful for her to wake up to.*

He left the light on in the kitchen and headed down the hallway toward the bedroom. Ron would be spending the night on the couch in the living room, but he wanted to at least see Amanda . . . see her lying in their bed, watch her breathe, and thank God that she was still a part of his life.

He wanted to wake her up and tell her that he was going to change. Do things right from now on, but he knew that no matter what he had to say to her right now she would never believe him. He'd said similar things dozens of times before and they always turned out to be nothing more than words. Empty words. This time they wouldn't be empty. He would say them to Amanda, and then back them up with deeds.

He pushed open the door to the bedroom and listened for the sound of Amanda breathing.

There was complete and utter silence.

No breathing.

No Amanda.

He flicked on the lights and saw that the bed was empty.

"Amanda!" he called out.

There was no answer.

Only silence.

A quick check of the dresser drawers confirmed she'd taken a bunch of clothes with her.

Maybe she really did leave this time. . . .

Amanda had walked out on him before plenty of times, but she had never really *left* him. She'd usually go away for a few hours and then return, mad as hell, but planning on sticking around and giving it another try.

But not this time.

She was gone.

"Shit!" Ron exclaimed, slamming an open hand against a wall hard enough to make a dent in the cheap fiberboard paneling.

He was angry . . . not with Amanda, but with himself. He'd had a good thing going with her—hell, he'd had a good thing going with his *life*—and he'd screwed it all up.

Hockey.

Amanda.

All of it.

Everything that was good had turned to shit.

And for what?

He didn't even have a reason.

He walked back toward the living room and caught sight of himself in the full-length mirror hanging on the wall to his left. His lip was bleeding again, there was a bruise over his right eye, his body was twisted from the pain in his ribs, his pants were dirty and torn, and he was wearing just one shoe.

"What a prize you are!" he said to his reflection.

He shook his head, not blaming Amanda in the least for walking out on him.

In fact, he'd do it himself if he could.

Chapter 5

~ 1 ~

She'd been walking backward with her thumb out to traffic for what seemed like an hour. She kept walking—or maybe backpedaling was a better word for it because that's what she was doing—at a decent clip even though she knew it wouldn't make any difference in the long run. It certainly wouldn't get her home any faster since the distance she'd walked could easily have been covered in minutes once she'd hitched a ride. However, walking still might get her a ride sooner than later. She knew that when she was riding in a car, she hated to see hitchhikers sitting on the side of the road just waiting for a ride. It just looked . . . *lazy*. If she walked in the direction she wanted to go she'd look more determined, a self-starter. That way, someone stopping to give her a ride would be *helping* her get where she was going instead of just *taking* her there.

It was all just a theory since nobody had stopped yet.

Or even slowed down.

So, in reality, the most important reason she was walking was to keep warm and to give her something to do. She'd tried just standing by the side of the road, but she found it too creepy. She'd felt as if someone, or something, had been watching her from the darkness. And the quiet between vehicles had spooked her. Without any sounds in the background, the slither and padding of animals by the side of the road had become heightened to the point where she was certain that she was seconds away from being attacked and eaten by something big and hairy with teeth the size of golf tees.

And so she walked.

The continuous crunch of gravel beneath her feet had a soothing effect on her, filling in the empty spaces between the roar of vehicles as they raced past her and on through the night.

Behind her in the distance, a truck was approaching. She knew it was a truck because after walking by the side of the road for so long she'd learned to distinguish the subtle differences between small imported cars and domestic vehicles, pickup trucks and big eighteen-wheel tractor-trailers.

She straightened her back, raised her thumb high off the road, and waited for the truck to pass.

As it neared, Amanda's hopes began to fade.

The sound of the engine continued to thrum at a steady rate. This driver wouldn't even be slowing down.

When the lights of the oncoming truck fell on her body Amanda froze, wondering a bit fancifully if she looked like a frightened deer.

Because she had reason to be afraid.

Not only wasn't the driver stopping, but it seemed as if he were veering slightly off the road.

She could hear the truck's tires sliding off the asphalt and grinding onto the gravel shoulder. The driver corrected the slip, turning the wheel sharply and managing to wrestle the truck back onto the highway. The van-trailer behind it began to fishtail and the driver seemed to have his hands full just keeping his rig on the road.

As it roared past her, Amanda could see into the cab

through the front windshield. The driver's hands and face were lit up by the lights of the dashboard, and even as he was frantically working the steering wheel to maintain control of the truck, he still had time to shake his fist at Amanda. Imagine that. He was shaking his fist at her as if she were to blame for his wild ride onto the shoulder . . . as if she had somehow caused him to drive off the road.

That was ridiculous. He probably didn't even see her until he was right on top of her. Driving off the road had been his fault. Her being there just meant he had to get back onto the road a little quicker than usual.

Moments later, with the truck now safely back on the road, the driver gave her a couple of sharp blasts on his air horn.

"Yeah, you too!" she said, giving him a pair of single-digit salutes.

She turned back around and resumed walking.

Maybe the driver hadn't seen her. Maybe that was why no one was stopping to give her a ride. It was dark out, and she was dressed in—she looked down at the clothes she was wearing—dark clothes.

No wonder no one was stopping. The only time anyone saw her was when they were too close to stop. No one was going to get into an accident trying to give a woman a ride. And realistically speaking, who was going to pick up a hitchhiker in the middle of nowhere, in the middle of the night?

Amanda sure wouldn't.

Who knew what kind of person you might be picking up?

A lunatic, maybe.

Or some kind of psycho.

Amanda braced herself for the prospect of not getting a ride till morning.

Which meant she'd have to keep walking through the

night. Or at least until she reached a rest station where she could sit and sleep until morning.

Just then she heard the sound of another truck approaching. It was an eighteen-wheeler like the last one.

She moved a little farther off the side of the road, just to be safe, and stuck out her thumb.

The truck was still a hundred meters off, but it was slowing down.

Slowing down.

Amanda would have thought the truck was too far away for the driver to know she wanted a ride, let alone see her walking on the side of the road. But somehow he'd seen her, and he was pulling over.

She stopped walking and waited for the truck to meet her. It was a newer truck. Big and black with plenty of lights and chrome on it. It looked like a comfortable ride, and warm.

The truck slowed to a stop next to Amanda, its right wheels on the shoulder, its left wheels still on the highway. When it was finally still, the truck let out a sharp blast of air as the parking brake was engaged and the vehicle was locked in place.

Amanda reached up for the door, but before her hand touched the handle, it turned and the door slowly swung open.

"Evening," the driver said.

"Hi." Amanda smiled.

"Where you heading?"

"South . . ."

"Me too."

". . . to Parry Sound."

"The hometown of Number Four, Bobby Orr." The man smiled. "It's right on my way."

It was then that Amanda noticed the stench coming from inside the cab. It was a strange smell, acrid and fetid, like something had died inside the truck. There was also a stink to it, like shit or something . . . like the driver was wearing a pair of Depends and wasn't stopping to change them until he'd reached his destination. And wafting up from underneath it all was the smell of disinfectant, or maybe an air freshener. Something like Lysol or Glade, that valiantly tried but ultimately failed to make the overall smell more palatable.

"You getting in?" he said, smiling broadly at her with a tight-lipped smile.

Amanda sniffed again, but the smell was either gone or she'd gotten used to it in the few seconds she'd been standing there. Whatever the reason, it didn't bother her anymore. She looked up at the driver. He was a funny-looking man, short and fat with a pale white head that was adorned by only a few wisps of gray-white hair. He was wearing jeans, a stained T-shirt, suspenders, and a dark leather jacket. She was uncertain about getting into the truck, feeling that there was something *not right* about the driver. After all, what kind of driver would stop in the middle of the road to give someone a ride?

A weirdo . . .

. . . or maybe just a nice man.

She studied him a little more closely. He looked normal enough; in fact he looked like somebody's goofy uncle, the one who always puts lampshades on his head at parties and carries a whoopee cushion in his pocket for laughs.

And the way he smiled at her . . .

It was as if he weren't all there, as if something was missing, like manners or a conscience.

Or maybe he was just lonely.

That was probably more likely.

After all, with his looks, he sure wasn't a lady-killer,

although there was a comforting quality to his eyes. They were big and bright . . . Soothing . . . Inviting.

Amanda grabbed hold of the door handle and pulled herself up into the cab.

It was warm and comfortable inside, and all traces of that wretched smell were gone.

"My name's Amanda," she said, closing the door. "Amanda Peck."

"I'm Konrad Valeska," he said, his voice tinged with a hint of an accent.

"Pleased to meet you."

His smile got bigger, exposing a couple of his teeth. "Likewise."

Amanda made herself comfortable.

Konrad shifted the truck into gear, and it began moving forward into the dark, dark night.

— 2 —

Constable Sharpe pulled off the northbound Highway 69 at Pointe au Baril, just twenty kilometers north of Parry Sound. He could use a coffee, but he was more interested in talking to the clientele that frequented the rest station there. They were mostly truckers running the route between Toronto and the northern Ontario cities of Sudbury, Sault Ste. Marie, and Thunder Bay as well as Winnipeg, Manitoba. Some of the more regular drivers drove the route between two and three times a week and would probably be up on all the latest news . . . as well as be privy to gossip and hearsay about what was really happening out on the highway.

Sharpe said hello to the two young girls working behind the counter and then walked past them to the washroom for a "rest break" of his own. It was funny how the stereotype of the *cop stopping for donuts* always focused on the donut part of it. The truth was that once you had that first cup of coffee, you were stuck stopping to relieve yourself every half hour or so throughout your shift. Then it was a case of as long as you were stopped, you might as well have a coffee while you were at it, which ensured you'd be stopping at some other place in another thirty minutes.

He came out of the washroom to find a fresh cup of coffee waiting for him on the counter. He fished some money out of his pocket to pay for it, but the girls refused to take it from him.

"No, that's okay," the taller one said.

The young girls appreciated a policeman stopping in every once in a while, especially at night when things could easily get out of hand, so they encouraged police visits with cups of free coffee. Sharpe was never comfortable with getting anything for free just because he was a cop, and he was even more uncomfortable about it when there was a roomful of people watching him get *no-charge* coffee.

"I insist," he said, dropping a five-dollar bill onto the counter.

The shorter girl took the bill, opened up the till, and gave him a toonie, two loonies, and four quarters in change.

Sharpe looked at the five dollars' worth of coins in his hand and realized he'd have to make a big fuss just to pay for his coffee, so he decided it was easier just to say thanks and be done with it.

"Come by any time," she said.

Sharpe nodded, picked up the coffee, and headed for a table where two men sat talking while they watched the traffic roll by on the highway outside the window. One of them was obviously much older than the other, but they both looked like truckers—although they were of two distinctly different generations—and if they were, Sharpe wanted to have a word with them.

"Mind if I join you?" Sharpe said.

The younger man shrugged, as if it didn't matter to him one way or another.

"Have a seat," the older one offered.

"Thanks," Sharpe said, settling in and quickly spooning sugar into his coffee.

The younger of the two, a man in his mid-to-late thirties with long hair and a beard to match, pushed the bowl of creamers toward him.

"I couldn't help overhearing your conversation," Sharpe said. "You were talking about the dead body that was found on the side of the highway the other day."

"Ain't that a shame?" the older man said. He looked to be in his sixties, with scraggly gray hair, a salt-and-pepper beard, and small brown eyes that were framed by an intricate set of crow's-feet. The Blue Jays cap on his head was worn and dirty, as if he'd got it on opening day back in 1977. "And I was driving through there just a couple of hours before that farmer found that body, too."

Sharpe sat up a bit straighter in his chair at this unexpected stroke of luck. "Did you see anything unusual?"

The man shook his head. "Nah. It was just another stretch of boring highway then. But the next time I drive by there . . . bet ya I get goose bumps all over."

The younger man sighed and gave a weak smile. "I felt worse than that when I drove by there earlier today. . . . I was near sick to my stomach."

"How many bodies is that now that've been found on this highway?"

Sharpe took a sip of coffee. "Five."

"Jesus!" said the old man.

After a few moments of silence, the younger man said, "Blood Road."

"What?" asked Sharpe.

"Blood Road," he said again. "That's what the drivers on the Trans-Canada are calling the highway these days . . . Blood Road."

It's a good name for it, thought Sharpe. And it wouldn't be long before newspaper and television news reporters heard the name and started plastering it all over the place. He could almost see the front page of tomorrow morning's *Toronto Sun*, the city's tabloid . . .

Fifth Victim
Found on
BLOOD ROAD

It was a great name for the highway, except that none of the victims had had any blood in their bodies when they were found. *Blood-less Road* would be a more accurate name, or maybe *Death Road*, or *Highway of the Dead*—

Sharpe stopped himself from pondering it any further. Catchy names were something for headline writers and television producers to think about. His job was to figure out who was doing the killing and stop them from killing again.

"These drivers on the Trans-Canada," Sharpe said, "they have any thoughts on who the killer might be?"

"Some say it's a monster," the young man said. "You know . . . like Bigfoot or something. But most are saying it's probably just some crazy trucker."

"No!" said the older man, shaking his head emphatically. "No way."

"Yes way."

"It can't be."

"Who else would be driving the highway five different times?"

The gray-haired old man put an elbow on the table and rested his head in his hand. "Used to be that driving a truck made you part of a brotherhood. You'd pass somebody on the road and you'd give him a wave. You stopped for a bite to eat and you could sit down with anyone in the joint and talk to him like an old friend." He paused a moment to shake his head again, only this time the gesture was barely perceptible. "It's not like that anymore . . . the trucking companies have squeezed a lot of the camaraderie out of the trucking business."

The young man let out a little laugh under his breath. "Hey, driving a truck for a living doesn't mean you've taken an oath and joined the Knights Templar."

"The what?"

Sharpe had heard of the Knights Templar—a group of religious knights who vowed military service against Arabs and other non-Christians—but he thought it best not to put himself in the middle of someone else's argument.

"Never mind," said the young man. "All I'm saying is that just because somebody drives a truck for a living doesn't mean he's agreed to live his life by some code."

"Well, it used to be like that."

"What if Charles Manson had been a truck driver?"

The old man seemed to become enraged. "Charles Manson could never have been a truck driver."

"Why not?"

"Because you've got to worry about people's safety to drive a truck and Manson wouldn't have cared one bit about that."

"He could have pretended to care."

"You can't pretend about something like that," the old man said, and judging by the conviction in his voice, it was obvious he absolutely believed it to be true. "You either have it in you or you don't."

Sharpe took another sip of his coffee, enjoying the lively discussion between the two men.

"That might be true, but he could have driven a truck just well enough so nobody bothered with him, and that would have left him free to kill people all over the country without anyone ever figuring out they were all done in by the same guy."

Sharpe felt a chill run the length of his spine. If someone in a coffee shop in the middle of nowhere could imagine such a scenario, then there was a good chance that there *was* a serial killer out there roaming the country in a truck, killing without the slightest thought of ever being caught.

And maybe he just happens to be working his way through Ontario at the moment, thought Sharpe.

The old-timer seemed ready to concede the other man's point.

"Okay, so maybe what you say is possible, but one thing's for sure, whatever is out there doing these killings, it ain't no member of the human race."

Sharpe wasn't sure why, but he had a feeling that what the old man had said was true.

Chapter 6

~ 1 ~

They'd been on the road for an hour and Amanda had barely said a dozen words to the driver, Konrad Valeska. He was perfectly willing to converse with her, but if she didn't speak he didn't feel any compulsion to fill the empty air between them.

That was fine with Amanda. She'd already ridden with two truck drivers tonight and they both had liked to talk, one about his family, the other about getting Amanda into bed. Riding in silence was a nice change of pace. But even though the ride was pleasant enough, she was starting to feel hungry. At the very least she could use a coffee and a donut to see her through till morning.

"Uh, Konrad," she said as a way of getting his attention.

"Yes?"

"How are you for gas?"

"Doesn't use gas," he said. "Runs on diesel fuel."

"Okay, how are you for fuel?"

"I need to top up, but I can go for another hour or so, why?"

"*My* tank's empty."

Konrad smiled at that, and his face took on the look

of an overgrown child. He was cute, she thought, in a grotesque sort of way. "Need something to eat?"

"A cup of coffee, maybe."

"Sure, sure. No problem. And let me get you something better than a coffee. How does a burger and fries sound?"

That *sounded* great, but Amanda had worked in a greasy spoon herself and knew how such things were prepared. She'd have a burger if that's all they had, but she'd probably give the menu a good going-over first. "Okay."

They drove on for several minutes before a rest station appeared on the side of the road. They pulled off the highway just before the town of Bigwood, south of Sudbury and still a couple of hours from Parry Sound and home.

Konrad parked his rig around back of the restaurant and they both went inside together. Amanda took a good long look at the menu and saw that they had salads and chicken sandwiches on sale, but those had been prepared earlier in the day—this day or maybe the one before it—while their burgers were being cooked on the grill *now*.

"I'll have a burger and fries," she said in the end. "And a Diet Coke."

"Can't go wrong with that," he said.

They waited another minute in line without being served. "Why don't you find a seat?" he said. "I'll bring you the food when it's ready."

"Okay." She found a table by the window and sat down, suddenly feeling exhausted. She'd been on the road several hours and had walked what seemed like miles. Her feet hurt, her legs were sore, and her clothes felt dirty against her skin. She was looking forward to getting home and slipping into a nice hot bath. She wasn't exactly looking forward to seeing Ron again. Showing up at the trailer after a failed attempt to run away would probably get him crowing like a rooster about how she couldn't do anything without him. But she wasn't going to buy any of that crap this time. She was going home just long enough to come up with a plan; then she'd clean out her bank account and leave for good. Maybe she might even leave Ron with a month or two of bills to pay, just so he'd know what it felt like to have the wolves at the door and not have anything to feed them with.

Konrad appeared at the table carrying a tray.

Her food was there, but there was nothing for him to eat, not even a coffee.

"Aren't you going to eat?"

He put his hand up as if to excuse himself. "I ate before."

Amanda stared at his hand a moment, noticing the extraordinarily long index finger, which was at least a half inch longer than his middle finger. "Before when?" she said at last.

"Before you got into the truck. Besides, I enjoy to watch you eat. Go ahead, it will make you strong."

Amanda picked up the burger and took a bite. She hated to admit it, but it was delicious, a lot better than the meat disks they served at the Big Wheel. Or maybe she was hungry. That always helped to make food taste better than it was. She took another bite and looked up . . .

And felt a chill come over her.

Konrad was watching her eat. But while there was nothing wrong with that—there wasn't a whole lot else for him to do—there was something very creepy about the way he stared at her. His eyes . . . his eyes were like two fires alight in the sockets, burning right through her. It frightened her and she wanted to look away, but she found that she couldn't. It was as if she were compelled to stare into his eyes until she were completely devoured by his gaze.

"How's the burger?" he asked.

"What?" she said, a bit dizzy and disoriented.

"The hamburger. Is it any good?"

"Oh, yes," she said, turning the burger around in her hands. "Very good. Thank you."

"No need to thank me. I like to see a woman with a good appetite."

Amanda took another bite of the burger and slipped a few fries into her mouth, eager to finish her meal.

A quarter of an hour later, they were stopped in the restaurant's adjoining service station topping up the truck's fuel tanks. The name on the trailer was TUCANA, each letter as high as the trailer wall and the word filling the side from front to back. The tractor was a Peterbilt, Amanda noted, and fairly new judging by the condition of it on the outside. There was plenty of chrome on it too. Amanda had seen plenty of trucks before, but this one seemed brighter and shinier than most.

Too bad it wasn't as clean on the inside.

When they'd come out of the restaurant and gotten back in the truck, Amanda had been struck by how bad the cab smelled. Like a dog had taken a dump in the back, or like someone had been killed back there and the mess had never been cleaned up. And there was dirt all over the place, especially on the floor, like the guy was a kid who dragged in mud every time he got in and out of the truck.

"All filled up," Konrad said. "Won't need to stop again for a long, long while."

"But I'm only going as far as Parry Sound" she said. "That's just a couple of hours from here."

"Right," he said, almost as if he'd forgotten.

Konrad went around the front of the truck, climbed in, and opened the door for Amanda.

Again she was hit by that same stench. The burger and fries she'd just eaten felt as if they wanted out. She put a hand over her stomach and took a deep breath through her mouth. Thankfully, the stink had already begun to subside.

Amanda climbed in and Konrad immediately started up the truck. It came to life with a great roar, then idled with a rhythmic, almost hypnotic metallic rattle.

He shifted the truck into gear and said, "Here we go!" as if they were riding a roller coaster and not an eighteen-wheeler.

After just a few kilometers, Amanda felt the exhaustion creeping over her body again. It was the middle of the night and she hadn't had a minute of sleep. The constant hum of the engine was making it hard for her to keep her eyes open and a couple of times she awoke abruptly after feeling herself nodding off.

"You can stretch out in the sleeper if you like," Konrad suggested. "It's quite comfortable."

Amanda looked over her shoulder. There was a curtain there separating the cab from the sleeper behind it. It would be nice to lie down and catch an hour or two of sleep, but the thought of making herself comfortable in this man's truck disgusted her. *That's where he sleeps.* And even though she had no idea what was behind the curtain, one thing that might be there was the source of the bad smell she experienced every time she got into the truck. That alone was enough to keep her in her seat for the rest of the ride home.

"I'll just stay here."

"I can wake you up when we get to Parry Sound."

"Thanks, but here's good."

"Suit yourself, but at least make yourself comfortable." He handed her a pillow from the floor between the seats.

"Thank you," she said, putting the pillow between her head and the window.

She rested her head on the pillow and closed her eyes and felt herself quickly drifting off to sleep. She opened her eyes one last time, and couldn't help noticing Konrad's face. The red lights on the truck's dashboard gave it an eerie sort of glow.

It was probably a result of exhaustion, or maybe the product of a wild imagination, but if she wasn't mistaken, the strange red lighting made Konrad look more like a demon than a man.

Amanda closed her eyes once more, and immediately drifted off into a deep, deep sleep.

— 2 —

Ron couldn't just sit around and wait for Amanda to return home. He had to do *something* about it, but what?

He knew he should go out looking for her, but she could be anywhere by now . . . a motel in town, some coffee shop out on the highway, maybe even on a bus to somewhere else. Even though it was unlike Amanda to run off for very long, Ron knew that if she decided she was going to leave, really leave, there was no telling where she might end up. And even if he looked for her, there was a chance that she didn't want to be found. If that was the case, he'd end up making an ugly scene somewhere trying to get her into the car and come home with him. That was the last thing Ron wanted right now, especially since it would remind Amanda of all the reasons why she'd left in the first place.

Looking for her seemed to be a dead end.

Ron sat on the couch, thinking.

But I have to look, he thought. *Even if I don't find her, at least when I tell her I looked for her it won't be a lie.*

He grabbed his jacket and headed out.

If nothing else, he could take a quick look around the trailer park. For all he knew, she might be sitting alone on some picnic table, looking at the moon.

It took him about twenty minutes to walk the park. He'd found a couple of teens drinking beer behind an empty trailer, and two younger girls smoking cigarettes out by the road, but there was no sign of Amanda anywhere.

As he headed back to the trailer, figuring he could make a call to the West Parry Sound Health Centre to see if she was there, he noticed that the lights were still on in Lisa Amato's trailer. Lisa was the closest thing Amanda had to a best friend, and if she was still awake there was a chance that Amanda had gone over there and was right now bitching and complaining to Lisa about that bastard Ron Stinson.

Ron knocked on the door.

"Come in."

Ron opened the trailer door and stepped inside. There was a light on in the living room, and another on in the kitchen. The air was filled with the smell of smoke, some of it tobacco but most of it weed. Lisa was laid-back on the couch, wearing a pair of tight jeans, a thin white T-shirt, and nothing on her feet. Judging by the press of her breasts and the clear outline of her nipples against the fabric of her shirt, she wasn't wearing a bra.

As Ron entered the room Lisa raised the beer bottle in her hand and said, "Hey, Ron, there's a cold one in the fridge with your name on it."

"Thanks," Ron said. "But not tonight."

"What? You turning down a beer?"

"It happens."

"Yeah, but not much. Are you feeling all right?" She laughed and took a slug of her beer, emptying it in a gulp.

"I'm looking for Amanda," he said. "Have you seen her tonight?"

"Don't tell me she's run off on you."

"She's just not home is all."

"Maybe she left you."

Ron felt himself wince at Lisa's suggestion. As drunk as she was, Lisa was able to figure it out. And it wasn't because Lisa was a genius, but because Ron was such an asshole and everyone knew that it was only a matter of time before Amanda got up the nerve to walk out on him for good.

"And maybe she's just gone out for a some fresh air."

Lisa laughed at that. "Right, and you'll be playing for the Maple Leafs next year."

Ron felt rage flair up inside him. People had been making that joke for years now and it still hurt as much as it ever did . . . even more with each year that went by. But Lisa was one to talk. She'd dropped out of school at seventeen to have an abortion and she'd spent the rest of her life waiting tables in every bar and lounge in Parry Sound. Some people even said she did tricks on the side. Ron didn't find that too hard to believe, but he'd never seen any proof of it either.

Ron wanted to stomp across the room and slap that silly grin off of Lisa's face, but he knew that wouldn't help anything. All he'd need right was to be arrested for assault and any hope he had of getting Amanda back would be gone right out the window.

"I hear they're short of hot dog vendors at the Air Canada Centre." Lisa laughed again.

Ron just looked at her, his face grim. "Do you know where Amanda is?"

"She's really gone, huh?" The smile was gone and all the playfulness seemed to have vanished from Lisa's voice.

"Yeah, she's really gone."

Slowly, the smile returned to Lisa's face. "As long as she's not around . . ." She grabbed the bottom of her T-shirt and began lifting it up, exposing her flat abs, and then her big right breast. ". . . why don't you stay awhile?"

Ron watched her touch the mouth of the beer bottle to

her nipple and was seriously tempted by the offer. But as much as he would have liked to stay, he couldn't. It'd be fun, but it wouldn't be right. He was supposed to be making a new start, after all.

"I'd love to, but I'm worried about Amanda."

"That never stopped you before," she said with a giggle as she slid her free hand down under the waistband of her jeans.

Ron had slept with Lisa a couple of times before, always after a fight. He'd never really had a problem with doing it before, but of course he was usually stoned or drunk when it happened.

"That was *before*."

Lisa looked at him critically. "Wow," she said. "I'm impressed. . . . What did Amanda do to deserve you?"

Ron wanted to answer her, but he couldn't think of a damn thing to say. Amanda had been good to him, a little too good in fact, and she deserved better than the likes of Ron Stinson . . . or at least a better version of the man that went by that name.

"If you see her," he said, "or she calls, let me know. All right?"

"Sure," Lisa said, waving him away and picking up the phone.

Ron turned to leave.

Behind him he could hear Lisa asking some guy named Lam if he'd like to come over.

— 3 —

The first thing she became aware of was the absence of movement. When she'd first dozed off she could remember the roll and hum of the truck as it moved down the highway . . . but now there was the familiar rattle of the engine, but they were no longer moving.

As if they'd stopped.

Pulled over to the side of the road.

Maybe we've reached Parry Sound, she thought.

If that was true, why hadn't he awakened her?

Amanda slowly opened her eyes. Her lids were heavy and it was a struggle to get them open, as if she were lifting a pair of lead weights.

It was still dark outside, still night.

Amanda tried to move but couldn't.

How could that be?

She closed her eyes and took a moment to try and orient herself. She was on her back, lying on her back with her arms and legs restrained. It seemed impossible, but she was strapped down so she couldn't move.

Her head too was secured by a thick strap bound tightly across her forehead. She could move her head from side to side and up and down, but just barely. She could hardly see the end of her arms, but her legs and feet were outside her field of vision.

What's going on? she tried to say, only to realize there was something big and round stuffed inside her mouth. She touched it with her tongue. A ball. What the hell was a ball muzzle doing in her mouth?

Just then, she felt a pinch on her left arm.

She flinched, but the straps prevented her from moving any more than a fraction of an inch.

The pain continued to burn in her arm as if something there was on fire.

She glanced down at her arm, pushing against the straps around her head with all the strength she could muster.

The driver . . . Konrad . . . had slid a needle under her skin, into a vein. The needle had a pale blue butterfly-shaped attachment and was connected to a thin plastic tube that was about a foot long. The tube ended with a sort of plastic cap.

That cap was open . . .

And there was blood leaking out of it.

At first, Konrad let the blood trickle from the tube, but when that proved too slow for him he began sucking on the end of it.

Sucking on the tube.

Amanda suddenly felt weak and drowsy.

This can't be happening, she thought.

It has *to be a dream . . .*

Only a dream . . .

She closed her eyes and drifted off to sleep once more, grateful that the horror she'd seen had been nothing more than a dream.

A nightmare.

Chapter 7

~ 1 ~

It had taken Constable Sharpe a while to get a map of the Province of Ontario that suited his purposes and that he could poke full of holes. There were plenty of maps that showed major roadways and exploded maps of major cities like Toronto, Ottawa, Kingston, and Brampton, but all of those maps had southern Ontario on one side, and northern Ontario on the other.

The province was just that big.

Americans always talk about how big Texas is, but Ontario puts that state to shame. Texas checks in at 266,803 square miles, while Ontario stretches out to 412,480 square miles, or roughly one and a half times bigger.

So Sharpe had to go looking for a map that had all of the major highways on it *and* the entire province on a single side.

When he'd found the map—made by Perly's and given away free at the Gino's Pizza in North Bay—he tacked it up on his wall so he could look at it easily when he needed to. Then he began sticking pins into the map in the locations where each of the five victims had been found.

He started with the fifth victim—Jane Doe 5—and

pressed a pin with a red head and tiny flag with the number 5 on it into the map on the west side of Highway 69 just north of Parry Sound.

Then he placed the other four pins in descending order.

Number four: west side of Highway 69, two hundred kilometers north of Parry Sound, just north of Estaire.

Number three: north side of Highway 17 near Spanish, 120 kilometers west of Sudbury.

Number two: south side of the intersection of Highways 101 and 144 southwest of Timmins.

Number one: north shore of Lake Superior near Terrace Bay, on the south side of Highway 17, two hundred kilometers east of Thunder Bay.

Jesus, thought Sharpe, *he couldn't have spread them out better if he'd thrown five darts up onto the wall at random.*

The pattern suggested that the killer regularly drove a route between Toronto and at least Thunder Bay, but more likely Toronto and Winnipeg, a three-day round-trip of over two thousand kilometers.

That's what the pattern *suggested,* but there was the nagging question about victim number two found near Timmins. Timmins was nearly three hundred kilometers off the route and was a six-hour round-trip. It was possible that the killer made a single trip up into Timmins and dumped a body while he was there, or maybe it was an unrelated killing that just happened to fit the pattern of the others.

Sharpe made a note to study the file on the second victim a little more closely.

And then he stared at the wall for a long, long time, hoping all the while that he wouldn't be needing any more pins.

— 2 —

There was light on her eyelids.

She opened her eyes, lifting the lids slowly until she could just make out her surroundings. The sky, she noted, was lighter than she remembered.

Almost dawn.

The truck was stopped. The engine was off, silent. Outside, some distance away, she could hear the roar of trucks and cars as they passed on the highway.

Must have stopped at a rest station, she thought.

She'd slept until morning but still felt tired. No, more than just tired. She felt weak, drained. Exhausted. She could hardly move her body and her arms and legs felt as if they were made of concrete and steel rather than flesh and blood.

And she ached. Her jaw was sore. Her arms and legs too. There were sharp pains burning across her rib cage and her forehead pounded with each beat of her heart.

What the hell happened to me? she wondered.

Then she opened her eyes more fully, realized where she was, and tried to gasp. The air wouldn't flow into her mouth and she had to choke and cough as the air slowly streamed into her lungs through her nose.

No dream, she screamed inside her head.

No nightmare.

She really was lying in the back of some man's truck, strapped down like a lab experiment, or maybe an exhibit at a fetish night at some downtown Toronto bar.

And there was a needle mark and bruise on her arm. . . .

My God, what's happening to me?

She twisted and turned against her restraints, slowly at first and then more and more forcefully. The straps cut into her skin, pressed hard against her bones, and the more she struggled the more pain they caused her. Frustrated, she suddenly flailed and kicked as hard as she could, but the straps remained steadfast and her situation only got worse.

She was out of breath and was frantically trying to get enough air into her lungs through her nose. Her nasal passages were clear, but she could barely keep up with her body's demands for oxygen. She was sweating too, which seemed to pull the straps even tighter against her skin. But the worst of it was that droplets of sweat were running off her forehead and into her eyes. It wouldn't have been much of a problem if her hands were free and she could wipe the sweat away, but she couldn't move and had to endure the lingering salty sting of her sweat as it burned against her eyeballs.

At last her breathing eased and she was able to lie still. It was obvious that remaining still and relaxed was the only way to make her situation even remotely bearable.

Her *situation*.

The word tumbled through her mind.

What kind of freak would do something like this?

The worst kind.

Amanda knew that lunatics and crazies passed through Parry Sound all the time, just like they did everywhere else in the world. But like most people she never expected her life would ever cross paths with one of them. Bad things always happened to other people—people you read about in the paper, or saw on television. When you read about them, or heard their story, all you did was take a moment, shake your head, and say, "What a shame." And then you went on with your life as if bad things were distanced from your own existence by hundreds of years and thousands of miles. And now, here she was in big bad trouble, feeling that same distance from the rest of the world with no hope of ever bridging the gap again.

Suddenly, she heard voices outside the truck. A man and a woman laughing.

She screamed, or tried to.

The ball gag was too full in her mouth, too tight against her lips, to let any air through. Her scream sounded like a muted moan and was caught and embraced by the curtains, pillows, and clothing surrounding her.

The voices faded, and then truck doors opened and closed. Then, nothing.

So close and yet so far.

Amanda lay still again, struggling to catch her breath.

Her struggles had made the inside of the truck warm and sticky. The sun was also getting brighter, shining beams of heat through the truck's windshield.

She was beginning to sweat just lying there breathing.

Where is he? she wondered. *Where the fuck is that asshole?*

The words tumbled over and over in her mind . . . until she drifted off into unconsciousness.

The sound of a door opening awoke Amanda sometime later.

A rush of cool air flooded the truck. It felt like winter against her skin, and smelled like spring to her nose and lungs.

She opened her eyes and blinked.

"Ah, you're awake," he said. "Good."

Amanda didn't move, didn't even try to look at him.

"I got you some breakfast," he said, lifting a bag of food into her field of vision.

She could smell it. Bacon and hash browns. Normally, she tried to stay away from such foods, but now the smell of them seemed like ambrosia to her. She began salivating and had to swallow to prevent herself from choking.

He removed the bag from view and showed her a tire iron.

"I'm going to take the strap from your head, and the gag from your mouth. . . ."

The man's breath was putrid, as if he'd eaten nothing but flies and dog shit all his life.

Amanda tried to hold her breath while he continued talking.

"If you call out, make any noise, or try anything funny, I'll smash your head in with this thing."

He paused and brought the tire iron closer to her eyes so she could get a good look at it. At first Amanda thought it was rusty, but there were tufts of skin and hair embedded in the grain of the steel, and what she'd first thought was rust was clearly dried blood—the blood of his previous victims, most likely.

"Do you understand me?"

She nodded as well as the strap on her head would allow.

"And even if you do everything I ask you, but do it too slowly or not to my satisfaction, I'll use it on your legs or hands so not only will you have to lie there, but you'll have to do it in utter agony. Do you understand?"

Again, Amanda tried to nod.

"Excellent." He raised his arms and undid the Velcro binding that held the strap tightly around Amanda's forehead.

When she was sure he'd finished talking, Amanda exhaled and took another breath.

He finished with the strap on her head and began work on the ball gag. Free of the restraint she tried to move her head, but it had been in one position so long it seemed to be locked into place.

As he worked to undo the ball gag, Amanda had the opportunity to take a long look at this man, Konrad Valeska, in the light of morning.

His face had the look and shape of a man's, but it was unnaturally long and slightly oval, like an egg with the larger part of it toward the back of his head. And he was not bald as she'd first thought. Not really. While his head was mostly bare, there were long wisps and tangled threads of pallid hair that virtually disappeared against the similarly pale white skin of his head and face. And his skin was *pale,* as if the man avoided the sun like some Victorian lady. And there was a sheen to his skin too, as if it was always cold and clammy no matter what the temperature outside. His nose was hooked and birdlike. Amanda remembered from a school lesson on eagles that the word to describe that nose was *aquiline.* His lips were pale too, only slightly distinguished from the rest of his face by a bluish purple tint. And when he spoke or smiled, Amanda could see that his teeth were a mess, scattered and ragged like a cob of corn that crows had had their way with. A few of the teeth had sharp points to them, but they looked rotten around the base as if they might fall out of his head the moment he bit into anything solid.

Finally, there were his eyes. They were a pale color, somewhere between green and yellow with a smattering of red dancing around the edges of the irises. And one of the eyes was slightly off center—maybe the right eye, maybe the left—making his eyes the kind that were absolutely impenetrable. You could stare into them for days, but they would never be a window to his soul. And it was so *easy* to gaze into them. They were glorious and horrible all at once, like a car crash or a bloodstain on the sidewalk—repulsive to look at, but mystically drawing your gaze until you were unable to look away . . . no matter how much you wanted to.

"There," he said, hanging up the ball gag on the hook above her. "Now you can eat."

"I'm not hungry," she said, mouthing the words slowly

so her stiff jaw and sore lips could say the words correctly. She actually was hungry, but didn't want to eat anything because she was afraid that he would use it against her, like she owed him something for providing her with food.

She knew it was a crazy thought. He had already kidnapped her, was restraining her against her will, and she had gotten a good enough look at him to be able to describe him to police or pick him out of a lineup . . . all of which meant he would probably kill her when he was finished with her. And here she was worrying about being indebted to him for a bit of food.

"Nonsense," he said. "You need your strength. You have to eat."

What do I need my strength for? she thought. *It doesn't take all that much to lie here. The straps make it real easy.*

He opened the bag and pulled out a small Styrofoam container filled with bacon strips. He popped open the container, lifted one of the strips with a pinch of his fingers, and held it over her face.

She kept her mouth tightly closed.

"Come on, eat!"

Amanda shook her head.

"Shall I get the tire iron?"

She thought about it a moment, then opened her mouth.

"Smart," he said. "The more you cooperate with me the longer you'll live."

Amanda felt a chill run the length of her body as she realized his plans for her definitely included murder. She'd suspected it before, but had been holding out hope that he would somehow let her go. Obviously that wasn't going to happen.

He dangled another strip of bacon over her mouth and said, "Again."

She opened her mouth and took the bacon a little more hungrily. If he intended to kill her, then there was only one thing she could do. She had to do as he said so she could live as long as possible, which would give her more time to figure out a way to escape.

She chewed the bacon slowly, thinking about it.

Escape.

It seemed impossible at the moment, but she'd come up with something. If nothing else, she'd have plenty of time to think. . . .

"Another one," he said. "It's good for your blood."

She ate the rest of the bacon quickly, then started on the hash browns. The potatoes were dry and she nearly choked on the second mouthful she ate. After that he helped her by lifting her head and putting a bottle of juice to her lips. She drank as much as she could before he pulled the bottle roughly away.

"More," she said.

"No!" he answered. "The more you drink the more you'll have to pee. It's too early to let you out."

Amanda didn't understand what he meant, but she figured that at some point he'd have to release her so she could relieve herself. If that was true, then there might be a chance for her to get away.

It gave Amanda hope.

He wrapped up the rest of the food and put it back in the bag, presumably for later.

She could have eaten more, but she'd had enough to tide her over for a while. She certainly felt better and stronger than she had just a few minutes ago. If she could keep her strength, then her chances of escaping would be that much better.

For a moment she felt confident she'd be able to get away. Somewhere along the line this man . . . this asshole of a man was going to make a mistake and before he knew what happened she'd be gone.

But her confidence quickly waned at the sight of the plastic package containing the needle and tube.

Christ! she thought. *Not again!*

He peeled open the package and took out the tube.

"Fresh needle every time," he said. "Better for you, better for me."

Amanda just looked at the needle and tube as he strung them out to their full length.

"You know, you can't buy these in drugstores. You have to be a company licensed to collect blood, like a laboratory or hospital." He laughed. "So I have to have them stolen for me."

When the idle conversation ended, the smile vanished from his face and he suddenly became all business. He tied off her arm with a rubber tourniquet and began prodding the underside of her left arm with his fingers in search of a vein. His touch was anything but gentle, especially since the arm was still tender and sore from the last time he'd poked her.

"Ah," he muttered.

He drew his finger in a line against her skin, presumably along the outline of a vein. And then there was a burning sensation in her arm as the needle slid through the skin and into the vein.

Amanda wanted to look away, but found she couldn't. She had to look down at her arm, and at him, to confirm what he was doing there.

He's sucking my blood out of a tube in my fucking arm! she screamed inside her mind. *Sucking my fucking blood!*

He took two, three, four long pulls on the tube, as if he were drinking soda through a straw.

"Ah," he said. "Excellent!"

Amanda felt as if she were going to throw up, but the

feeling passed as her body suddenly felt weak. Her eyelids had become heavy and she could barely keep them open.

How could that have happened so fast? she wondered. *How much blood did he take from me?*

As she drifted in and out of consciousness, she was aware of the needle being pulled from her arm, and the tube and the needle being put away in what sounded like a steel box below her. Then there was movement inside the cab as he moved into the driver's seat and got the truck started.

The rhythmic rumble of the truck made it even harder for Amanda to stay awake. She fought against her body's natural desire for rest long enough to be aware of the truck moving. But then it stopped a short time later and was shut off completely, as if it was being parked for the day.

In moments the entire cab had been blacked out and the inside of the truck was shrouded in darkness.

There was movement again as he joined her in the back, above or below her, she couldn't be sure.

And then . . . silence.

He was asleep, breathing oh so slowly.

She fought to stay conscious for a little while longer, but it was obvious to her that he'd be sleeping through the day and if that was the case, then she might as well get some rest herself.

As sleep slowly overtook her, she marveled at the irony of her situation. As a result of her hurried attempt to get away, she'd become more trapped than she'd ever been in her life.

Chapter 8

~ 1 ~

Ron lifted his head and looked at the digital clock on
the stand next to the bed. The red numbers blinked *12:00.*
. . . They'd been doing that for days since he'd never bothered to set the clock after the power had gone out in the
trailer park last Monday. He reached over for his watch
and saw it was just after seven. He rolled onto his side
and set the clock. Then he lay back and said, "Amanda?"

He hoped to hear her voice answering him from the
kitchen where she'd be making coffee, or breakfast or
maybe just reading the paper. But there was no answer.

You really did it this time, didn't you? he thought as he
stared at the ceiling. *She's gone this time, and she ain't
coming back.*

Ron wondered how long he'd be able to live in the trailer
without Amanda around to handle the bills. Not long. The
landlord didn't care for him all that much. He *loved*
Amanda, always had a kind word for her, but he absolutely
despised Ron. But Ron didn't blame the guy. It didn't take
a genius to see a bruise over Amanda's eye and figure Ron
was the bastard who did it. Once the man learned Amanda
was gone, he'd be chasing Ron out by the end of the month
whether he had the rent money or not.

But it would be harder for him to get rid of you if you

had the money, he thought. That meant getting a job. Ron wasn't thrilled by the prospect of finding work, but he knew he had to. Besides, if Amanda ever came back, she'd be impressed by the fact that he was working steady. Might be just the thing to bridge the chasm between them, or at the very least, give her a sign that things had changed.

A job.

Ron had worn out his welcome at most places around town, but there were still a few people who might be willing to hire him back on. Minor league coaches mostly, who would expect him to help coach their teams come winter. Ron wasn't interested in coaching kids since that was something you did in your forties and fifties. But he needed a job now and he'd worry about the conditions of employment after he began working.

He washed up, got dressed, and headed out to the Double-B Landscaping company on the edge of town. The owner of the company, Bobby Bloxam, was a long-time minor hockey coach in town. Ron had played for him in his peewee year, taking the team all the way to the provincial championship. It was the only championship season Bloxam had ever had, and the man had always been grateful to Ron for giving him an All-Ontario title.

When he got to the Double-B yard the men were all out in the lot drinking coffee and smoking cigarettes before they got onto the trucks and headed out for the day's jobs.

"Bobby around?" Ron asked one of the men.

"Still in the office."

"Thanks."

The office was a small room set to one side of the garage where the company's trucks and equipment were serviced and stored. It was full of plows and snowblowers in the summer, lawn mowers and grass trimmers in winter. It smelled of oil and grease and just a little bit like cut grass.

Ron knocked on the open door and stepped into the office.

"Bobby?"

The man looked up from the paperwork on his desk. He was a small, round-headed man with thick glasses. Ron had worked for the man for a few weeks one summer about four years ago, but his face looked a lot older than Ron remembered. It was deeply creased and etched by the passage of years. He was wearing a faded Parry Sound Minor Hockey Association baseball cap that had sweat stains all around the bottom band.

"What are you doing here?"

Ron was a little surprised by the question. He'd expected something more along the lines of *Hey, Ron, how ya doin'?*

Ron smiled. "Lookin' for work."

Bloxam nodded slightly and ran his tongue over one corner of his mouth while he looked Ron over. "That so?"

"Yeah."

"Shouldn't you be playin' hockey somewhere?"

Ron hadn't expect this kind of reception, but he understood why it was happening. Bloxam loved hockey, and he'd seen kids give everything they had to the sport only to be let down by their lack of talent. And here was Ron Stinson, the best player to come out of Parry Sound since Bobby Orr, and he'd pissed it all away. The man probably looked at what Ron did with his gifts as a slap in the face to anyone who ever dreamed of playing in the NHL.

Ron said nothing, but it was obvious the man wanted an answer. "Yeah, I should be, but I'm here looking for work, instead."

"You know, the last time you worked for me, you ruined a lawn mower by running it over a pile of rocks. Cost me three hundred in parts to get it working again."

Ron just stood there. He couldn't remember ever doing that, but he knew that it was possible that he had. He'd been drunk on the job plenty of times, and the fact that he'd been working cutting machinery wouldn't have stopped him. He was Ron Stinson, after all—*the* Ron Stinson—and his charmed life wasn't going to end in some accident while he was cutting grass.

"I'll do better this time around."

Bloxam looked at him.

"How bad you need a job?"

Ron looked at his shoes. He wasn't used to squirming. When something like this happened before he'd throw his hands in the air and say, "Fuck this!" and walk away. That was the easy thing to do. This . . . this was hard.

"My girlfriend walked out. There's going to be bills . . ."

Bloxam just looked at him.

Ron felt compelled to say more. "And I got to do something to turn things around."

The man's expression didn't change. "You'd say anything to get a job right now, wouldn't you?"

"Probably, but it also happens to be true."

Bloxam smiled, but only for a moment. "I've got a couple of guys off sick this week. You can fill in for them if you want, but I haven't got any full-time work right now. Understand?"

Ron nodded.

"Fine, you can start tomorrow."

"How 'bout today?"

Bloxam was silent a moment while he studied Ron.

"Hardeep!" he called out.

A few seconds later a tall, wiry East-Indian man with a beard came into the office. He was pretty young, maybe even still in his teens.

"Yes?"

"This is Ron. Take him on your crew today."

"Sure," said Hardeep. Then he turned to face Ron and a look of recognition crossed his face. "Hey, aren't you Ron Stinson, the hockey player?"

Ron nodded humbly, almost embarrassed to be recognized.

Bloxam was shaking his head. "He was Ron Stinson the hockey player, now he's Ron Stinson the grass cutter."

Hardeep had a confused look on his face, like he didn't know what to make of Bloxam's comment. "Oh, okay."

"Now get out of here."

Hardeep left the office without another word.

Ron looked over at Bloxam and said, "Thanks."

"If you want to thank me," he said, "don't screw up."

Ron nodded, then followed Hardeep out of the office.

– 2 –

Constable Sharpe pulled back the chair, set the Tim Hortons cup down on top of the desk in the constable's room at the detachment, and had a seat. Once he was settled in, he cracked the plastic cover on his coffee, trying to tear and fold it back neatly, but making a mess of the job. Finally, he just tore the tab off and sipped the coffee through a large hole in the cover. Although getting to the coffee could sometimes be an ordeal, the coffee itself was great as usual. He couldn't imagine starting his day without a medium double-double.

With his morning coffee warming his insides, Sharpe switched on the computer and waited for the machine to boot itself up. He'd sent out a description of the victim to other police jurisdictions across Canada and the United States and was hoping for some kind of help in identifying her.

He scrolled down the list of messages, but they were

mostly internal memos along with a few personal e-mails, including one from the sergeant inviting him to go for a run on their lunch hour. Sharpe could use the exercise, but the sergeant's idea of a run was five kilometers, which always left Sharpe drained for the rest of the day.

He was about to click on *reply* and say, "No, thanks," but he decided he'd rather just speak to the sergeant on his way out of the detachment. That way he'd be able to let him know what was going on with the case *and* tell him he couldn't make the run all at the same time. The computer was a great tool, especially for those who knew how to use it, but for old-timers like Sharpe, there was no substitute for good old-fashioned human contact.

Sharpe put aside the keyboard and cleared the desk so he could spend the morning going through the files pertaining to the other victims found along the highway. The crime bureau investigators working the northern murders had sent down copies of their files overnight so Sharpe could bring himself up to speed on the investigation. The idea was that Sharpe would conduct the investigation in and around Parry Sound while they continued working on the earlier murders. All the while they'd be in close contact with each other, speaking at least once a day to confer and compare notes on each new development.

The files were about a foot thick and would take Sharpe the better part of the day to wade through them all. He slipped on a pair of reading glasses and opened up the first file.

"Hey, Sharpie!" someone called from across the room.

Sharpe looked up and saw one of the newer constables—a short, squat block of muscle named Sean Boneham—approaching with a sheaf of papers in his hand.

Why was it all the rookies looked like Schwarzenegger? he wondered. When he'd joined the force Sharpe had weighed 185 pounds, and had been one of the biggest in his class at the Ontario Police College. These days he was dwarfed by the majority of recruits, including some of the women.

"Fax for you from the California Highway Patrol."

"California?"

Boneham shrugged, his shoulders barely moving up on his short, thick neck.

"Thanks," Sharpe said, taking the papers.

He flipped quickly through them, then began reading the cover letter. The fax was from a liaison officer from the highway patrol letting him know that the description of the latest victim sounded like a good match for a young girl who'd been missing from northern California for several weeks.

If this turned out to be correct, then Jane Doe 5's name was Yvonne Parker. She was from San Francisco and had been spending the summer hitchhiking across the country. She'd been checking in with her parents every few days, either by phone or by mail, but the contact had stopped two weeks ago, the last letter bearing a Winnipeg postmark.

It was only a probable match at best, but Sharpe had a strong feeling that this was the girl they'd found on the roadside. To prove it, they'd faxed a set of dental records, which Sharpe could bring to Dr. Casey's office so she could make a positive ID.

Sharpe put the fax aside and took another sip of his coffee. Somehow it had gotten cold while he'd been reading.

Identifying the victim was a good piece of news, but it didn't do much in terms of helping Sharpe catch the killer. If anything, the news extended the killer's operating area all the way into Manitoba. In theory, the victim could have been picked up anywhere between Winnipeg and Parry Sound—a route over 3,400 kilometers long.

Sharpe let out a sigh. These things were supposed to help him catch the killer, not make it more difficult for him.

But at least it wasn't all bad.

If nothing else, identifying the victim might bring closure to the missing girl's family, as well as give them some remains to bury in a proper funeral ceremony.

Not much of a bright side, but it was the best he could do under the circumstances.

Sharpe finished his coffee in a gulp, pocketed his reading glasses, and gathered up the faxes to bring to Dr. Casey.

— 3 —

Ron had dropped by the Big Wheel on his way home from work to see if Amanda was there. Stephen, the short-order cook, told him it was her day off and he hoped she was spending it relaxing.

"She's a good worker," he said. "She's earned it."

Ron smiled at the man and left, hoping that since it was her day off, she hadn't really left for good. She'd probably come back that afternoon, or at worst maybe late tonight, still in plenty of time before work the next morning.

Yeah, that's probably what she did.

He arrived at the trailer around six-thirty but there wasn't a single light on in the house.

"Amanda," he said through the open doorway.

No answer.

In fact, the trailer was exactly as he'd left it. There was no sign that anyone had been there all day.

Ron closed the door behind him and dragged his feet into the living room. He'd been excited about getting home and seeing Amanda again, but now that he knew she wasn't there, his body began feeling the effects of the day's hard work. His ankles ached, his hands were raw, and his shoulders felt as if someone had shoved a knitting needle right through the muscles. And his ribs burned. He probably had a cracked rib or two, or maybe a bit of cartilage between the ribs had been torn. Whatever it was, it would heal in another day or two, but working for a landscaper wasn't going to make the healing process any easier.

He walked over to the fridge, opened it up, and instinctively reached inside for a beer, stopping himself short as he realized there weren't any. *One day of hard work and you're already looking for a beer,* he thought. *No, thanks.* He picked up the half-empty two-liter bottle of President's Choice Cola and drank it straight from the bottle.

It wasn't beer, but it wasn't bad.

He began searching the fridge for leftovers.

After eating, Ron surfed up and down the television dial but couldn't concentrate on any one show for more than a few minutes. His mind kept coming back to Amanda.

Where could she have gone?

She'd run off before, but she'd always come back in a few hours after she let off a little steam. It just wasn't like her to stay away this long. If anything, she should have called him to rub his nose in it, asking him how it felt to be alone and suggesting he get used to it. That would be more like Amanda, but this silence . . . it was all wrong.

He wanted nothing more than to just go to bed and not

worry about it, but he couldn't. He wanted to be confident that Amanda would be crawling back home to him
any minute, but he wasn't. That was stuff the old Ron
would have done. The old Ron would have borrowed or
stolen some money, bought a case of Export, and drunk
it all waiting for Amanda to walk through the door. Ron
didn't know why, but he just couldn't bring himself to do
that anymore. He had to do something more responsible,
something more grown up.

I could go to the police, he thought. That was the right
thing to do. She might be in trouble, after all.

Ron got up off the couch and headed out to the OPP
detachment on Bay Street.

He'd never been inside it before, but it wasn't for a lack
of trying. He'd been drunk and disorderly plenty of times
before, even been in a bunch of bar fights, but the fact
that he'd been a hockey star in town had saved him from
ever being locked up. Ron liked to think the police always spared him for his sake, but something in the back
of his mind told him that they did it to save the Town of
Parry Sound the embarrassment of discovering their latest hockey star was little more than a drunken bum.

There was a civilian on the other side of the door, a
custodian or maybe a cleaner, locking it up for the night.

"Can I help you?" the woman asked.

"Yeah, I'd like to, uh . . . report a missing person."

The woman pulled the door open a crack and said,
"What did you say?"

"My girlfriend's been gone for a while now. I want to
report her missing."

The woman opened the door fully and let Ron inside.
"Have a seat," she said. "I'll get somebody to come talk
to you."

Ron sat down on a stiff wooden bench. While he
waited he glanced around at the walls, reading the posters

about community initiatives organized by the police, like Toys for Tots, and others warning about the dangers of drinking and driving.

A few minutes later a short, stocky young constable came out to meet him. Ron immediately recognized him as Constable Boneham. He'd played against Boneham in bantam hockey and the guy had had no talent at all. He'd hung on to his dream of turning pro by playing tough, managing to get a Major Junior tryout in Ottawa only to find that there were plenty of tough guys in Major Junior, most of whom could also skate and score goals as well as fight. He'd obviously bulked up over the years, and looked like he could bench press a cruiser if he put his mind to it. Boneham was the last guy Ron wanted to see at the detachment since he'd have an opinion about Ron and how he'd wasted his talent.

"Hey, Ron, what's up?"

"I, uh . . . want to report a missing person."

The officer nodded. "Tell me about it inside," he said, turning around and heading back into the detachment.

Ron followed the man to a desk in the middle of a large room that had several desks for officers to work at.

"Who's missing?"

Ron had to look at his hands to say the words. "My girlfriend," he said. "Amanda Peck."

"How long she been gone?"

"Since last night."

Boneham looked at Ron for a few moments, as if studying him. "You guys have a fight?"

Ron's first instinct was to lie, but his first instincts had always turned out to be wrong. Instead, he told the truth. "Yeah," he said at last.

"Were you drinking?"

Again, "Yeah."

"Did you hit her?"

He didn't want to answer that question, because he couldn't really be sure. He knew he'd been physical with her, but he couldn't recall if he'd hit her or not. "I might have pushed her around a bit."

The look of disappointment on Boneham's face was obvious. Ron got ready to hear some kind of speech, knowing he deserved it . . . and worse. But instead, the constable continued with his questions.

"She's left you before, right?"

Ron sighed. "Plenty of times."

"And she's always come back?"

"Always, but not this time."

Boneham put down his pen and stopped talking notes. "Look, Ron, women run off all the time. That don't mean they're missing. From what you just told me she had every right to leave. Smart thing to do, if you ask me, since she might eventually end up in the hospital and you in jail."

Ron lowered his head. "I know."

"Besides, based on what you told me, I can't really consider her missing for a few more hours. And even then, I'd be hard pressed to classify her as missing."

"I understand," said Ron. "But even if she was gone for good, she would have told one of her friends, or maybe even called *me* up to let me have it. Hell, I know I deserve it. But there's been no sign of her."

Boneham was silent, listening patiently, as if he was seriously considering what Ron was saying. Ron hated to admit it, but whatever Boneham thought about him personally, he wasn't letting it get in the way of him doing his job.

"And the thing is, Amanda doesn't have a car. So if she's gone anywhere, she probably hitched a ride out on the highway. Normally that wouldn't bother me, but with the body they found out there the other day . . . well, I'm worried about her."

Boneham's face had changed. He wasn't just listening anymore, but looked gravely concerned.

"She was hitchin' a ride?"

"Yeah, probably."

Boneham got up from the desk. "Follow me."

Ron followed the officer across the room.

"Sharpie," he said, as they neared a desk occupied by another, older constable that Ron had seen around town but didn't really know all that well.

"Yeah?" the man said, looking up from the papers on his desk.

"This is Ron Stinson," Boneham said.

"Ron."

Boneham turned to face Ron. "This is Constable Sharpe. I want you to tell him everything you just told me."

Ron nodded. "Okay."

Then he sat down in a chair and told his story again.

Chapter 9

Amanda opened her eyes.

It was dark inside the cab.

Dark outside too.

They were moving.

She tried to speak, but found that the ball gag was back over her mouth.

Her jaw muscles ached.

She let out a grunt, trying to get the driver's attention.

"Ah," he said, glancing over his right shoulder. "So you are now awake."

Another grunt, and a kick of her leg. The leg was too firmly strapped down to move more than an inch, but the straps themselves made loud *cricking* noises as they stretched taut against her leg.

"Full of energy this evening, I see."

Fuck you! she screamed inside her head.

"Don't waste your strength trying to free yourself. You'll only grow more weak."

She stopped squirming, if nothing else than to give the appearance of cooperation.

The truck slowed as the driver, Konrad Valeska, geared down with a rev of the engine between each shift, and gently applied the brakes. When the truck was safely stopped on the shoulder, he left the engine idling and crawled back into the sleeper to undo her gag. "I've found that it's always better to have someone to talk to," he said.

"Fuck off!" she spat.

He shook his head in disappointment. "Such language. Am I supposed to be shocked, or offended?"

"Go to hell!"

A smile broke across his face and his teeth, his ugly rotten teeth, became exposed. "My dear girl, what makes you think I haven't already been there?" His voice trailed away in a laugh that gave Amanda the creeps.

"Now," he said, holding up the gag. "You'll either speak to me with a civil tongue or not at all. Understand?" He lifted the gag a bit higher to emphasize his point.

She nodded as best the head restraint would allow. She remembered drifting off to sleep without the strap being bound across her forehead, but he must have replaced it—as well as the ball gag—while she slept.

"And I won't hesitate to use the tire iron to break your bones if you get unruly." It was a statement more than a threat, but it was just as effective as any warning.

"I'll be good," she said, even though the words made her feel sick.

"Excellent," he said. "And to show you that I can be kind, I'll free your head so you can be more comfortable. If nothing else, it will make it easier for you to speak."

He undid the strap. Amanda tried to move her head, but her neck was too stiff and sore to allow any range of movement. There was also a cool feeling across her forehead, as if the skin there had become raw and covered with bloody sores that were now drying in the cool night air.

"Better?"

"Yes, thank you."

He gave a satisfied nod, put away the gag, and got back behind the wheel.

In minutes they were back on the road.

Amanda wondered where they were going, but that question was way down on the list of things she wanted to know. Number one was, "Why are you doing this to me?"

There was no response from Konrad for the longest time; then he said, "There is no *why* to it. I simply *must*."

Amanda didn't understand his answer, but she wasn't about to waste time pondering it. "If, if you let me go, I promise I won't tell anyone about this."

"Not your boyfriend?"

"No."

"Not your family?"

"No."

"And not the police?"

"No, of course not."

"Liar!" he said. "The moment I let you go, you'll go straight to the nearest police station and, what's the term? Ah . . . spill your guts to them." He laughed under his breath at that.

"No, I swear I won't."

He put a hand up to silence her. She didn't exactly want to stop talking, but his hand seemed powerful somehow, commanding, and for a moment she was unable to say anything more.

"Please," he said, a hint of exasperation in his voice. "I suggest that you not treat me like one of your small-town redneck buffoons. I might look like a fool in your eyes, but I assure you, I am not."

Amanda had a feeling he was right. "Sorry," she said.

They continued on for several minutes with neither of them saying a word. There were a million questions whirling through Amanda's mind, but she couldn't just ask them as they came to her, she had to be more specific with her queries so his answers couldn't be so evasive.

"Why do you stick the tube in my arm?" she asked at last.

"Because my teeth are all rotten."

She didn't understand. "What's the needle for?"

"For your blood."

"What do you want with my blood?"

"I need it to survive."

"What, like a vampire?" she asked.

"No, not *like* a vampire. I *am* a vampire."

Amanda felt the tiny glimmer of hope she'd been holding on to slowly trickle away. She'd been praying the man was just a little bit crazy, but now it was obvious that he was an A-1 nut bar.

A psycho.

In-*fucking*-sane.

"A vampire?" she said, a bit of a laugh edging her voice.

"Yes."

"Driving a truck?"

"Why not driving a truck?"

"Well, because vampires . . . they live in castles and—"

"And they are all counts and barons, right?"

"Yeah."

"Or rock stars all dressed in black, wearing mascara and nail polish, screaming about being damned for all eternity?"

Amanda said nothing. He'd basically outlined most of the mental images she had of vampires, at least the ones she'd picked up from movies and television.

"And good-looking, too. Right? Vampires are supposed to be good-looking. Noble and regal. Not fat and foolish like me."

She'd obviously struck a nerve. The man was on a roll and it didn't look as if he was about to stop until he'd thoroughly vented his spleen.

"It's all Hollywood bullshit!" he cried. "Bram Stoker described Dracula as a *tall old man, clean-shaven save for a long white moustache*. Sure, he was dressed in black from head to foot, but he was also *without a single speck of color about him anywhere*. Does that sound like Bela Lugosi to you? Or Christopher Lee, or Frank Langella, or Gary Oldman, or even Tom Cruise? He played a vampire too, you know. Feh!" He paused a moment and Amanda could almost picture him shaking his head in disgust. "Max Shreck . . . now there was a vampire."

"Who's Max Shreck?" Amanda said.

He sighed. "You see, the greatest, most accurate portrayal of a vampire on film and you don't even know who he is."

"Sorry."

"I suppose you haven't read many books."

"A few." Amanda said. She'd read a few paperbacks by the more popular authors like Stephen King and Dean Koontz, even a few by . . . "I've read some Anne Rice."

"Oh, yes. The woman who wrote her *Vampire Chronicles* to find out what it might be like to be a vampire . . ." His voice trailed off and Amanda couldn't be sure if he was laughing or crying. "More than a dozen books and she still hasn't got a clue."

"I liked the books I read."

"Of course you did, they are fantasies. Good stories, but hardly what it's like, what it's really like to be a vampire."

He went silent again, but Amanda knew he was just resting up for another rant.

"The vampires of fiction are all rich of course, as if all one had to do was deposit a dollar in the bank and watch it grow over the centuries. But bank tellers are suspicious of customers whose accounts are active for more than a hundred years. The truth is, money makes the mortal world go around so vampires have to work to earn money in order to be able to live among mortals."

"That's why you drive a truck?" Amanda asked.

"Yes-s-s, but that's not the only reason. You see, in the books, it is oh so easy for vampires to find food, sometimes feeding on three or four mortals a night. Ha! You mortals can be stupid, but even you get curious when someone goes missing. Can you imagine three or four people a night, gone! Why, there would be police on every corner . . ." He paused, and resumed speaking in a softer voice. "It was easier in the old days. People were isolated from one another. You could ravage a town and move onto the next before the news even got there. Or for a few coins you could have someone bring you a mortal to feed upon. Now . . . now people are connected by radio and television, cell phones and the Internet. A child goes missing on one side of the country and they are looking for her on the other side before the sun goes down. Don't get me wrong, it's not *impossible* to feed, it's just very difficult. You have to know what you're doing. You can't always give in to blood lust. It's a constant battle just for survival, and to win it, you have to be cold and calculating . . . smart."

"And you're smart?" Amanda said, knowing he was crazy.

"Yes, I am. You think it silly for a vampire to drive a truck, but as a truck driver I am always on the move. I can feed on a mortal every few days, then leave them on the side of the road thousands of kilometers apart so the authorities never connect the victims. And thanks to the more depraved of your species, there are bodies turning up on the sides of roads all over the world that are not of my doing. And even if my presence arouses suspicion, I can simply move along and start feeding somewhere else."

"So why here, in northern Ontario?"

"Why not? I have to be somewhere. . . . Besides, the nights are very long here at this time of year. And the farther north I go, the less daylight I have to worry about."

Amanda hated to admit it, but the nights were pretty long in the fall and winter, which would suit a vampire—a real vampire—perfectly. "Sounds like you've got it all figured out."

"It's a hard life. Almost the opposite of the lives of the vampires you read about. Fictional vampires always operate above the law, roaming freely from country to country for hundreds of years without a care in the world. While we do live for hundreds of years, it's a life that's above nothing. Because of our longevity, and because of our thirst for blood, we are forced to live at the bottom of the ladder, not the top."

Amanda could almost taste the bitterness in his words.

"Try getting a new driver's license every sixty years, or a new passport every century. People get suspicious when you don't grow any older in twenty-five years, when they never see you during the day, or they can't remember you ever eating a fruit or a vegetable."

Or see you suck the blood out of somebody's arm, Amanda thought.

"But I've survived. My kind always does." His voice was quiet now, almost wistful. It was as if his anger had run its course and he'd become exhausted from spitting such vitriol. "I don't mind being a truck driver, not really. The money's okay, and there's always someone looking for a ride so there's never a shortage of mortals to feed on . . . all I have to do is stop, open the door, and smile."

The words sent a chill down Amanda's spine. *Which is exactly how I ended up in this predicament,* she thought.

They rode along in silence for several minutes.

"What are you going to do with me?"

"Oh, feed off of you for a few more days, maybe a week."

No mention of sex. Amanda took that to be a good sign. "And what will you do with me after you f-feed off me?"

"Why, dump you on the side of the highway like the others. What else?"

Chapter 10

It was her second night strapped in the back of the madman's truck. She'd had a bit to eat and drink but she hadn't relieved herself in close to twenty-four hours.

"I have to pee," she said.

"Sorry, but I'm not stopping."

"Please, I really have to go."

"You're going to have to hold it for a while."

"If you don't stop I swear I'll do it in my pants."

He let out a little laugh. "What makes you think that will bother me? You'll be the one that's all wet."

Shit! Amanda thought. *No wonder it smells so bad in here.* Dirt, old blood, and fresh piss were one potent combination.

She really did have to go to the bathroom, but that wasn't the reason she was pressing him so hard. She'd been thinking of ways to escape, and going to the bathroom, or even relieving herself by the side of the road, seemed like a real possibility. It would get her unstrapped and out of the truck, which were two things she'd never be able to do on her own.

And so, she was giving it a try.

"I've got to do the other one too," she said, matter-of-factly. That was a lie, but *what the hell!* "I suppose that won't bother you either."

He was silent for a while, then said, "There's a rest stop coming up in a few kilometers. You can do your business, but if you're thinking about getting away, think again."

Of course he was suspicious of her, but what was he going to do, follow her into the stall? Amanda thought about that for a while and came to the conclusion that he might just do that. At this time of night there wouldn't be many people around and he could almost walk her into a bathroom with a leash around her neck if he wanted.

Still, it was a chance. . . .

"I just have to go to the bathroom."

"Fine."

A few minutes later the truck began to slow. She could feel the vehicle pulling to the right and slowing further as it—she hoped—made its way through a parking lot.

Finally they came to a stop.

He engaged the parking brake and a shriek of air cut through the night.

He climbed into the back and stood over her. He began undoing the straps on her feet and legs—*rip! rip! rip!*—then stopped to look at her.

Amanda turned her head so she wouldn't have to look at his face and gaze into his eyes.

But he grabbed her head and turned it back so she was staring right at him. He held her there for a few moments, then let go of her head. As much as she wanted to turn away, even close her eyes, she found that she could not.

She just *had* to look at him.

And the longer she did, the more dizzy she felt.

"I will help you to the bathroom. On the way you will speak to no one. When you get to the bathroom you will go directly to a stall. There, you will do what you must, and as soon as you are finished, you will return to me. I will help you back to the truck and you will return to your place here . . ." His voice trailed off, but the words seemed to continue to creep into her mind, into her body, into her soul.

"Do you understand?"

"Yes," she said, even though she wanted to tell him off. "I understand."

"Good." He resumed undoing the straps.

When her legs were free, she tried to move them. They ached something fierce. She could barely bend her knee and it hurt even to move her ankle. Then came the arms. She wanted nothing more than to raise her hand up and scratch his eyes out, but she couldn't do it. *Something* wouldn't allow her to do it. Her arms felt as if they were weighed down by rocks and cement. She lifted her arm at the elbow and the joint crackled like a piece of year-old kindling.

How can I escape, she thought, *when I can't even move?*

He put a hand behind her neck to lift her into a sitting position.

She could feel his bare hand against the skin at the back of her neck. *It's so cold,* she thought. *As if he were dead.* He slid a hand under her knees and lifted her up. Then he turned around and placed her in the passenger seat. Without a word he climbed over the driver's seat and got out of the truck.

This is it! she thought. *I could get up, run away . . . or maybe just lock the doors so he can't get in, then honk the horn until someone notices, comes running to save me. Save me!*

She tried lifting her hand . . .

The lock to the door was right there, less than a foot away. All she had to do was raise her hand and push the button, just touch it with one of her fingers, and the door would be locked and he wouldn't be able to get in.

. . . but her hand wouldn't move.

She knew what she wanted to do, but she couldn't do it.

He's got some kind of power over me, she realized. *He gave me instructions about what I must do and locking the doors wasn't in there. I can't get away . . . because he won't let me.*

She wanted to cry, but the tears wouldn't come.

The door suddenly popped open.

He reached up and lifted her out of the seat. Lifted her out of the seat as if she weighed little more than a dog. She even felt light in his arms, as if she could fly away if she were given half the chance.

Gently, he eased her down onto her own two feet. Her legs felt like wet noodles and it took several tries before she could even stand on her own.

His hand slid across her back and under her right arm.

"This way," he said, guiding her toward a building that housed a set of men's and women's washrooms.

As Amanda slowly put one foot in front of the other, she glanced around to try and get a sense of where she was. It was no rest stop she recognized. There was a service station across the lot, and the building they were headed toward looked like a restaurant, but they were approaching it from behind. The washrooms were just inside the door, meaning no one would be around to see her enter the building.

And then, as if by some miracle, there was a man coming out of the restaurant through the rear doors. He was a tall and powerfully built black man who looked as if he could take care of himself, and rescue a woman in distress. Best of all, he was staring at her and Konrad with a curious look on his face.

Amanda tried crying out, screaming, but her jaw was

slack and her tongue numb. The words bubbled out of her lips like slurred baby talk.

"You okay?" the man said.

Konrad shook his head in dismay. "I had a bottle of wine in the truck," he said. "She said she was just going to have a sip, but I guess she had a few, you know . . ."

The man smiled, and held the door open for them.

You idiot, she tried to say. *He's kidnapped me.* But it all sounded like incoherent drivel.

"You must have knocked a few back," he said with a laugh. "I hope you don't feel too bad in the morning."

"Thanks," Konrad said.

And then the man was gone.

When the door closed behind them, Konrad said, "You will go directly to a stall. There, you will do what you must, and as soon as you are finished, you will return to me."

Amanda recognized the words as the very same ones he'd said in the truck. Maybe the words were important. Maybe they played a part in his control over her.

"Do you understand?"

"Yes," she said, amazed that she was able to say that word properly.

"Go then."

He released her, and to Amanda's surprise she could stand on her own. She wasn't about to run anywhere, but she was able to walk on her own.

Maybe he's hypnotized me, she thought. *I can walk now because I need to get to the stall. But once I'm done I'll be helpless again and I'll need him to help me walk back to the truck.*

He pushed the washroom door open for her, and she stepped inside.

She wanted to stop and look at herself in the mirror, but she couldn't.

Something was making her go straight to the stall.

She entered the stall nearest the sink so she could speak to anyone washing their hands. But the bathroom was empty and silent. And if someone did need to use it, Konrad would be out there in the hall telling them the bathroom was out of service.

And they'd believe him.

One look into his eyes and they'd believe him.

Amanda unbuckled her belt, undid her pants, and sat down to relieve herself.

Turned out she really *did* have to go.

As she sat there, she looked around the stall. It was covered with graffiti, everything from phone numbers to screeds about bastard truck drivers who left broken hearts scattered along the highways.

And as she read it all, a thought occurred to her.

I could write something on the wall. Leave a message. Let someone know what's happened to me.

She looked around the stall and patted the pockets of her pants ringing her ankles, looking for something to write with. A pen, pencil, anything.

She traced a finger against the wall hoping she could smudge the ink from a previous message.

It didn't work.

She could write with her finger, but needed something to make a mark.

Blood!

She could write her message in blood.

It was so ironic, the thought of it almost made her laugh.

Need to cut myself, she thought. *Need to draw blood.*

She began running the fingernail of her right index finger over her left arm. Although the nail was long and sharp it wasn't doing anything but leaving red lines on her skin. She needed something sharper that could cut flesh.

Her belt buckle might do the trick. The clasp was rounded, but the tongue inside it was thin and sharp. She reached down between her legs and brought her pants up to her knees.

It was sharp.

She pressed the tongue against her left arm, but stopped herself. *He'll see it there.* She switched hands and lifted the sleeve of her shirt. If she did it high enough the sleeve would hide the wound from him.

A deep breath.

And another.

Then she stabbed the tongue of her belt buckle into her right arm. She clenched her teeth to keep from crying out, then pulled the tongue out of the skin.

A drop of blood bubbled up out of the hole she'd made. She touched her left index finger to the crimson bead . . .

And wrote on the wall—

HelP!

The blood went on red, then turned slightly brown as it dried.

She read the word she'd written. *HelP!*

Then what?

She needed to leave some information.

A dozen words went through her mind, most of them too long and unspecific. She was running out of time.

She jabbed the metal tongue into her arm again.

Am CAPtIve

Blck Ptrblt

Pllg TUCANA

Her arm was a mess. She was feeling weak and she was out of time. It would have to do. Hopefully the police knew she was missing and would be looking for her. But . . .

Amanda realized the police wouldn't know who left the message.

She jabbed her arm one last time and wrote—
AmAnDA.

Satisfied it was as good as she could do under the circumstances, she cleaned herself up and pulled up her pants. She flushed and exited the stall. Again she wanted to look in the mirror, but found she couldn't deviate from the path between the stall and the door.

"What took you so long?"

She tried to answer, but her mouth was already dysfunctional.

It's only a matter of time now, asshole.

He put his arm around her and led her back to the truck. Amanda felt exhausted and, although she hated to admit it, was looking forward to lying down.

He opened the door (there was that god-awful smell again) and lifted her up into the seat. Moments later he was laying her down in the back of the truck.

The straps went on in no time at all.

And as the last one was secured into place, she felt his control over her beginning to fade.

"Comfortable?" he asked.

"Like my mother's womb," she said.

He looked at her strangely for a moment, then laughed. "Such spunk," he said. "I'll be sad to see you go."

She didn't believe that for a second.

He brought out the tube and stuck the needle into her left arm. No blood. He tried it again a few times, unable to find a decent vein. "Already running low?" he said, reaching down below her for the thick rubber band he used as a tourniquet. He tied off her arm and tried the needle again. "Eureka!" he said, finding blood immediately and quickly lifting the tube to his mouth.

She watched him feed for a while—feeling weaker by the second—until she was unable to keep her eyes open any longer.

Amanda drifted off to sleep, looking forward to the help her little bathroom message would bring.

In the morning.

— 2 —

The police officer, Constable Sharpe, had seemed pretty interested in Amanda's whereabouts. He'd asked a million questions, some of which Ron wasn't too happy about answering (like if he drank, and if he and Amanda fought, and if he'd ever hit her), but he'd answered each question as honestly as he could and the man seemed to appreciate it.

He'd even asked Ron for a picture of Amanda. Ron had one in his wallet, and gave it to the cop gladly. Anything to help track her down. The cop hadn't made any promises, but he'd said he'd do his best, and Ron believed him.

And now that he was done with the police, Ron wasn't looking forward to heading home alone. The trailer seemed empty without Amanda around, and he was too wound up to go home anyway. In the past he'd usually unwind with a few beers, but he couldn't do that now.

Not if he wanted Amanda back.

So maybe he could go out looking for her. He could visit a couple of the bars in town where Amanda and her friends sometimes hung out and ask if anyone had seen her. He knew he was probably asking for trouble visiting bars when he was trying to keep from drinking, but he thought that if he just looked for her—and didn't stop for any drinks—then maybe he'd be all right.

Everything worked out well . . . for a while.

He checked out the After Dark without much trouble. There were only a few people he knew in the place, and after he asked them about Amanda none of them seemed to want much to do with him, as if he'd maybe killed her or something. They all promised to keep an eye out for her, but unless she showed up in the bottom of a bottle of Molson Canadian, it wasn't going to be much of a search.

After the After Dark, he decided to check out KJ's Billiards on John Street. It was a bit of a long shot since it wasn't exactly one of Amanda's usual hangouts, but there was still a chance she might be there. Besides, if she'd been frequenting any of the usual places, Ron would have heard about it by now.

The inside of the place was dark and there were only a few people there working the pinball machines and video games, and a few others shooting pool. There was a businessman in a suit and tie at the electronic blackjack machine, and a group of middle-aged roughnecks playing pool off in the corner. He didn't recognize any of them and figured they all must be from out of town.

Ron made a circuit of the place, just to make sure he hadn't overlooked anyone, when he bumped into one of the guys who'd been playing pool.

"Oh, sorry, pal," he said.

"You sure are," the man said.

"What?"

The man ignored Ron, and looked over his shoulder at someone in the shadows instead. "Hey, Hamm, you ever think you'd run into this guy again?"

Hamm? Ron thought. *The guy from the poker game.* He looked at the man he'd just bumped into and realized it was the grip.

"Uh, I gotta go," Ron said. He tried to get past the grip, but the guy suddenly seemed six feet around. Not only that, but now there was a buddy on either side of him.

"Well, well, well," said a voice behind him. "This *must* be my lucky day."

Ron slowly turned around . . .

Just in time to see Hamm walking toward him. Not really walking as much as limping.

Must have kicked him harder than I thought, thought Ron.

"Hi, Hamm, how ya doin'?" Ron said. "If I knew you'd be here, I would have brought the money I owe you."

"Yeah, right."

"No, it's true. In fact, I'll just go home now and get it for you. I'll be right back. You'll be here, won'tcha?"

He turned to leave but the men behind him grabbed him by the arms. He squirmed once and then realized they weren't letting him go anywhere.

"Here," Ron said, holding up his left hand. "Take the ring. You won it fair and square."

Hamm chuckled at that. "I don't want the ring. And I don't want your money, because I know you haven't got any."

"What *do* you want, then?"

Hamm pointed a beefy finger in Ron's direction. "You!"

"W-wait," he tried to say.

But before he even got the word out, Hamm's boot had slammed into the junction between Ron's legs. They must have been steel-toed boots, because Ron was already seeing stars.

The men holding his arms let go of him then, but he wished they hadn't. He was having trouble staying up on his feet and the floor looked very hard and awfully far away.

Closer in were Hamm's fists.

They hit him twice in the face, and three times in the gut. The floor began to rise up . . .

Or maybe Ron was falling.

Either way, it didn't really matter.

Ron was unconscious long before he hit the floor.

Chapter 11

— 1 —

They had been off the highway for a while.

The constant hum and thrum of the truck had lessened; then they came to a stop. After that it was stop-and-go, left turns and right turns as they made their way through a city—and a fairly large one at that.

Amanda could make out the glow of the streetlights as they shone down into the truck. They were spaced fairly close together and their light was interspersed with colorful reds, blues, and greens from business signs lining the street.

If I could get away here, Amanda thought, *I might have a chance of escaping.* There had to be places to run to, and places to hide in. Abandoned buildings, dark alleys, parked cars. If only she could get out of the truck.

Konrad made a wide turn and stopped the truck. Then he struggled with the shift lever for a few moments before finally selecting the proper gear. Then they were moving backward. She knew they were moving in that direction because the lights shining into the cab were now sliding the other way. A few minutes later there was a slight bump against the truck and the parking brake came on.

Konrad shut off the engine and Amanda's world was

filled with utter silence. It seemed unnatural for there *not* to be any noise after hearing it for so long.

"Where are we?" she said.

Without answering, he climbed into the back and took out the ball gag.

"No, please don't," she said.

Undaunted, he strapped the gag over her mouth. Then he secured her head, pulling the straps so tight the back of her skull began to throb in pain.

"I'll be back," said Konrad.

I'll be here, Amanda thought.

He crawled out of the truck, and closed the door after he got out. Then he locked it, which surprised Amanda because he'd never taken such a precaution before.

And then she knew why.

She could hear voices outside the truck. Konrad was talking to someone at length. About what, she didn't know. The words were too muted by the locked door of the truck, but the tone was that of jovial conversation, the kind of thing you might hear between two people chatting about the fortunes of the Toronto Maple Leafs, different makes and models of trucks, or maybe even the weather.

Eventually the sound of the voices faded.

Some time later she could feel the truck shake slightly. There was a *clank* and a *screech* and she guessed that the back doors to the trailer were being opened. After that there was a slight but continuous rumble as the contents of the trailer were being unloaded.

Then, voices again.

A key in the door's lock.

The door opened.

"Hey, buddy," said a voice.

Amanda could hear it clearly through the open door.

"Where you gonna be today in case we need you to move your truck?"

"In the sleeper," he said.

The other man didn't respond. Amanda imagined he'd nodded, then walked away, but he didn't.

"Jesus," he said. "Is that your truck that stinks like that?"

Amanda felt her heart begin to race. She tried to scream, to kick, to make a sound, *any* sound, but the door was suddenly slammed shut and the words between the two men instantly turned into mumbles.

The moment was gone.

No one would be hearing her pitiful cries.

Amanda lay still.

Tears began to well up in the corners of her eyes. Her body began to shake and shudder, and the tears streamed down the side of her head and over her ears.

The door opened again.

Konrad got into the truck and climbed into the back with Amanda.

"Close one, eh?" he said, a smile on his face.

Amanda looked at him, through wet, watery eyes.

"But don't get yourself too excited over it. If he'd caused me any trouble, I would have killed him."

Amanda sighed, having no trouble believing what he said to be true.

He produced the needle again and tied off her arm, then waited for the veins to rise up against her skin.

He must have had trouble finding a decent vein, because he began to flick his finger against the skin in an attempt to coax a vein to show itself.

"Ah," he said at last.

There was the same sliver of fire in her arm, and then the drowsiness set in.

Amanda closed her eyes.

It seemed so hopeless . . .

Yet there was still some hope.

The sun was starting to rise. People would be on their way to work, moving from place to place and stopping for coffee at the rest stops all along the highway.

Someone would surely see her message, and then it would only be a matter of time before help would be on its way.

— **2** —

Charles Bou-Najm checked his watch.

It was still five minutes to seven, but he figured the sooner he started work, the sooner he'd be able to go home.

It was a funny thing, that.

He was paid by the hour, but he never punched a clock. Every day he earned eight hours' pay, even though he rarely spent more than six on the job. And the best thing about it was that his supervisor didn't mind one bit. As long as all the bathroom stalls were clean and the garbage cans inside and out were changed each day, he never said a word about Charles heading home early.

When he'd first started the job two months ago, Charles had thought the boss didn't care about the hours because Charles did such a good job. But over time he realized that he didn't care what Charles did because it was a shitty job that no one else wanted. So, six hours or eight, as long as the work was done, what did it matter?

Charles snapped his plastic gloves on his hands and grabbed a spray bottle and roll of paper towels from the supply closet. He always began his day by cleaning out the women's washroom stalls first. There were usually few women using the bathrooms that early in the morn-

ing and he was able to get in and out without having to
make too many people wait for him to finish.

He began at the far end of the row of stalls, wiping
down the walls and toilets of each one whether they
needed it or not. The women's bathrooms were usually
cleaner than the men's except when someone tried to
flush a pad down one of the toilets.

That always caused a mess.

But even those messes were tame compared to some of
the shit-wads he had to clean up in the men's room. Just
thinking about it made him feel sick.

No wonder the boss doesn't care what time I leave,
thought Charles.

He got to the last stall, the one by the sink, and stepped
inside it. The toilet was pretty clean and just needed a
quick wipe.

He flushed the toilet and took a look at the stall walls.
There was all the usual graffiti that his regular cleaning
liquid wouldn't take off, but there was also something
new.

Words written in . . .

It looks like blood, he thought. *Or maybe something
else.*

The writing was brown, and blood was supposed to
be red.

Charles stared at the wall, reading the words.

HelP!
Am CAPtIve
Blck Ptrblt
Pllg TUCANA
AmAnDA.

He couldn't make any sense of them.

The *help* was clear enough, but what was *am captive*
supposed to mean? And the rest of it seemed like nonsense.

Graffiti.

Well, he couldn't do anything about the stuff people wrote on the walls in permanent marker until they let him paint over them, but he could sure as hell clean this new writing off the wall.

Charles raised his bottle up to the level of the words and squeezed the trigger. The fluid burst from the nozzle in a fine mist and in seconds the words on the wall began to bleed.

Rivulets of reddish brown began running down the wall and the words and letters soon became illegible.

Charles pulled a fresh paper towel from his roll and wiped the wall with a wide sweep from right to left.

A moment later the writing was gone.

Charles gave the other walls a quick wipe, even though they didn't need them, and stepped out of the stall.

He checked his watch and was pleased to see he was making good time. If the rest of the day went as well, he'd be home by noon.

Chapter 12

— 1 —

Constable Sharpe shut off the engine of his cruiser and turned the photograph over in his hands.

Nice-looking girl, he thought. *Young. Pretty.* She didn't look like much of a match for that washed-up hockey player Stinson. That guy had had so much promise, the rink used to fill up with people just to watch him play bantam hockey. That's what probably drew her to him—the expectation of greatness.

Or maybe she loved him.

The guy seemed pretty shaken up by her disappearance, and he'd looked sober. That was a good sign. Sharpe knew that if a nice girl like that had left him, he'd probably have hit the bottle pretty hard himself, at least for a little while.

Sharpe looked at the picture again, hoping he'd find her to give two young people a second chance.

He pocketed the photo, grabbed a stack of papers off the passenger seat, and got out of the cruiser. Across the lot was the rest station situated just south of Parry Sound on the southbound side of Highway 69. He'd had plenty of coffee this morning and needed to make a deposit in the station's rest room. But that was just one of the reasons he'd stopped here. After he finished relieving himself, Constable Sharpe started making the rounds of the restaurant, showing the woman's picture and asking everyone in the place if they'd seen her.

He approached a table where two men sat sipping coffee. One was in his mid-thirties and round-faced, while the other was thinner, younger, and wore wire-rimmed glasses.

"Hey, fellas," Sharpe said.

"Hi, ya," one said.

The other nodded.

"Wondering if you've seen this girl in your travels. You know, thumbing a ride. Maybe in a rest station somewhere?"

The round-faced driver yanked his Labatt Blue hat off his head and ran his fingertips over his bald pate. Then he replaced the cap and shook his head. "Nah, sorry. Would've remembered runnin' into a cutie like that."

"Lemme see that," the younger man said.

Sharpe gave him the photo.

"Yeah, I seen her."

"Where?"

"She's a waitress at the Big Wheel outside of Parry Sound."

Sharpe sighed. "That's right."

"Something happen to her?"

"She's missing. She might have even hitched a ride on this highway."

"No," said the older man.

"Ah, shit!" said the younger.

"I'd appreciate it if you kept an eye out for her," Sharpe said, giving each man one of the flyers that had been made up by the force's Records and Registration Section. A lot of times the family of the missing person would take up the initiative and make up the flyers themselves, but Amanda Peck had no real family in Parry Sound and the hockey player had probably done as much as he could just by reporting the woman missing to police.

"Can I have a couple more of those?" the younger one asked.

"Sure, but there's other officers distributing them up and down the highway."

The two men studied the flyer closely, reading the information under the photo of Amanda Peck.

The older man looked up first. "I hope you find her," he said, then added, "alive."

"So do I," Sharpe answered.

After that, Sharpe continued making the rounds. A couple of other people recognized her from the Big Wheel, but other than that no one had seen her out on the highway.

Sharpe was about to leave and head down the highway to the next rest station to the south, when a tall black man came out of the bathroom and noticed everyone in the place studying the flyers Sharpe had just circulated.

At the nearest table he asked if he could take a look, and pulled the flyer out of the hands of a gray-haired woman in a plaid flannel jacket.

Sharpe watched the man's face as he studied the flyer. His jaw dropped and his eyes went wide.

"Have you seen her?" Sharpe said, hurrying over to the man's side.

"Yeah," he said, his voice a little shaky. "I think."

"Where?"

"A rest station north of here, outside of . . . of, uh, Wawa."

Sharpe could feel his heart start to pound, his blood begin to race. "Was she alone?"

The man shook his head. "No, she was with this guy. See, I was sleeping in my truck in the lot when I woke up needing to use the bathroom. I did my business, got a juice from a vending machine for the morning, and I was headin' back to my truck when this woman"—he pointed at the flyer—"was coming into the building."

"Was she all right?"

"She was drunk. That's what the guy carrying her said. He said she'd had one too many out on the road."

Sharpe could feel a bit of anger starting to rise up inside him. "What did this guy look like?"

He shrugged. "I don't know, like a short, fat, bald guy."

"That's it?"

"Well, yeah, except . . . he wore a pair of suspenders that made him look kinda silly, and a leather jacket."

"He was carrying her along and you didn't do anything?"

"I held the door for him."

"Great," Sharpe felt the anger starting to creep into his voice, but was unable to do anything to stop it.

"Hey, how was I supposed to know there was a problem? This is the first I've seen or heard she's missing. If I'd seen this yesterday, maybe I *could* have done something."

He was right. If they'd got the message out sooner, maybe things would have been different, but the boyfriend didn't report her missing until last night and even then they couldn't be sure she was really missing. Sharpe felt his anger begin to subside. It wasn't this guy's fault she'd been kidnapped.

"I understand," Sharpe said, his voice calm again. "And you're being a big help now. But I need you to try and see if you can remember anything else from last night."

"Sure," the man said.

They sat down at a table away from the others and talked.

— 2 —

The crews were already sitting in the trucks when Ron pulled into the Double-B Landscaping lot.

He'd somehow awakened in his own bed with bruises and aches all over his body. He was scratched here and there too, but nothing too serious. At least nothing was broken.

Ron got out of his car slowly, his legs and ribs burning with every tiny movement.

"Holy shit, look what the cat dragged in!" Bobby Bloxam said as he walked across the lot toward the waiting trucks.

"Morning," Ron said, with a little wave.

"You're late!"

"Crews haven't left yet."

Bloxam said nothing for a moment as he stood looking Ron over. Finally, he said, "Out drinking last night?" The disappointment in his voice was unmistakable.

"No, sir." Ron wasn't sure why he'd used the word *sir*, but he felt it was appropriate here.

"Bullshit!"

"I haven't had anything to drink in a couple of days."

Bloxam shook his head. "One of the boys said he saw you coming out of the After Dark last night. We weren't expecting you to show this morning."

"I was there," Ron admitted, "but I wasn't drinking."

"No?"

"I was looking for Amanda. She's missing."

"Shit."

"The cops are looking for her now, too."

Bloxam was silent a moment. "So what the hell happened to you?"

"After the After Dark, I went to KJ's and ran into some guys I owed money to." Ron shifted on his feet and winced as a new pain shot up his side.

"You can't work today, not like that."

"I came here to work." Ron said. He was hoping he'd feel better once he got moving and his body warmed up. The more he stayed still, the more everything hurt.

"All right." Bloxam nodded. "Your decision, but I don't want you asking to go home at lunch. And if anyone complains you're not doing your share, don't bother coming back. Okay?"

"That's fair."

Bloxam assigned him to a crew.

And as he turned and limped over to the truck, Ron wondered how the hell he was going to get through the day.

— 3 —

A check of the rest station near Wawa proved to be a bust. There wasn't a sign of the girl having been there and no one working on the night shift remembered seeing either the girl or the driver whom he described to everyone as a "short, fat, bald guy wearing suspenders."

"That's about every other driver who walks in here," said a woman behind the counter in the restaurant.

Sharpe felt the excitement he'd been feeling begin to fade after that. He'd found a lead but it had turned cold, and the more he asked around the colder it seemed to get.

He decided to quit searching the rest stations for a while and see if the flyers turned up anything useful.

After all, they were reaching out to thousands of people up and down the highway every hour. If he was holding the woman hostage—which seemed likely since a body hadn't turned up yet—then she'd have to eat something or go to the bathroom again and there'd be another chance for someone to recognize her.

What he really needed, though, was a make and model of the truck the killer was driving. It was one thing to hide a woman and travel the highway inconspicuously, but it was another thing altogether to make a trailer invisible. First of all, big trucks could only run on major highways and the trailers they pulled behind them were like moving billboards. If he knew the company the killer drove for, he could narrow the search and maybe even get a name.

It was worth a try, especially since there were plenty of other people out there searching for the girl.

There were Ontario Ministry of Transportation weigh scales all along Highway 17, with one just a short drive from Wawa. Sharpe thought he might as well start there since he was probably going to want to ask the officers manning the scales all along the highway the same questions anyway.

"Afternoon," Sharpe said, nodding in the direction of the man and woman sitting at the desks overlooking the highway.

They both wore uniforms that were a mix of tan and khaki. Technically, they weren't police officers, although they were responsible for enforcing many laws and regulations pertaining to road and highway safety. They could pull a truck off the road and could levy fines, but they could not lay criminal charges against a driver or vehicle owner.

"What can we do for you?" asked the man. He was a big man, probably in his late forties with a bit of a pear shape to him. He had a big walrus-style mustache and his hairline had receded halfway to the top of his head.

The woman kept watch out on the highway.

Sharpe identified himself and showed his badge, then said, "I'm investigating the death of the woman found on the highway the other day, and I'm looking into the disappearance of a Parry Sound woman that may or may not be connected."

"That her?" said the man, pointing to the flyer that was already up on their wall.

"Yes," Sharpe said.

"I hope you find her," said the woman without turning around.

"That's why I'm here. I'm looking for some help figuring out who the driver is and I thought you might be able to help me."

"I will if I can."

Sharpe nodded and got out his notebook and walked over to the huge map of Ontario they had on the large wall directly opposite the window. "See, the bodies have been found outside of Parry Sound, of course," and he pointed to the location on the map, "then north of Estaire, near Spanish, outside of Timmins, and near Terrace Bay."

He looked over at the man to see if he'd followed. He was still staring at the map, so perhaps he had.

"We think the killer is a driver who's been driving the same route for several weeks. Our first thought was that he was driving between Winnipeg and Toronto, but the body outside Timmins doesn't fit with that route . . . so, I thought I'd check with you people for some ideas on this guy's route and the company he works for."

The man shrugged. "Hey, buddy, there are hundreds, sometimes thousands of trucks that drive through here every day. We can't check them all, and we sure as hell don't know where every one of them is going, or what they're carrying."

Sharpe felt kind of stupid standing there listening to the guy rant. He was just asking a few questions, but this guy was going off as if he'd asked him to solve the case for him.

"It was just a thought," Sharpe said, working hard to remain professional and treat the man with respect. "No harm in asking, right? Never know, I might just get lucky."

"This one's overweight, Danny," said the woman. "I'm bringing him in. Make sure you take a good look for other defects, will ya?"

Danny looked over his shoulder at the woman, then sighed. "Right." Then he put on his jacket and headed out to meet the truck that his partner had just pulled off the highway.

When the door closed behind him, the woman got out of her seat. She was a petite younger woman with short red hair and a bright wide smile. Her uniform was clean and pressed, as if she took her job very seriously.

"He's a nice guy, but sometimes Danny can be a pain," she said.

Sharpe liked her immediately.

"My name's Roberta, by the way."

Sharpe nodded.

"Show me again on the map where the bodies were found."

Sharpe pointed out the locations again.

After a few moments studying the map, she said, "Danny was right about one thing. There *are* thousands of trucks on this highway every day, working for almost as many companies."

Sharpe felt like he should say something, but realized she was more thinking out loud than initiating a conversation.

"If the bodies were just found between Toronto and Winnipeg I'd say you'd be looking at dozens of companies with regular routes between the two cities. Canadian companies like Laidlaw and Challenger, even American outfits like Schneider and J.B. Hunt heading back for the border. But Timmins, that's out of the way. . . ."

Now this is more like it, Sharpe thought. The woman was using reason and logic to make an educated guess. She could turn out to be wrong, but there was no harm in trying.

"If I were you, I'd ask around at a couple of the companies that specialize in northern routes like Manitoulin, Bison, or maybe Tucana Northern."

Sharpe wrote the company names down in his notepad. When he was done he said, "Thanks for your help, Roberta. I appreciate it."

She flashed him a smile, then said, "Would you provide me with a reference letter if I apply to the OPP?"

Sharpe was caught a bit off guard by the request. He didn't really know the woman, but a letter recounting her help with this case wouldn't be out of line. "Yeah, sure." He dug in his pocket for a card and gave it to her. "Not enjoying the work on the highway?"

"The truckers call these booths chicken coops, and some days it feels like that, especially with Danny. I've had enough and I want out."

"No problem," Sharpe said. "Just let me know when you need it."

The door opened then and Danny stepped inside. "Wasn't a thing wrong with that rig," he complained. "Wasn't even overweight."

She flashed a knowing smile at Sharpe then, and he realized that she'd sent Danny out to check the truck just so he wouldn't be in the way when they talked.

Sharpe gave the lady a nod and a wink, thinking that she'd make a terrific constable some day.

— **4** —

The day was done.

Ron thought he would never see the end of it.

With the summer season over, the landscaping crew had spent the day reshaping the lawn around a tony waterfront home on Parry Sound Harbor. Most of it was earthmoving work handled by a couple of guys in small tractors, but there was still plenty of detail work that required wheelbarrows and shovels. That's where Ron came in. While Bloxam might have given him a break because he knew how and why he'd received his injuries, none of the guys on the crew gave a shit. To them, Ron was just another hand, and the most junior one at that. As a result, he ended up doing all the grunt work and would keep doing it until someone else, someone newer, joined the crew.

Ron leaned out of his car and nearly fell from the driver's seat onto the ground. He'd been all right at the end of the day when his muscles were hot from the day's work, but after they'd had a chance to rest on the ride home, they were stiff and ached something fierce.

With an extended groan, Ron rose to his feet and nudged the car door closed with a slight hip check.

Then he leaned up against the car and rested.

The trailer door was less than fifteen feet away, but it seemed like more than that, way more.

He took a step with his right foot, then followed with his left, walking—he thought—like Boris Karloff in *Frankenstein*. The movements were the same, but the difference between the two was that the monster had his creator, Victor Frankenstein, to blame for his misery, while Ron had no one to blame but himself.

After a few steps he stumbled forward and the trailer door came up on him quickly. Putting a hand out to save himself, he grabbed the door handle and it turned. He'd left the door unlocked just in case Amanda came home and didn't have a key, and also because there was little of value inside the trailer for anyone to steal.

"Mandy?" he said as he pulled opened the door.

There was no answer.

He wasn't surprised.

Amanda hadn't just run away anymore. Something had gone terribly wrong and she was in trouble, he was sure of it.

Ron wanted to do something to help find her, but he was in no shape to help himself, let alone anyone else.

He moved down the trailer hallway, keeping in contact with the walls on both sides with his fingers to keep himself upright, then turned left at the bedroom.

A couple of steps into the room and he fell face-first onto the bed.

Relief washed over his body.

Just *not moving* felt good.

As he closed his eyes and drifted off to sleep Ron remembered a time not too long ago when he was in terrific shape. Pro athlete kind of shape. He'd work a job in the summer, then do weight training in the evening. Sometimes he'd even wake up early just to go for a run.

Those days were long gone . . .

Or so it seemed.

If anything, this job might help get him back into shape.

There's a positive side to everything, he thought.

Amanda had told him that plenty of times when they first began living together. She said it less and less after a while, then never said it at all in the weeks before she left.

Ron's last few conscious thoughts were about Amanda. *Where is she?*

And . . .

What's the positive side to this one going to be?

— 5 —

Amanda's eyelids fluttered open and she slowly awakened to greet the tail end of the day. The sun had already begun to set, but the inside of the truck was still warm and humid from the sun that had shone through the windshield all day long.

As she became more aware of her surroundings, Amanda realized her clothes were soaked with sweat. And as she blinked, drops of sweat ran off her forehead into her eyes, burning them like acid.

She blinked her eyes several times to fight the sting, then coughed. To her amazement, the ball gag popped out of her mouth and came to a rest on her lips. She turned her head to the side and spat the ball away.

"Help me," she said, loud enough for Konrad to hear her, but not enough for anyone outside the truck to notice. She was still fearful of the tire iron, especially since she still had hope for escape, to which her legs would likely play a major role.

There was no answer.

Surely he's up by now, she thought. *The sun's almost down and we should be on the road soon.*

"Konrad," she tried again. "Are you there?"

Still no answer.

Great! He's gone somewhere and left me here to die of heat exhaustion, or thirst. Or maybe I'll just starve to death. Her stomach growled as if providing a running commentary on her thought process.

Or maybe he's still asleep, waiting for the sun to set completely. But that didn't make sense. He was always up and about at dawn and dusk, using that time to prepare himself for the light of day or dark of night. He had to be up somewhere other than inside the truck . . .

Which gave Amanda an idea.

"Help!" she shouted as loud as she could, which didn't seem very loud at all. "Help me! I'm in here!"

If he caught her, he'd probably break her legs, but it was still worth a try. Hell, it might be her only chance, and she wasn't going to let fear stop her from taking it. She was going to die anyway, the only question left was how painful her death would be. However painful, a chance at life was worth the risk.

"Help me-e-e-e!" she screamed.

She paused a moment and suddenly felt exhausted.

And then the futility of it all came home to her. Her eyes welled up with tears, washing away the sting of her sweat. As the wave of frustration ebbed, she took a deep breath and tried to relax.

The driver's-side door suddenly popped open.

Amanda gasped, partly in surprise, but also to suck in some the deliciously cool and fresh air from outside the truck.

"I loosen the gag so you can breathe easier and that's the way you repay me, by calling for help?"

"I had to try."

"You're a fool," Konrad said in a low voice. "Do you think I haven't had this truck soundproofed?"

He was bluffing, Amanda was sure of it. She'd often been able to hear voices outside the truck, so why wouldn't someone outside be able to hear her? It was possible to soundproof a vehicle, but it was an expensive proposition, and money wasn't something Konrad seemed to have a lot of.

And so Amanda began to wonder what other aspects of his control over her might be built on lies and deception. *Maybe he isn't as smart as he thinks he is . . . or as powerful.* The thought seemed to buoy Amanda, hinting to her that escape wasn't as hopeless a notion as he'd like her to believe.

"You try that again," he said, getting out the tire iron, "and I'll mash your legs into a bloody pulp."

An idle threat, Amanda realized now.

If he hurt her, she'd bleed all over the truck and that would be a waste of her blood. There was also a chance her wounds would get infected, which might make her blood taste bad. It might also finish her off more quickly than the surgical removal of her blood. And that was something Amanda was sure he didn't want. As easily as he'd preyed on his victims so far, picking up hitchhikers and disposing of their dead bodies was probably more difficult than he'd made it sound. He wouldn't want to get rid of her before he absolutely had to, since that would attract even more suspicion from the authorities than his usual mode of operation.

For some reason, Amanda felt a little less helpless than she had up until now. Konrad might not be human; hell, he might even be a vampire, but he wasn't infallible. He'd make a mistake somewhere along the line and Amanda would be ready to take advantage of it.

And get away.

Be free.

It seemed like such a simple thing, yet it was so far away.

Konrad put down the tire iron and a smile flashed across his face. "Here," he said, pulling his hand out of a brown paper bag. "Do you like donuts?"

Amanda hadn't eaten for what seemed like days. Of course she liked donuts. She liked anything right about now.

He held the donut out for her and she took a bite. It was a sugared donut, covered with soft white powder that seemed to melt on her tongue. She swallowed and took another bite.

"You wouldn't happen to be diabetic, would you?" he said, holding the donut in mid air while she chewed. There was something like hope in his voice.

Amanda shook her head, then swallowed. "No."

"Ah, that's too bad."

Amanda wanted another bite of donut, but she was too curious not to ask the question. "Why?"

"I once had a diabetic woman and after she'd gone without her insulin for a few days her blood sugar level was so high it was like eating candy, cake, and ice cream for breakfast, lunch, and dinner." He paused a moment and something akin to regret crossed his face. "I tried to keep her alive as long as I could, but I enjoyed her blood so much I couldn't drink it in moderation."

Couldn't drink it in moderation? Amanda wondered. *That meant he must have gorged himself on the woman.*

Amanda felt her stomach begin to heave. She fought against the urge to throw up, knowing that if she did she'd risk choking on her own vomit.

She took another bite of the donut. It tasted foul now, but she continued eating, knowing she needed her strength.

Konrad must have noticed her struggling to keep the donut down. "A real fighter, eh?" He nodded, impressed. "That's good because I'm getting old and I could use your strength."

She took another bite, finishing the donut and wanting another.

To her surprise, he reached into the bag and pulled out a another donut for her. This time it was a chocolate-glazed, usually one of Amanda's favorites, but now just a source of carbohydrates.

She ate this one a little more slowly, and near the end she was almost able to enjoy it.

Then, just as she was finished eating, Konrad tied off her arm and brought out the needle.

"You know, with that kind of attitude you might just live longer than the others."

Amanda wanted to know just how long that would be, but she knew it didn't matter because she was going to make it. She was going to survive this ordeal, and then the son of a bitch was going to pay.

Chapter 13

~ 1 ~

Constable Sharpe was putting in plenty of overtime, but the detective superintendent who headed up the Criminal Investigation Bureau had made sure that all of it would be approved. There was a serial killer on Ontario highways and a woman was missing, but hopefully still alive. Whatever it cost to catch the killer and save the woman's life was a small price to pay compared to the alternative.

Besides, Sharpe didn't mind the work. When he'd first joined the OPP as a newlywed, he hated when shifts went overtime and was always in a hurry to finish up and get home to his wife.

Twenty years of marriage had cured him of that.

Over time he realized that the job took as long as it took and he had no control over how and when his shifts went long. He also discovered that after a shift it took him a couple of hours to unwind, usually with a few beers, and his wife—ex-wife now—had never approved of that. Sometimes she'd even be waiting for him at the door, expecting him to turn right back around and head out to the mall, or to visit friends. When he told her he needed some downtime, she chided him, laughed it off, and expected him to "leave it at work." That had been one

of her favorite expressions and it came to grate on his
nerves like fingernails on a chalkboard.

After a few years, he thought children might help the
situation by giving the woman something to do with her
time, but that's not the way it worked out. She expected
him to be home earlier and more often so he could be
with the kids, but without much seniority he didn't have
the luxury of picking his hours, or working anything resembling nine-to-five.

The strain of it all eventually took their toll and she
filed for divorce. She was good about giving him access
to the kids and that's all he wanted anyway. After he
moved out, he became more relaxed at work, slept better
at night, and his health began to improve.

After a while he and his ex even got together every
couple of weeks for sex, neither of them being much interested in playing the field.

That had been ten years ago.

Now his daughters had grown up and moved on. The
ex-wife had found someone new and seemed to be happy.

Sharpe was happier too, his life being far less compli-
cated than it had ever been in the past.

The only trouble now was that there was a killer on the
loose, and his next victim was a woman just about the
same age as his youngest daughter.

That hit close to home, and made Sharpe vow to work
around the clock if that's what it took to save the
woman's life.

He checked his watch as he pulled into the Manitoulin
Transport yard on Dixie Road in Mississauga, a city of
over half a million situated directly west of Toronto.

He'd already paid a visit to a similar yard in Mississauga that was home to Bison Transport, one of the
bigger trucking companies servicing western Canada, but
the dispatcher there said that while they had trucks going

between Winnipeg and Toronto all the time, they hadn't transported anything into Timmins for at least a month. While that sounded strange to Sharpe, considering that Bison was such a big company, the dispatcher told him that there was the odd truckload that went into Timmins, but those were usually snapped up by smaller companies and local owner/operators. "We've got more routes than we have drivers," he'd said, showing him the full-page color ads they ran in trade magazines like *Truck News* each month, "so we couldn't take once-in-a-blue-moon loads even if we wanted to."

Scratch one trucking company.

The Manitoulin Transport yard was smaller than the one used by Bison, but it seemed to be just as busy with trailers lined up at the loading docks and idle tractors parked in a row along the fence on Dixie Road, giving the impression that the company was bigger than it actually was.

Sharpe got out of his unmarked cruiser and started toward the loading docks. Halfway across the yard a shunt driver in a yard mule that was used to move trailers to and from the loading docks stopped and slid back the small window on the left side of the driver's compartment.

"Can I help ya?" he asked.

"I want to talk to somebody in charge, maybe a . . ." He paused a moment, trying to think of the right word. ". . . a shipper or a dispatcher?"

"Night man's in the office," the driver said. "Through the door at the end of the loading dock. He'll be able to help you."

"Thanks," Sharpe said, giving the man a friendly nod.

The driver drove off, the tiny tractor he was driving zipping away as if it were being chased by a much bigger truck.

Sharpe continued toward the loading docks and entered the warehouse through the door to the right of them. The office was set a dozen feet back from the entrance, and was filled with empty desks cluttered with mounds of paperwork. A lone man was sitting at one of the desks in the middle of the room reading a copy of the *Toronto Sun*.

"Excuse me," Sharpe said, badge in hand.

"What?" The man looked up from the paper slowly, but he snapped straight in his chair when he realized Sharpe was a policeman.

"Working hard, I see?"

"I'm on break."

Sharpe nodded. "Well, I won't take up too much of your time, then."

"What can I do for you?"

Sharpe identified himself, explained why he was there, showed him the small map he'd made indicating the locations the bodies were found, and asked if his company ran regular routes through northern Ontario.

"Sure, all the time," he said. "On any given day we probably have a dozen trucks on the road between here and Winnipeg. We've even got trucks going farther west all the way to Edmonton and Calgary."

"What about Timmins?"

The man's eyes squinted halfway shut and he began shaking his head. "We did have a contract with a sawmill up there. When we started it was two loads into Toronto every week, which was fine, but then they wanted one load into Montreal, and then a few weeks later one load into Ottawa. . . . After a while it was getting to be too one-load-here, one-load-there. We never had time to arrange for a load from where they were sending us so our drivers were having to bobtail it around the province half the time."

"Bobtail?"

"Drive without a trailer," he said.

"Ah."

"Anyway, that contract ended three weeks ago." He shrugged. "It's better for everyone, anyway. We've got less headaches and can spend more time on our better customers, and they've got their pick of any gypsy driver in the area."

Sharpe hated asking since it would seem as if he didn't know anything, but the term "gypsy driver" seemed interesting for some reason. "What do you mean by 'gypsy'?"

"That's a driver who will haul a load to any destination, and usually works for all kinds of carriers."

Sharpe took out his notepad and wrote that down. "These gypsies, they ever work for a company for a few weeks, maybe a couple months, then move on?"

The man laughed under his breath. "All the time. They start working for some outfit, and everything seems great, but then after a few weeks you learn more about the guy and it becomes obvious why he doesn't have regular work. Most of 'em are nut bars."

"How so?"

"They'll have one kind of problem or another, like depression, or be obsessive-compulsive, or who knows what? Sometimes they're just lousy drivers."

"You have anybody like that working for you at the moment?"

He shook his head. "We don't hire anybody who's got a resume that looks like a checkerboard. We like to see people working for the same company for a few years before they come to us. It's harder to get drivers that way, but it's worth it in the end."

"I see," Sharpe said. He was done here, but there was one last thing the dispatcher might be able to help him with. "If I were a gypsy trucker looking for a regular route for a while, where would you suggest I go?"

"Easy." He shrugged. "Tucana Northern. Those guys'll hire just about anybody who can fog a mirror."

Sharpe smiled.

Tucana Northern was the last company on his short list.

Finally, something seemed to be falling into place.

— 2 —

They'd been on the road for a while now.

Amanda didn't have a clue where they were, but it really didn't matter. She was inside a madman's truck at the moment and she wanted to be outside it, wherever outside might be.

"I have to go to the bathroom," she said.

"Again?"

Amanda nearly laughed at that. "Yeah," she said, "I like to relieve myself at least once a day."

Konrad let out a long sigh. Obviously, he wasn't pleased. "How long can you hang on?"

Amanda had no real concept of time anymore, but she said, "Ten minutes, maybe half an hour."

"I'm not taking you to a rest station again," he said. "You'll have to go by the side of the road."

This didn't sound good to Amanda. She had hoped to visit a rest station, maybe to leave another message, maybe to escape outright. Doing her business by the side of the road in the darkness wasn't going to give her much opportunity to get away. And to top it all off, Konrad would probably watch her the whole time, so she'd have to do *something* or he'd know she was just looking for a way out.

"I don't want to go on the side of the road," she said at last.

"I don't care. It's the side of the road, or nothing."

"But why?"

"You're too weak to use a rest station. You won't even be able to walk on your own."

Amanda couldn't be sure how strong she was since she'd been strapped in place for days. Still, getting out of the truck would surely present her with some opportunity to better her situation. She had to give it a try.

"All right then, I'll do it on the side of the road."

Almost immediately, the truck began to slow.

She could feel her heart begin to race, pressing hard against the straps across her chest. She tried to keep her breathing slow and regular but the anticipation of her moment of freedom was too much for her to remain calm.

He must have sensed her excitement.

After he turned on the truck's interior light, he stared directly into her eyes and said, "Don't even think about escaping. You're too weak. I'm too strong. It's dark out, and I can see better at night than you can see during the day."

She tried to look away, but he forced her to gaze into his eyes. "You will relieve yourself, and then *look forward* to getting back into the truck. It is your home. You like it here. . . . Do you understand?"

She tried not to nod her head, but she was helpless against him. "Yes."

He began to unstrap her. As the bindings were ripped away she wanted to jump up, beat him with her fists, run away as fast as she could, but she found she couldn't even lift her own leg.

Am I that weak? she wondered. *Or does he have some sort of control over me?*

When she was free of the straps, he slid his arms beneath her and lifted her off the table.

As he lifted her up, Amanda's left arm fell away.

Something touched her fingertips.

She grabbed at it, pulled.

It was hard and prickly . . . like one of the bindings he used to strap her down.

An extra strap.

It was in her hand now.

She closed her hand around it, fingers desperately trying to fold the dangling ends into her palm.

He lifted her out of the truck and carried her down to the roadside.

They went about five yards onto the grass by the side of the highway, and then he put her down.

"Go ahead," he said. "Now."

She turned her back to him and pulled down her pants. She'd been worried that she wouldn't be able to do anything, but her body decided on its own that it wasn't going to miss the chance to purge itself.

"Here," he said, handing her a few tissues.

She cleaned herself, pulled up her pants, then slid the strap down her leg between her thigh and her pant leg. Finally she zipped up and secured the button at her waist.

The moment she was done, she practically fell into his arms.

He carried her back to the truck, lifted her inside, and strapped her back onto the table. The straps were looser now and she could wiggle around a bit beneath them. Perhaps she'd lost weight, or maybe there just wasn't any need to strap her down very securely anymore. He probably thought that even if she could get out of her bindings she wouldn't be able to get very far.

He was probably right, but Amanda wasn't about to give up hope.

As the truck began moving again, a smile slowly broke over Amanda's face.

She could feel the extra strap securely hidden in her pants.

She didn't know what it might be good for, but just the thought of having something he didn't know about gave her a feeling of power.

Somehow she'd use the strap to get away.

At the moment she didn't have a clue as to how she might make that happen, but if she had anything it was plenty of time to come up with a plan.

— 3 —

The Tucana Northern yard was located in an industrial area near Dixie Road and Steeles in Brampton, the city north of Mississauga and northwest of Toronto. It wasn't easy to get a good sense of the yard in the dark, but compared to the yards of the first two companies, this place was a dump.

Old dead trucks had been lined up against one wall, their lights pulled from their sockets, mirrors ripped away from their mounts, whole fenders gone, and rusty doors hanging off their cabs at odd angles just waiting for a strong gust of wind to tear them away. Presumably the truck carcasses were being cannibalized for parts, but it was an ugly sight and it begged one to wonder about the quality of the trucks these vehicles had so valiantly given up their lives for to keep them on the road.

There were as many lights burning in the yard as there were burnt out. The mishmash of lighting created odd patches of light and dark on the asphalt and gave the place the look and feel of a cemetery, or perhaps an auto graveyard.

The place looked deserted, but one of the five loading

doors facing the street was open and a faint light shone out from inside the warehouse, like a large square moon.

Sharpe drove up to the open door, got out of the unmarked cruiser, and used the steel ladder on the right to climb up onto the loading dock.

"Hello," he said into the warehouse.

He paused and listened, but there was no answer.

"Hello," he tried again, this time cupping his hands around his mouth so the sound of his voice would carry farther.

Silence.

Then, from somewhere deep in the warehouse, "Whaddya want?"

"Hello!"

"We're closed," said the voice, closer now. "First loads get picked up at seven in the mornin'."

Sharpe headed for the sound of the voice, stretching his neck to look down the aisles as he walked deeper into the racks. "I'm not here for a load," he said.

"Whaddya want?" the voice said again. This time it was very close, probably just another aisle over.

Sharpe took a few steps, then looked left. Approaching him at what seemed like a snail's pace was a large man carrying a broom. There were boots on his feet that he seemed to drag across the floor like slippers. His hair was cut short, but somehow looked wild and unrestrained, as if the man had just gotten out of bed. He had on a pale green jacket and faded green work pants, but the two failed to meet at his midsection, a band of which was clearly visible between the two.

When the man was close enough to see the badge hanging out of Sharpe's jacket pocket, Sharpe extended his hand and introduced himself. And since the name on the patch of the man's shirt read *Ray,* he began by saying, "Well, Ray—"

"My name's Jimmy," he said. "Jimmy Paul. The wife picked up the shirt at the Goodwill for work."

Sharpe sighed. The man had two first names and neither one of them was the name on his shirt. "Okay then, Jimmy . . . I was hoping there might be a dispatcher working. I need to ask a few questions."

"I do some dispatching," Jimmy said.

Sharpe looked at the worn-down bristles of the man's broom and said, "Chief cook and bottle washer, eh?"

"What?"

"Never mind. You do some dispatching here, do you?"

"Night stuff, sometimes. When there's loads going out at night, I'm the dispatcher."

"What about when there aren't any loads going out?"

He lifted his broom. "Then I clean up."

"Well, I've got some dispatcher-type questions for you."

"Shoot!"

Sharpe reflexively pulled out his notebook and black pen, then said, "This company run loads between Toronto and Winnipeg on a regular basis?"

"Plenty."

"What about Timmins?"

"Sure. See, that's why the company's called Tucana *Northern* . . ."

Sharpe resisted the urge to smack the man.

". . . we carry a lot of loads into northern Ontario . . . although not a lot of stuff goes into Timmins. It's not that big a town and there's not a whole helluva lot up there, so we end up doing a lot of LTL loads into there."

"LTL?"

"Less-than-a-truckload," he said. "Say a company has just a couple of skids they need delivered, we'll carry the load for them, but we'll charge them more because the trailer's only half full. When we can find 'em, we fill the space with other freight going to the same town. Seems to work well for places like Timmins."

Sharpe suddenly felt as if he was about to make some kind of breakthrough on the case. His heart began beating faster in anticipation.

"This company hire a lot of *gypsy* drivers?"

"We call 'em independent owner/operators."

"Any of these independent owner/operators have criminal records?"

The man shook his head emphatically from side to side. "We check them out as best we can, and if we find out they've got a record, we don't hire them."

"*If* you find out they have a record?"

A shrug. "It's hard to check out everybody, especially when you usually have to hire somebody, like, yesterday."

Sharpe nodded, understanding that what he was saying was they hired just about anybody who had an AZ-class license and a truck that ran. "Let me ask you this, then. Are any of your drivers . . . oh, I don't know, *strange* in any way?"

Sharpe realized there was a small amount of irony in asking Jimmy this question, but the man seemed oblivious of it.

"Oh, boy," he said. "We got a couple of wackadoos, but every company's got its share, if you know what I mean."

"Is there one of them that stands out in your mind as being really weird?"

The man looked to the ceiling, his eyes half closed and his mouth severely twisted from the strain of concentration. "If I had to pick just one guy, it would have to be a guy by the name of Valeska."

"Oh, yeah, what's so strange about him?"

A little laugh. "You might as well ask what's normal about him, we might not be here so long. . . ."

Sharpe remained silent, giving Jimmy the chance to ramble.

"First of all, he only picks up stuff at night. Not just at night, but after dark. Makes his deliveries that way, too." A sigh. "That's why the company's got me working nights."

"That all?"

"No. His truck stinks, and he stinks pretty bad, too."

"Like he needs a bath?"

"No, it's worse than that. It's like he shits his pants, or maybe it's dried blood, I don't know, but it smells something awful."

At the mention of blood, Sharpe felt the hairs on the back of his neck stand up on end.

"Anything else about him that's odd?"

"I don't really know him that well. See, he doesn't talk to anybody other than to get his load, and if you ask me I don't think he even likes anybody in this place. Hell, he don't even seem to like himself half the time."

"Sounds like a great guy to have working for the company." This time Sharpe edged his words with a bit of a sarcastic tone so the guy would know he was being funny.

"Day bosses here, they tried to get rid of him a couple of times already."

"What happened?"

The man shrugged. "He's got a way of changing your mind."

"How so?"

"I don't know . . . he just does." He was quiet a moment, as if thinking. "Like one time I came in early because I heard they were going to fire him for starting a fight with one of the other drivers. So the boss gets him into the office . . ." He began shaking his head. "And I don't know how he did it, but he walked out with an increase on his per-mile rate and better loads."

That didn't fit. From what Jimmy had been saying, this guy was an asshole, and from what the guy who ran into him in Wawa said, he was basically a big, fat slob. But from this it sounded like the guy was Prince Charming, able to smooth out every wrinkle with a smile and a song. But the more Sharpe thought about it, the more sense it made. How else would a man be able to continue kidnapping and killing if he didn't have an innate ability to make people go against their better judgment, even bend them to his will? Sharpe looked at Jimmy a moment, then said, "And I bet your boss isn't the kind of guy who's easily persuaded, right?"

Jimmy nodded. "You got that right. That's why it's the strangest thing."

Sharpe wasn't sure how or why he knew it, but he was certain that this was the driver he was looking for.

"Where can I find the man?"

"I'm not really sure," Jimmy said.

Sharpe prepared himself for a letdown, expecting to be told that Valeksa had already moved on.

Then Jimmy smiled. "But maybe I can find out for you."

Sharpe followed Jimmy into the office, where they looked up the information on the driver, Konrad Valeska.

"He's got one of our trailers right now," Jimmy said. "It's one of the new ones. Says *Tucana Northern* on the side of it in big red letters." He winked. "Looks real cherry."

"What kind of truck does he drive?"

Jimmy looked at the file. "Peterbilt 379 . . . Black." He turned over the paper. "It's all it says."

"Where is he, right now?"

"Right now, I don't know."

"Don't you guys keep track of your trucks with some sort of satellite tracking system?"

"We do, but Valeska's transmitter is broken."

Of course it is, thought Sharpe. *And this outfit probably isn't too worried about getting stuff like that fixed.* Then he was struck by another thought. *Probably why Valeska happens to be driving for* this *company.*

"And he's doing a lot of LTL deliveries along the route too . . . so best I can tell you is that he's somewhere between here and Winnipeg at the moment and he should be back this way in another day or two."

Sharpe looked at Jimmy without saying a word.

Jimmy shrugged. "Sorry, but it's the best I can do."

"Thanks," Sharpe said. "It's still a help."

Moments later he was headed for his cruiser, thinking about what to do next.

First, he'd put out the word all along the highway, and with any luck they'd have him in custody in no time, probably by morning. After all, how hard could it be to spot a forty-eight-foot-long truck that had the words *Tucana Northern* painted on the side of it in big red letters?

And if they didn't catch this guy in the next day or two, then Sharpe would be personally waiting for the asshole to roll through town.

Chapter 14

— 1 —

Dawn was near.

They were making a delivery to who-knows-where, and Konrad seemed pretty agitated. The sun would be rising soon and there didn't seem to be anyone around to start unloading the truck.

Would he have to be exposed to daylight if they didn't start unloading before the sun came up? Amanda wondered. That would be great, to see him wither under the sun's rays, shrivel from the heat of the day.

"Where are they?" he said.

She'd never seen him like this. He seemed worried, frightened about the prospect of running late. It looked good on him, she decided.

"They've never been this late before," he said, taking another look at his watch as if that might hurry things along.

He glanced out the window again, then looked into the mirror toward the end of the trailer and the loading dock it was backed up to.

"I'm going to need my strength," he said under his breath.

And then he crawled in the back and took out a fresh needle and tube.

Amanda felt weak just looking at the tube. She'd been drained several times in the past few days and she knew that she couldn't survive much longer at this rate. Surely, one or two more bloodlettings was all her body could stand.

He wrapped the rubber tourniquet around her arm and began searching for a vein. He flicked at her arm with his finger—as if he were trying to knock an insect off her skin—but her veins were slow to respond.

He kept at it for several more seconds and slowly, the look on his face began to change.

"Ah!" he said, like a child who'd just been offered some candy.

He pressed the tip of the needle against Amanda's arm. . . .

"Hey!" called a muffled voice. "Anybody in there?"

Konrad suddenly put away the needle, removed the rubber hose from her arm, and climbed up into the front of the truck.

He cracked open the window. "I'm right here!"

"Well, let's get going, pal," said the voice, standing just on the other side of the door. "We haven't got all day to wait around for you to wake up."

Amanda realized this was her chance to cry out, to scream. She tried, but she was too weak to make a sound that was anything more than a squeak.

Konrad ignored her attempt to make some noise. He wasn't the kind who took a jab or slight kindly and he had to set this guy straight. He opened the door and climbed out of the cab. "Listen, *pal*—" she heard him say, before everything went quiet when he closed the door behind him and hurried back to the end of the trailer to get them started unloading.

This was her chance.

She wriggled and jerked her right arm and found that

there was a bit of play beneath the straps. If she were whole and healthy, it would have been a simple matter of pulling her arm free and getting out of the bindings.

But she was weak, very weak.

It seemed to take forever to move her arm a few inches, and each new inch seemed to take twice the effort as the one before.

But she was determined.

Her life was at stake and this was likely her last chance to save herself before Konrad finished her off.

She kept moving her arm, and helped it along by moving her fingers spiderlike up the side of her body.

One last try and . . . she was free.

There had been one strap across her wrist, one at the elbow, and another just below the shoulder. The wrist strap had been the most difficult to get out from under, and now that her hand was free it was easier to move her arm. She drew her hand across her body and the strap over her elbow fell away.

Her arm was free.

Great, she thought, *now what?*

Although she could unstrap herself now, there was no point in doing it because even if she were free she'd never be able to get out of the truck on her own.

Her thoughts drifted toward the strap in her pants. It was still there. She could feel it pressing against her thigh as if reminding her of its existence.

During the long hours on the road Amanda had thought of several possible ways of using the strap to escape. None of them were very good, each with countless ways in which they could fail . . .

But she had to try one.

She slipped her right hand down into her pants and retrieved the belt that was hidden there. It was long and thick, but hopefully it was flexible enough to do the job.

Amanda could hear voices outside the truck getting closer.

Adrenaline began to flood her system and she found that she had slightly more strength now than she'd had just moments before.

She lay the belt across her chest and reached over with her right hand to pull the sleeve of her T-shirt away from her left arm. Then she threaded the tongue of the belt between her arm and the side of her body until it came out the back. Then, holding the belt in place with the left side of her chin, she reached down and pulled the belt around her arm and slid it through the thick steel buckle on the end.

Keeping tension on the loop around her arm with her chin, Amanda pulled on the belt as hard as she could.

The belt constricted around her arm, tighter and tighter until she could feel it squeezing the flesh, compressing it firmly against the bone.

But was it tight enough?

She'd taken a St. John Ambulance first-aid course in high school once. In the class they'd explained that in order to cut off the blood flow to a person's arm, you had to tighten the tourniquet so that the compression of the blood vessels in the arm was higher than the systolic pressure produced by each beat of the heart. Normally that would be a difficult proposition, but after losing so much blood, her body's systolic and diastolic blood pressures were probably at an all-time low.

Amanda let out a tiny laugh under her breath. How could she be smart enough to know that, but still dumb enough to find herself in this situation? Maybe there were different kinds of smart. If she wasn't smart enough to stay out of trouble, maybe she was smart enough to get away from it.

With grim determination, she firmed her grip on the

belt and pulled again, this time not stopping until the pain in her left arm forced her to stop.

It was as tight as the belt was ever going to get.

Hopefully it would be tight enough.

With little wasted motion, she pressed the two sides of the Velcro against each other, securing the belt in place. Then she wrapped the excess of the belt around her arm, using the Velcro to secure the entire length of it in place around her arm.

The voices outside the truck were louder now, but still muffled. She was sure Konrad would be back inside the truck in moments.

She pulled the sleeve over the belt on her left arm and then slid her right arm back under the straps along her body.

When everything was back in place, she took several deep breaths, trying to calm her racing heart.

And then, just as the door opened, she realized that she'd put her arm back in place under the strap on her wrist but *over* the strap on her elbow.

Seeing that, Konrad would be sure to know something had happened while he'd been out of the truck.

Too late now, she thought, desperately trying to slow her breathing.

"Lazy bastards," he said. "Said if I wanted the truck empty before the sun came up, maybe I should help them unload it. . . . Human scum! They're lucky I'm letting them live to see the sun."

Amanda let out a deep breath. Her breathing was better now, but her heart still felt as if it were pounding.

Her arm sure seemed to be throbbing. She'd secured the belt around it as tight as she could, the only limitation being the strength—or perhaps the weakness—of her pull. But it must have been enough because her arm felt pinched off and she was already beginning to lose feeling in several of her fingers.

Konrad got out the rubber tourniquet again and set to work tying off her arm. "The next time I'm down this way I think I'll come by early and make a little snack of the one with the big mouth. . . ." He laughed at that, as if the mere mention of feeding off a smart-ass human was enough to make Konrad feel superior.

She watched him slide the needle into her flesh. It was a strange sight, especially when there was no feeling in her arm to accompany it. It was just as if he were piercing someone else's arm. . . .

And that's when Amanda felt that her plan might actually have a chance.

Konrad sucked on the tube.

There was a bit of blood at first, but not the usual spurt that he'd enjoyed in the past.

"Already," he said, throwing the tube down onto her chest. "She'd been such a fighter, held so much promise . . . and she only lasted half as long as the others."

It worked! Amanda screamed inside her head. *He thinks I'm drained, that I'm dead.*

But then the straps began coming off around her legs, and she felt him undoing her jeans and pulling them down around her ankles.

What now?

— 2 —

By the time Constable Sharpe got back to Parry Sound, he was eager to get to the constable's room and check his mailbox to see if anything had come through on his request.

Before he'd left the Tucana Northern yard in Brampton, Sharpe called Constable Boneham in Parry Sound and asked him to type up an alert broadcast for the CPIC system, which would put out a BOLO (or a *Be On the Look-Out*) for Valeska's truck. Then he asked Boneham to run the name Konrad Valeska through the American NCIC and Canadian CPIC systems and the database of the Ontario Ministry of Transportation—or MTO for short.

There was a very small chance that the man had been licensed by the Province of Ontario, but Sharpe was more interested in doing a search for all of North America. Normally Sharpe would do the search through the computer himself, but Boneham had a few minutes before his shift ended and was happy to help out Sharpe by preparing the BOLO and running the Valeska name through the system. With any luck, Boneham would be long gone and the information he wanted would be waiting in his box by the time he got back from Brampton, a ride of just over three hours.

After getting off the highway at Bowes Street, Sharpe stopped at the Tim Hortons on Mall Drive. He'd just wanted a coffee for himself, but he knew that if he walked into the detachment with a fresh cup of coffee, there would be plenty of guys there giving him a rough time about not picking up coffees for them. He hadn't been sure how many officers were on duty, but he bought four medium coffees, which would fill up a tray and make it look like he had his hands full as he walked through the door.

"Hey, Sharpie!" the officer at the desk, Constable Zoe MacKinnon, said as he entered. MacKinnon was an old-timer with almost as many years on as Sharpe

Sharpe lifted the tray to eye level so the officer could see that he'd brought coffee for everyone.

"You're the best," MacKinnon said, then added, "What, no donuts?"

Sharpe gave the woman a cold stare.

Moments later, two other officers, Sergeant McSherry and Constable Allen, arrived at the front desk, as if they'd been able to smell the fresh coffee from the rear of the detachment.

"Did you remember cream and sugar?"

"Sugars are in the bag," he said.

The officers began preparing their coffees.

Sharpe cleared his throat.

"Thanks," said Constable Allen.

"Yeah, thank you," echoed Sergeant McSherry.

"You're welcome, Sarge," said Sharpe.

The sergeant was in charge of the shift, but didn't remind you of it every minute of the day. He never acted like another one of the guys, but he was friendlier than most sergeants Sharpe had known over the years. However, when the situation required it, McSherry could come down on you harder than a freight train at midnight, and as far as Sharpe was concerned, that was exactly how it should be.

With everyone busy preparing their coffees, Sharpe took a look in the direction of his desk and asked, "Did Boneham find anything for me?"

"What sort of info were you looking for?" asked MacKinnon as she stirred sugar into her coffee.

"I'm not sure. A driver's license maybe, probably out of province, possibly American."

MacKinnon shrugged.

"I think he had something on that," said Constable Allen. "Hold on." She left the front desk and headed for the back of the constable's room.

Moments later she returned with two sheets of paper in her hands. The top sheet was a handwritten note and the other was—he hoped—the information he was looking for.

"This it?"

Sharpe took the papers from her and quickly read the note from Boneham, written in a barely legible scrawl.

> *What kind of game is this???*
> *If this is your idea of a joke, you can do your own grunt work next time.*
> *Boner . . .*

Sharpe slid the cover sheet behind the second and stared at the paper in disbelief.

"Ontario?" he said under his breath, looking at the enlarged blue Ontario Driver's Licence—or *Permis de Conduire* as it was called in French—printed on the page in his hands.

He searched the rest of the license and saw that the name on it was indeed Konrad Valeska. There was an address on the license too, for a location on Clifton Hill in Niagara Falls, Ontario. Finally, there was a photograph of the man, which bore absolutely no similarities to the description the witnesses and the Tucana Northern dispatcher had given him.

The man they'd described was a short, fat, bald guy who looked "strange" and almost "inhuman." The man in the photograph was good-looking, even handsome, as best as Sharpe could discern such things about men.

Most importantly, the man in the photograph looked *familiar*.

"Clifton Hill," Sharpe said aloud.

"What?"

"Clifton Hill," he repeated. "In Niagara Falls . . . Why does that sound so familiar?"

"That's the huckster's street near the Falls where they

have all those freak shows and museums," offered Constable Allen. "You know, Dracula's Haunted Castle and things like that."

Sharpe was beginning to get a bad feeling in the pit of his stomach about this. "Dracula's Haunted Castle?" he said.

"Or maybe it's called Castle Dracula. It's been a while since I've been down there."

Sharpe stared at the license again, worried that there was a very bad reason why the man in the photo looked so familiar.

"Hey, Maggie," he said to Constable Allen. "You recognize this guy?"

She took the sheet from him and looked at it for a second.

"Course I do. That's Brad Pitt."

"Brad Pitt?" Sharpe said, feeling sick.

"Yeah, you know, the actor."

Sharpe took the sheet from her. "Did he ever, uh . . ." He paused, not sure how to phrase the question. "Has he ever played a vampire in a movie?"

"You bet," said Constable Allen. "*Interview with a Vampire*, with Tom Cruise . . . Now there are two vampires I wouldn't mind sticking my neck out for."

The rest of the officers laughed.

All except Constable Sharpe.

He stood there mumbling, "Funny, very funny."

— 3 —

He's going to rape me! Amanda thought. *Even though he thinks I'm dead, he's going to fucking rape me!*

She wanted to kick and scream, to tear his eyes out . . .

But she couldn't move and she couldn't make a sound.

She couldn't do anything to stop him because then he would know she was still alive. She just had to lie there, playing dead and letting him do whatever he pleased with her body.

Just the thought of it made her sick.

How was she ever going to handle . . .

He began by running his hands up and down her bare thighs.

His hands were so cold. Amanda was afraid that he'd feel her body heat and know she was still alive, but so far he didn't seem to notice.

Maybe *dead* and *near dead* were virtually the same thing to him. Maybe his thing was to have the actual moment of death come while he assaulted his victims. *Isn't that what they call the orgasm anyway, the little death?* Maybe he got off on killing his victims with sex. After all, if they're going to die anyway, why not have a little fun with them before they go?

Amanda fought hard against the urge to vomit.

His hands moved to her inner thighs, pushing against them and spreading them apart. Although she desperately wanted to fight him, she offered no resistance.

Then a finger was inside her, one of his filthy dirty fingers.

She felt like crying, but did nothing more than let her head fall to the side. It was the best she could do to disconnect herself from the horror that was occurring down between her legs.

Another finger slipped inside her.

And another.

She could feel herself being stretched apart.

Penetrated.

Invaded.

Violated.

Bastard! she screamed inside her head. *Fucking bastard!*

His fingers began sliding back and forth, moving in and out without the aid of any sort of lubrication.

It was the most pain she'd ever experienced there in her life. Her inner lips and the walls of her vagina were quickly becoming sore, rubbed raw by his disgustingly rough and foul hands.

After another minute, he stopped and removed his fingers from inside her.

Amanda took a slight breath and let it out slowly, careful not to let her chest rise or fall more than was absolutely necessary.

And then she heard the *zip*.

There were dozens of things she hoped the sound was indicative of, but she knew it could only be one thing.

He had unzipped his pants and was about to . . .

It felt cold and clammy inside her.

An image of a pale white snake slithering up inside her body began to haunt the dark corners of Amanda's mind.

And that's when she made the decision . . .

Simple freedom wasn't enough anymore.

She *would* get away from him. Of that, she had no doubt. In fact, she was more determined to survive now than she had been in days.

But she wanted more than just to survive.

She wanted to *kill* him for what he was doing to her.

Kill him slowly.

Inflict pain upon him.

Make him suffer.

As she was suffering now.

He made several more strokes, then pulled out.

For several moments nothing happened. No movement, no sound.

And then she felt something cold and wet splattering onto her thighs, her belly, her chest . . .

Even across her face.

The smell of it was putrid, like rotten meat, or tainted blood.

A drop of it ran down Amanda's cheek, nestling into the corner of her mouth.

It tasted foul, like a potent mix of darkness and evil, but Amanda didn't flinch.

"Excellent!" he said between heavy breaths. "My wolfen brothers will have no trouble finding you now."

Chapter 15

He didn't bother strapping her back in.

Moments after he'd done his business, Konrad was back in the driver's seat and pulling away from the loading dock.

He drove the truck quickly, erratically, as if he were in some sort of mad race against time.

Maybe he is, thought Amanda. It would be light out in a little while, and if he didn't dump her body somewhere soon, he'd have to keep her inside the truck for the entire day . . . where she would begin to rot.

One more thing to stink up the truck.

He turned a corner a little too quickly and the right side of the truck seemed to come away from the asphalt. The tires on the left side cried out in complaint over the extra workload.

A hard jerk of the wheel righted the truck.

Amanda bounced and slid around in the back of the truck trying to discreetly grab hold of something to keep herself from falling off the table and in between the seats.

And then the ride smoothed out.

A highway.

He couldn't travel for long on this road since the sun

would be up in a quarter of an hour and by the time it did he had to be parked somewhere safe for the day.

Amanda smiled at the thought.

Wherever he dumped her off, she would be within at least a fifteen-minute drive of *civilization*. It was a strange word, but it was just what she needed. A place where there were other people, and a telephone, and a newspaper, and police, and restaurants, and a hospital . . .

The truck began to slow.

This is it! she thought.

She took several deep, deep lungfuls of air knowing she'd have to hold her breath while he lifted her out of the truck.

The ride got bumpy as the right side wheels pulled onto the gravel shoulder of the highway. A slight touch on the brakes and Amanda felt herself rolling forward.

Finally the truck came to a complete stop.

Amanda rolled back flat onto the table and let go her grip on its corners, playing dead once again.

The truck's engine continued to rattle and roll.

Konrad jumped out of the truck, leaving his door open as he ran around the front of the truck toward the passenger side. The door there opened quickly and a gush of cool predawn air blew through the cab. Amanda could feel goose bumps beginning to rise up on her flesh, but was powerless to stop them.

And suddenly, she was gripped by panic.

He's going to notice, she told herself. *I'll have gotten this far, only to have my own body betray me.*

Her flesh continued to tighten. She could almost picture the hairs on her arm beginning to stand up on end.

His hands were on her.

Unlike the times he'd lifted her out of the truck before, this time he was rough with her, taking little care to get her out of the truck neatly.

Her head hit one of the walls of the sleeper, twice.

But she didn't cry out.

And when her foot got tangled up in one of the belts he merely pulled harder on her leg, nearly separating her foot from the rest of her body.

And still she remained silent.

Maybe I'm already dead, she thought. *Who knows, maybe this is what death is like . . . experiencing pain and being unable to do anything about it.*

Moments later she was outside and could feel the sharp edge of the predawn cold against her skin.

Her nipples began to condense and pucker now as well.

But she wasn't worried that he'd notice anymore. If he hadn't noticed anything by now, he wasn't going to notice anything, period. Why would he notice, anyway? He'd already decided she was dead and he'd desecrated her body; now all that was left was to dispose of it, like the wrapper your food came in after you've finished eating.

The thought made Amanda want to laugh.

My body is just the wrapper his food had come in.

He adjusted his grip on her, then began swinging her back and forth, back and forth.

What now? she wondered, but before she could answer her own question she was suddenly weightless.

Soaring through the air.

Free-falling.

Free!

The moment seemed to stretch out in time. She could feel herself tumbling and spinning, rising at first, and then definitely on the way—

Whumpf!

She landed on her side, the impact knocking the wind out of both ends of her body. Then she bounced back into the air, coming down a second time on her head. It slammed against a rock and for a few moments her world was nothing but the searingly bright white spikes behind her eyes.

When the spikes were gone and the roar of the truck was fading in the distance, Amanda finally allowed herself to ask, *Is it over?*

Her body was wracked with pain.

And she could barely move.

But she could smell the grass around her.

And feel the cool wind blowing gently through her hair.

She opened her eyes . . .

And saw a huge silver-gray wolf staring her down, its fangs sharp, wet, and bare.

— 2 —

Ron rolled over onto his side, saw the numbers on the digital clock by the bed, and shut off the alarm.

He wouldn't be needing its help today.

That's because he was already awake and—strange as it seemed—eager to start the day. The first couple of days of landscaping work had been hard on Ron's body, but he'd survived. That was a good word for it because he'd only just *survived* on the job, barely making it to the end of each day. His muscles had ached in protest, as if asking why they were being made to work so hard again.

Ron didn't blame them for complaining. He hadn't used them much in the last couple of years, and now he was asking them to perform again, harder than they used to.

Early on, he'd wondered if he was still capable of doing any hard physical work, but his body seemed to be responding nicely. He could feel a toughness returning to his muscles, something he hadn't known since his last year of junior hockey.

Maybe it *was* possible for him to get back into shape.

Another few weeks of this kind of work and he'd be down twenty pounds and zeroing in on his playing weight. As long as he kept working hard and stayed away from the beer, there was a really good chance that some of the old Ron Stinson would come shining through.

If only Amanda was here, he thought. *She'd be proud of me.*

Ron turned his head and looked out the bedroom window. It was getting brighter outside as the sun started to rise on yet another day without her.

Where the hell is she?

— 3 —

Amanda put her arms up to shield herself from the wolf, but only her right arm moved.

Her left arm . . . well, her left arm felt as if it weren't even there. She reached over with her right hand to feel for the arm. There was something there that she knew was her arm, but she couldn't feel it being touched. It was as if something foreign was connected to her body, hanging off her shoulder like a cold dead slab of meat.

The tourniquet!

She followed the thing by her side up to her shoulder and found the belt still wrapped tightly around her arm.

The wolf glared at her, growling softly as if wondering what was going on here. She was supposed to be dead and an easy meal for the wolf, but instead she was moving around. Alive. Amanda doubted if that small detail would matter much to the wolf since she wasn't much of a match for anything on four legs in her present condition, much less a full-grown wolf.

She tried to move away from the animal, but it was impossible to do anything with just three working limbs. She had to get the tourniquet off her arm.

With a couple of tugs, she managed to tear the Velcro free.

The ripping sound startled the wolf, but only momentarily. After a quick step backward, it took two tentative steps forward, getting closer and becoming less wary with each passing moment.

The belt came loose and blood ran back into Amanda's arm.

She let out a scream as feeling returned to the limb.

The arm was ice-cold, and as the nerves were revived by the flow of blood, thousands of tiny pins seemed to needle at her flesh. On top of it all the arm was broken. She'd probably landed on it when she hit the ground, cracking the major bones, and dislocating several fingers, judging by the pain.

Now each small movement sent shocks of pain racing up and down her arm.

But at least she could move it.

Amanda looked up and saw that the wolf had moved in closer.

Instinctively, she backed away from the animal, only to realize she was also moving *away* from the highway, with the wolf matching her progress step for step.

And so she carefully began moving in a wide arc that would eventually get her turned around and pointed back in the direction of the road.

But the wolf wasn't going to wait for her to make the circle.

Without warning, it began snapping at her feet, its jaws only narrowly missing the end of her right shoe.

"Get away," Amanda said weakly, resisting the urge to kick at the wolf. "Shoo!"

The wolf ignored her taunts and it became obvious to Amanda that she'd need to save her breath for other, more important things than shooing away a wolf—things like staying alive.

The strap around her upper arm finally came loose, sliding down the length of her arm and into her hand. It had a steel buckle on its end and Amanda wondered if it could be used as a weapon. She removed the strap from her arm, picked it up, and extended it between her hands to its full length.

It'll have to do, she thought, swinging the belt in the direction of the wolf.

The steel buckle at the end of the belt caught the animal on the snout and it pulled away, and this time it didn't regain its ground as quickly as it had before. Instead, it stayed back, watching Amanda patiently.

I'm going to get away, she thought, still crawling awkwardly backward on her hands and feet, but now making a beeline for the highway.

And that's when she heard the second wolf behind her. It was growling more tenaciously than the first. Amanda turned her head slightly for a look over her right shoulder. The wolf was there, a big brown and gray beast, waiting for her to come to it.

Where the hell did they come from? she wondered.

And that's when she remembered the words Konrad had said in the truck.

My wolfen brothers will have no trouble finding you now.

It was his blood, she realized. The blood he'd ejaculated onto her body was the thing that was calling out these wolves.

But how could she get away when the stuff was all over her arms and legs, and her clothes?

Her clothes . . .

Without another moment's hesitation, Amanda dropped the strap and pulled her top off over her head.

It came away from her body inside out and she had to waste precious seconds righting it to get the bloodstains back on the outside.

"Is this what you want?" she said aloud, spinning the shirt over her head as if she were at some rave.

The wolves' eyes followed the shirt for a moment.

And then she flung it as hard as she could.

It landed on the grass to her right about fifteen feet away.

The wolves bounded toward the shirt and immediately began to tear it apart.

Amanda knew the shirt would keep them busy for only a little while, and then they'd be back for her, even more bloodthirsty after having a taste of the vampire's blood.

She rolled over so she was on her hands and knees with her face and chest facing the ground. She began crawling toward the highway, and after a few yards somehow found the strength to lift herself up onto her feet.

She stumbled through the bushes and over the grass until she felt hard gravel beneath her feet.

The highway.

She'd made it.

But there wasn't a car in sight.

Behind her, she could hear the wolves fighting over the last remnants of her shirt.

Then silence.

They'd be coming for her now.

In the distance, a pair of pinprick lights winked into existence on the crest of a hill.

Amanda began running toward those lights, desperately trying to keep one foot in front of the other . . .

. . . in front of the other . . .

. . . in front of . . .

There was still some distance between herself and the lights, but she could go no farther.

She was too weak.

Too tired.

And in too much pain to continue.

This was as far as she could go.

Hopefully it would be far enough.

She took one last step, and stumbled.

Her legs folded beneath her like a pair of deck chairs.

She put out her hands to break her fall. The right one hit the asphalt and helped break her fall, but the left one crumpled on impact, sending jolts of electric pain shooting up her arm and causing her to roll left across the highway.

She closed her eyes and waited for the wheels of whatever was approaching to run her over.

The lights grew bright against her eyelids.

The sound of the vehicle began to roar in her ears.

It was a truck.

Amanda held her breath and waited for the end.

But before it came, there was a long, loud screech of rubber tires shuddering against the pavement.

The truck came to a stop.

Its lights were upon her.

Two doors opened and closed in quick succession.

"It's a half-naked girl," said a voice.

"You got your cell phone on you?" said another voice.

"Yeah."

Silence for a moment.

"Well, use it to call 911, dumb-ass!"

Chapter 16

– 1 –

They'd found her on the road, literally crawling along Highway 69 in the northbound lanes between the exits to Coldwater and Fesserton.

When he heard the news, Constable Sharpe jumped into his cruiser and headed south down the highway, driving as fast as the traffic would allow, and then some.

This was an incredibly lucky break for the investigation, not to mention the girl. She'd be able to give them a description of the man, his truck, and all kinds of information about how he operated, which with any luck would ultimately lead them to the man's capture.

After almost an hour on the road, Sharpe found himself passing through Crooked Bay where Highway 69 joined up with the much larger Highway 400. With two lanes now in both directions, Sharpe was able to up his speed by twenty kilometers an hour, which would eventually shave more than fifteen minutes off his ETA.

There was no question he would be able to interview the girl when he arrived, but the investigators working on the murders farther north would also be flying down to interview her as well, and Sharpe wanted to make sure he had the opportunity to interview her first before she grew too tired to answer any more questions, or just plain tired of answering the same questions over and over again.

The hospital in Midland was unimaginatively named Huronia District Hospital, which the locals had shortened to the equally boring HDH. Sharpe parked out in front of the hospital behind the other cruisers there, and entered through the building's front doors. Unfamiliar with the hospital's setup, Sharpe approached the information desk in the lobby and asked where he might find Amanda Peck.

The old man behind the desk looked at Sharpe for several moments, then blinked. "Is that the girl they found naked on the highway?"

"Yes, that's the one."

"There's already police with her. Lots of 'em."

Of course there would be OPP officers from the Midland and Orillia detachments with her. They'd probably asked her all kinds of questions already, but they'd be working toward wrapping up a missing person case, while Sharpe on the other hand was still investigating a murder.

"Well, I need to speak to her on another matter," he said, wondering why he had to explain himself to the old-timer.

"Just through those doors there," he said, pointing. "Look for the policemen. . . . Like I said, there's plenty of 'em."

"Thanks."

Sharpe went through the swinging doors and saw at least four constables milling about. *They all look so young,* he thought. *Young enough to be my sons*.

"Who's the officer in charge?" he asked one of them, a blond-haired young man with a jutting square jaw.

The constable pointed to the sergeant standing outside a doorway down the hall.

"Thanks."

Sharpe headed down the hallway, glad to see that the sergeant was a man closer to his own age, maybe even a little older. The name tag on his chest read KNOWLES.

"Sergeant," he said, shaking the man's hand. "I'm Constable Sharpe from Parry Sound, I'm here to—"

"They told me you'd be coming," he said. "You can interview her if you like, for all the good it'll do you."

"Is she unable to speak?"

The sergeant shook his head. "She speaks just fine . . ." He paused as if he was thinking just how to put it; then he said, "Just check with the doctor before you go in."

Sharpe turned around and saw another young man standing behind him. Although he was obviously a doctor, he looked even younger than the constables in the hallway, as if he were just out of high school.

Or maybe, thought Sharpe, *I'm the one who's getting older.*

"Can I see her?" he asked.

The doctor took a moment to look Sharpe in the eye, then said, "If you make it short."

"How is she?"

The young man took a deep breath and sighed. "She's lost a lot of blood . . . and I mean *a lot* of blood. It's actually pretty amazing she's still alive."

"Is she conscious?" Sharpe asked.

"It was touch-and-go there for a while. We didn't dare do much to her until we got some blood and plasma into her. She's on her fourth bag now." He shook his head, as if in disbelief. "It's the last one of that blood type we have on hand."

Drained of blood, Sharpe thought. *Just like the others.*

"Anything else?"

"Plenty. We still don't know if there'll be any permanent damage to her arm."

"Her arm?"

The doctor let out a little laugh. "She said she had to tie it off to get away." A shrug. "There isn't a lot she's saying right now that makes much sense."

"Such as?"

"Needle marks up and down her left arm . . . She said she was raped too, but while we found some evidence of penetration, we didn't find any semen, just blood." The doctor raised his hands, palms up, as if he was at a loss to explain any of it.

"Her blood or somebody else's?"

"So far we haven't been able to tell. We did all the usual hematology tests on the samples we took from her body and clothing, but so far we haven't been able to nail down a specific blood type."

"Hmm," Sharpe said with a sigh.

"What is it?" the doctor asked.

"When I heard she'd been found alive, I thought it was going to make my job easier."

— 2 —

In a busy yard just outside of Barrie where hundreds of trucks were being loaded and unloaded throughout the day, a black Peterbilt pulling a Tucana Northern trailer was wedged in between two bright orange Schneider rigs.

Inside the cab of the Peterbilt, Konrad Valeska slept.

Inside Konrad Valeska, the insatiable need for human blood continued to gnaw at his belly.

— 3 —

Sharpe was glad to see the girl was awake. A pretty girl, especially considering what she'd been through the past few days. She was dressed in a hospital gown and her left arm was in a cast that went from her wrist to just above her elbow. Her right arm was bare, and set up with a couple of intravenous tubes, one for saline and another for blood.

There were no flowers in the room. In fact, there were no decorations of any kind.

"Hello," he said.

She looked over at him and rolled her eyes. "Not another cop," she said. "I've already answered every one of your questions, three times."

Sharped ignored the comment, hoping to smooth things over with some small talk. "I'm Constable Sharpe," he said, "from Parry Sound."

"Yeah, so?"

He'd hoped the mention of her hometown would mellow her out a bit, but it looked as if nothing like that was going to happen. And after all she'd been through, he guessed he shouldn't blame her. So instead of trying to make himself a friend, Sharpe decided it would be best just to get straight to the point. "What happened to you?"

"I already told the other cops what happened to me. They didn't believe me, so why should you?"

"I'm working a different case than they are."

She looked at him through slightly narrowed eyes, as if sizing him up.

A few moments later she shrugged as if to say, "What the hell?" and began talking.

"I was out for a walk by the side of the road. I must have wandered out onto the highway, because I got hit by a car. When I woke up I was dazed, disoriented, and started wandering through the forest. It took me all that time to find the road again and that's when those two men found me and called for help." She punctuated the end of her story by turning her head and looking out the open window.

"How about the real story now?"

"That *is* the real story."

Sharpe shook his head. "You don't show any signs of exposure, and the only thing broken is your arm, which means you were either knocked off the highway by a go-cart, or you're lying to me . . . for what reason, I don't know."

"I'm already in the hospital," she said. "I don't want to be put in a mental ward."

This was all wasting too much time. Sharpe needed to grab her attention.

"Is his name Konrad Valeska?" he said.

Her eyes opened wide and she looked at him as if he'd just named the winning numbers for that night's Lotto 649 draw. "How do you know that?" she asked.

"I've been investigating the last murder . . . and looking for you."

"Well, you found me, and that's the name of the guy who did it."

"Was he holding you for sex?"

"No. He wasn't interested in that at all, not until the very end, anyway. When he thought I was dead."

"You faked your own death?"

"Played dead's more like it."

"And that's when he had sex with you?"

She said nothing in response.

"Is that when he raped you?" he prodded.

"Yeah, that's right, asshole," she shouted. "I was his little dead fuck-doll!"

Sharpe looked over his shoulder at the doorway. All he needed was for the doctor to come in and send him out of the room, citing the patient's need for rest. He stared at the door for several moments, but only a couple of the constables had been curious enough about the noise to poke their heads into the room.

"Sorry, about that," he said, realizing he needed to be a lot more compassionate if he was going to get her to open up to him. "I'll tell you what. Let's try it again, only this time why don't you just tell me what happened to you from the beginning?"

"And I won't have to repeat myself?"

"I'll only ask you questions at the end, and just about the things that I'm unclear about."

"All right," she said, taking a sip of apple juice from the cup on the tray in front of her.

Sharpe got out his notepad and a pen.

"It all started when Ron wanted money. . . ."

— 4 —

Ron Stinson was hard at work digging a trench two feet deep and a foot across. The work was giving his arms an excellent workout, but the shovel handle was murder on his hands and he swore he could feel the blisters forming while he worked. A few of the other guys had suggested he get himself a good pair of gloves, and that was first on his list of "things to buy" when he got his first paycheck. Another thing on the list was a bunch of flowers for Amanda, just as soon as she came home to see them.

"Hey, Ron," said another one of the guys in the crew, a teenager named Jerry Boimstruck.

"Yeah!" Ron said, not stopping his work.

"Are you the same Ron Stinson who was a star in junior?"

"That's me."

"You played for the Brampton Battalion, right?"

"That's right. Won the Memorial Cup and everything."

Jerry shook his head. "I remember watching you play midget. I thought you were headed for the NHL for sure."

"Yeah, me too."

"So what the fuck happened, man?"

Ron stopped digging and thought about it. *What did happen?* He wanted to say it was bad luck, or maybe blame it on Europeans taking his spot on the big team, but that was all bullshit. Sure he'd been injured, but he'd done it to himself, drunk himself right out of hockey.

"Things just didn't work out," he said. "That's all."

"Yeah, but what are you workin' here for? I mean, what are you doing here when you could be playing pro hockey somewhere else?"

That was a good question.

"I hear they've got pro leagues in Italy, Germany, France, Sweden, Switzerland, France . . . They've even got pro teams in England, for cryin' out loud."

He was right. So what if he didn't catch on in the NHL? There were plenty of other places to play hockey around the world. Maybe he'd look into it.

"I'll keep that in mind," he said. "Thanks."

— 5 —

". . . and that's when the truck stopped and I heard someone named Dumb-ass call 911."

Constable Sharpe had listened to her tell her story from beginning to end without interrupting once. It all seemed so logical . . . *if* you were willing to believe her assertion that the suspect, Konrad Valeska, was a blood-drinking vampire.

Seemed impossible, but there was actually a pretty strong case in favor of it.

For example—

The marks on her arm were made by the needle he used to draw her blood. . . . *He used the needle because he was an old vampire and his teeth were shot.*

He drinks the blood of his victims. . . . *All the bodies had been drained of blood.*

He had no trouble lifting her in and out of the truck. . . . *Vampires are said to have the strength of ten men.*

He has power over the people he works with, making them change their minds and bend their will to his own. . . . *Vampires are supposed to have hypnotic eyes that they use to transfix their victims.*

He ejaculated all over his victims to summon the wolves. . . . *Vampires are said to be able to control wolves, even change forms and become wolves themselves if they need to.*

He's awake and drives only at night, sleeping all day long. . . . *Ditto for vampires.*

But in order to buy all that, Sharpe would have to disregard the fact that there's never been any documented physical evidence anywhere in the world since the dawn of time that vampires actually exist. He would also have to believe that vampires have been able to elude detection and capture throughout the centuries and only now, Constable Sharpe of the Ontario Provincial Police was on the trail of the first vampire in history who was careless enough to let one of his victims get away.

It was incredible.

Unbelievable.

It was all so . . . *X-Files.*

Crazies he could understand. He'd seen enough of them over the years to know that people who were mentally unstable were capable of anything, but a *vampire*. That was just too much to believe.

"Did he ever actually refer to himself as a vampire?" he asked.

"Oh, yeah. He went on and on about it, complaining about how Hollywood depicts vampires as being so handsome and regal when it's actually the opposite that's true."

Sharpe thought about Valeska's driver's license, with a Clifton Hill address and a photo of Brad Pitt. It was another connection, or maybe just a very clever criminal having a bit of fun with the system. After all, he'd met plenty of crazy people who were quite smart. A few of them might even have been geniuses in a strange sort of way.

"Look, Amanda," he began. "I don't doubt any of the things you've told me—"

"Bullshit!" she said, cutting him off. "I can hear it in your voice. You don't believe a word I've said."

"Yes, I do. I think you believe everything you've told me is the truth. I just think that this man, Konrad Valeska, is a sick, sick individual who *thinks* he's a vampire."

A strange sort of smile crept over her face and she looked at him with something akin to pity. "You keep thinking that, Constable," she said, "but if I were you I'd be filling my hollow-points with garlic paste. Just to be sure."

Sharpe thought her suggestion was ridiculous, but managed not to let it show. "Thanks," he said. "I'll keep it in mind."

Chapter 17

~ 1 ~

Orest Rojik had four hundred kilometers to go before home, but he was wishing it was more like *fourteen* hundred.

He'd been driving a week, delivering farm equipment from Winnipeg to some distributor in Fredricton, New Brunswick, and then picking up a load of auto parts in Halifax headed for Winnipeg, a round-trip of more than 2,400 kilometers. Normally, Rojik would be ecstatic to get back home again, especially after such a long haul. There wasn't a better feeling for a long-haul driver than pulling into the driveway after an extended road trip, family playing out in the yard, the smell of home-cooked food wafting out from the kitchen window.

But that was before . . .

The last time Rojik had returned from taking a load out to the East Coast, he pulled up into the driveway in time to see a half-naked man running barefoot through his backyard. Then, inside the house, he found his wife in bed . . . at four in the damn afternoon.

The next morning he was in a lawyer's office in downtown Winnipeg getting divorce papers drawn up. Trouble was, the divorce would take a few weeks to be finalized—at the very least—and he'd agreed to let

Enid stay in the house until she could arrange to move in with one of her boyfriends.

One of her boyfriends.

That had been the real kick in the nuts. It was bad enough to come home to find out your wife had been riding every rail in town, but it was a whole 'nother pile of shit to learn that there were at least six guys in town getting it from your wife more often than you were.

Of course, he'd have to sell the house now. Not only was he a cuckold, but he was the laughingstock of the town.

Maybe I'll just live out of my truck for a while, he thought. *See where the road takes me.*

It wasn't such a bad idea. Rojik was a loner to begin with and living out of his truck would save him the mortgage payments he'd been paying on a house he hardly ever lived in. If he needed a shower or a bed to sleep in, he could always get a hotel room, and if he ever found himself lonely, there were enough lot lizards working the nation's highways that he'd never have to know another lonely night.

Just the thought of some of the lot lizards he'd seen over the years brought a smile to his face. Sure, plenty of them were drug addicts and who knows what else, but a few of them were pretty good-looking. And young too. At forty-five and a tad heavy around the middle, Rojik didn't see a lot of young girls looking his way. But with a bit of money here and there, he could at least be treated like a king every once in a while. It wasn't that much different an arrangement than he'd had with his wife, except this way at least he knew he was getting exactly what he was paying for—

Just then something darted out onto the highway in front of Rojik's truck.

"Shit!" he said.

He hit the brakes hard, hoping to hell he wouldn't knife the truck and end up on his side.

The wheels of the tractor locked.

The trailer wheels locked up too, shuddering under the light load of an almost empty trailer.

Rubber screamed in protest.

Rojik screamed in terror.

The truck was slowing, but not stopping.

Up ahead, a deer was caught in the beams of his headlights.

It was just standing there, staring at Rojik, as if it were dumbfounded to find a truck out on the highway at this time of the day.

Rojik pulled on the air horn's lanyard.

The deer was startled, but didn't run.

It just kept on standing there, watching Rojik getting closer, waiting for it to—

WHAM!

Rojik slammed into the deer still doing fifty.

Blood splashed across the windshield.

And then the truck began to skid across the asphalt as if there'd been nothing more in its way than a cardboard cutout.

The skid seemed to last forever, and then all of a sudden it was over and the truck had come to a complete halt.

The engine of Rojik's Freightliner rattled rhythmically under the hood, just as it always did.

Rojik let out a sigh, relieved he was still breathing. Still alive.

He doubted he could say as much for the deer.

After a quick check of his mirrors, Rojik shifted his rig into first and slowly pulled over onto the right shoulder of the highway.

He wondered for a moment if he should turn off the engine, or keep it running in case he couldn't get it started again, and decided on the latter.

With his warning lights flashing, Rojik got out of the truck and started toward the front of his rig.

"Shit!" he said again as he turned the corner.

The deer's head had gone through the front grill as if it had been shot out of a cannon. Luckily it was just a young stag and its antlers hadn't been long enough to puncture the radiator. Still, it was going to be bloody hell working the tangled branches out of the metal grill.

He grabbed the deer's haunches and tried to pull the animal away from the truck.

It wouldn't move.

He took a closer look at it and realized that its right rear leg had gotten wedged in between the front bumper and the bottom of the grill.

He grabbed the leg and pulled.

It was stuck in there good.

Might have to cut the leg out, Rojik thought.

Luckily he kept the head on the axe handle he used to test for tire pressure on his circle check sharp. A couple of whacks with that and the leg would come away no problem.

He went back to the cab to get his axe.

― 2 ―

With the missing girl in the hospital and her body on the mend, Constable Sharpe decided to go home for a few hours' rest. There was still a CPIC wide-area broadcast out for Konrad Valeska's truck, and with any luck, someone on the highway would spot him soon. Sharpe wanted to be fresh and ready when it happened.

That's when he got the call on the radio about the trucker outside of Still River. He asked the dispatcher if there was a more detailed description of the man and when she gave it to him, everything Sharpe knew about the case seemed to fall neatly into place.

"He's short, about five-foot-five, stocky build, ball cap, and jacket, and . . . he's covered in blood."

"10-9 on that last part?"

"He's covered in blood," the dispatcher said. "The woman who called in said . . ." There was a pause, as if the dispatcher had to reference some notes. ". . . there's blood all over him. His clothes, his shoes, his face, his head, everywhere except his hands. They look like they've been cleaned, but . . ." Another pause. ". . . his fingernails are black."

"She say anything else?"

"Isn't that enough?"

Amanda Peck had said the guy was a vampire. When asked to make a guess, Dr. Casey had said the killer was a vampire. Even the OPP's own profiler had made the connection between the nature of the killings and the way vampires prey on their victims. So, if this was the killer, was there something about him that was different? That said, *I am vampire?*

"Did she say there was anything, I don't know, *weird* about the guy?"

"The man's covered in blood," the dispatcher said in a tone that suggested Sharpe might be an idiot. "How much more weird would you like?"

Sharpe ignored the comment. "But she said it was a man?"

"Yeah, a man."

"10-4."

That's got to be him, Sharpe thought. *It has to be.*

The description was pretty close to the one Amanda Peck had given him.

And he was just a man. Not a vampire. A man.

Even the location where they found him was a pretty good fit.

The Tucana Northern shipper had said that Valeska was making deliveries in Winnipeg and would be back through Ontario in a few days. And though he'd dropped off the girl on the southbound side of Highway 69, halfway between Barrie and Parry Sound, the town of Still River was north of that point, and south of Sudbury. The only thing that didn't fit was that Still River was *only* a couple hundred kilometers south of Sudbury and enough time had passed since they'd found the girl for him to put many hundreds, perhaps even thousands of kilometers between himself and the last victim.

Who knows, maybe he's even fled the country by now.

Still, there was a good chance this was the guy and Sharpe hoped he could get up there in time to be in on his capture, and if not that, then at least he'd be able to question him after they had him in cuffs.

There was just one thing he needed to check on before he made the run up to Still River.

With the battery on his cell phone out of power, Sharpe pulled into a rest station just before Pointe au Baril and put in a call to Jimmy, the shipper working nights at Tucana Northern.

"Jimmy?" he said. "This is Constable Sharpe, I spoke to you earlier about one of your drivers—"

"Valeska."

"That's right."

"What about him?"

"Have you seen him? Has he been in for a load?"

"I would have called you if he did," Jimmy said. "I mean, that's why you gave me your card, right?"

"That's exactly right," he said, feeling a bit sorry that he hadn't put more faith in Jimmy. "I'm just checking."

Sharpe said good-bye, and ordered a double-double for the ride up to Still River.

Once inside his cruiser and headed north on Highway 69, he hit the lights, switched on the siren, and put his foot down hard on the accelerator.

With any luck he'd be in Still River in less than an hour.

— 3 —

The look on the face of the girl behind the counter had been something else.

Like she'd seen a ghost, or maybe a monster.

Even now, everyone in the place was *looking* at him, like he'd done something wrong.

Orest Rojik picked up the tray with his burger, fries, and coffee and headed for a secluded corner of the restaurant. He'd hoped that people might ignore him there, but he could feel their eyes on him, following him across the room as if they expected him to do something.

That's right, he thought, *I'm the guy whose wife's been sleeping with everyone in town. I'm the one.*

He slid into the booth farthest from the counter and resumed eating. He hunched up his shoulders, wanting to disappear inside his coat, and looked around for a newspaper. There was one on the table in front of him, so he got up, picked up the paper, and brought it back to his own table. It was a day-old copy of the *Toronto Sun* but it would do the job.

He folded the paper so he could hold it with one hand, and then raised it up to eye level so that people around him couldn't stare at him anymore.

"At last," he said under his breath. "Maybe now I can eat in peace."

He took a bite of his burger, washed it down with some coffee, then picked up a French fry and dragged it through the pool of ketchup he'd squirted onto one side of his plate. The fry was cold, and a bit under-cooked, but it was tasty enough.

"Put down the paper, slowly," said a voice.

"What?" Rojik said, without looking up.

"Put it down slowly," repeated the voice. "And keep your other hand where I can see it."

Slowly, just as he'd been instructed, Rojik lowered the paper.

Directly across from him was a large man, dressed for the most part in black, pointing the biggest gun Rojik had ever seen directly at his forehead.

"What is it?"

He glanced around, there were others surrounding him, all dressed in black and looking a little bit like commandos.

"Put your hands down on the table and slide out of the booth."

"What's going on?"

"Just do it!" the man shouted.

Rojik wasn't sure what was going on, but he tried to do what they were asking. He was trying to get out of the booth, but his legs were trembling and his arms were shaking and he just couldn't seem to slide out from behind the table.

Obviously he wasn't moving fast enough.

A hand grabbed his jacket and pulled.

Then there were other hands on him, holding him down.

Rojik felt something warm and wet running down his leg.

"Why are you doing this to me?" he said.

"Why are you all covered in blood?" the man asked.

Suddenly, Rojik understood, and he smiled with relief.

"Something funny?"

"No, sir," he said, removing the smile from his face. "It's just that I hit a deer about twenty-five klicks up the highway."

The tension in the room suddenly began to dissipate.

"You can check my truck if you want. There's a hole in the grille and blood all over it. . . . I know it looks like hell, but the rig is still okay to drive."

"Aw, shit!"

"Geez."

Rojik smiled again.

A few of the other truckers in the restaurant were having a good laugh, but none of the police officers around him seemed to appreciate the humor of the situation.

Maybe it would be one of those things that they'd laugh about later.

Rojik was sure looking forward to getting back into his truck and having a good guffaw.

Constable Sharpe tried to follow the situation in Still River on the radio as he headed north, but it was difficult to know what was going on because things were happening on-scene that weren't necessarily being reported over the radio.

From what he could gather, an OPP Tactical Response

Unit was being considered, but it would likely take too long for them to arrive on the scene to be of much use, and as far as Sharpe knew there had been no mention of a weapon. A more likely scenario would see the officers on the scene apprehending the suspect on their own, hopefully without a problem or anyone getting hurt.

Sharpe had hoped to reach Still River before they went in for the capture, but there were other people in the restaurant and the conventional wisdom was that taking him early and by surprise was the best way to avoid a standoff.

When he pulled into the rest station parking lot, Sharpe noticed there were a couple of rigs that had the Tucana Northern logo on the sides of their trailers.

"We got him!" Sharpe said out loud, pulling to a stop just outside the restaurant.

But when he got out of the cruiser, there was something wrong with the scene. He had expected everything to be tense, but instead, there were officers milling about, laughing and joking with each other, and looking as if they'd just completed a training exercise, not just apprehended a serial killer.

"Who are you?" someone asked Sharpe.

"Who's the Officer in Charge?"

Just then an older man, a sergeant from the looks of it, stepped out of the restaurant. His eyes caught Sharpe's almost immediately. "It's not him," he said.

"What?"

"It's not the Valeska character you're looking for."

Sharpe wanted to rush into the restaurant and see for himself, but he knew that such action was unnecessary. Of course it wasn't Konrad Valeska. The pattern and timing was wrong by a day or two. The man should have picked up a load in Toronto by now, but he hadn't so it was likely that he was somewhere far, far away, hunting along some new stretch of highway.

"That's too bad," Sharpe said.

"It's not *so* bad. It's not every day you catch a deer's killer so, uh, red-handed."

The officers near the sergeant laughed.

Everyone's a comedian, thought Sharpe, wondering if he was the one who would have the last laugh.

— 4 —

Outside the rest station.

As the crowd began to form around the entrance to the restaurant, wondering what was going on inside . . .

As the flashing lights of the police cars blinked on, looking more and more like fireworks with each passing second . . .

And as the mobile news van from the *New VR* switched on its high-powered television lights to bring the news to the rest of the province . . .

A Tucana Northern trailer being pulled by a shiny black Peterbilt began to move.

It slithered across the parking lot, then glided onto the highway, like a snake slipping into a river.

Moments later it had merged with the flow of traffic, and was gone.

Chapter 18

Ron learned that Amanda was alive when he got home from work and found the OPP constable who was investigating her disappearance, Constable Sharpe, parked outside their trailer.

Initially he had figured it to be bad news and took forever to get out of his car. Although his body had firmed up from the days of hard work, when he finally did exit the car he found it difficult to walk the few steps to the constable's cruiser.

But somehow, he reached the man's car.

The constable rolled down his window.

Ron put a hand against the roof of the car, leaned forward, and waited to hear the bad news.

"We found her," Sharpe said. "Alive."

Ron's heart and body suddenly felt lighter, but despite that, his knees went weak and he had to lean more heavily against the cruiser to remain on his feet.

"How is she?"

"She's in bad shape, but she'll live."

"Where is she?"

"Hospital in Midland." A pause. "Want me to take you there?"

Ron considered it. He might not be in the best shape to

drive a car that far, but he didn't want to spend an hour riding with the cop just to get there, and then another hour with him on the way back. Seeing Amanda again was going to be a personal thing and Ron didn't want to have to go over their meeting with the cop on the way home.

"Thanks for the offer, but I'd rather drive myself."

"Sure, no problem."

That had been an hour and a half ago. Since then he'd had a shower, a couple of peanut butter and jam sandwiches, and had driven the hundred or so kilometers into Midland. Now he was circling the hospital looking for a place to park for free. Parking in the hospital lot itself was free, but it would take a toonie to get out of the lot when he was done at the end of the night. He had a few dollars on him, but he wanted to hang on to them to buy some flowers in the hospital gift shop for Amanda.

He eventually found a place to park on a nearby side street, wedging the car between a pickup truck and a minivan, then walked ten minutes to the hospital.

The lobby of the place was like every other hospital lobby he'd seen, with a reception area, coffee shop, and gift shop. There was a small refrigerator in the gift shop with preprepared flower bunches. There weren't any prices on them, but he picked one he liked and headed for the cash hoping for the best.

"Six fifty," said the old woman behind the counter. Her hair was thin, and her skin wrinkled. She looked tired, maybe even bored, and was counting the minutes until her volunteer time was over and she could go home.

Ron pulled out his change pouch. It was a small red leather sack with two steel bands at the open end. He squeezed the bands at the ends, opened the pouch, and poured the loose change into his palm. There was a toonie, two loonies, three quarters, and a few dimes, nickels, and pennies.

Not even close to six fifty.

Ron sighed.

He slid the change back into his pouch and picked the flowers up off the counter.

As he turned to bring them back to the refrigerator, the old woman said, "How much you got?"

"Not even five bucks," he said.

"Close enough," said the old woman.

Ron turned to look at her and saw she was smiling. The smile changed the whole character of her face. She wasn't a mean-looking old lady anymore, but a kind-hearted matron who lived to help people in need. Or maybe people who just needed a little help in their lives.

"Thanks," said Ron, emptying his change purse and sliding the coins across the counter.

"You're welcome," she said, still beaming.

As he left the shop, Ron wondered if she would have been as kind to the person he was a week ago.

Probably not.

And if she hadn't, he more than likely would have tried to steal the flowers.

If the woman in the gift shop had noticed a difference in him, then maybe Amanda would too.

He pushed the elevator button and waited.

Full of hope.

— 2 —

Traffic on Highway 400 heading south into Toronto was light, even for a weeknight.

Valeska needed blood, but hadn't come across any hitchhikers since he'd set out at sundown. There was no reason to expect he'd come across any heading south in the middle of the week, but you could never be sure how things would play out.

Like the last one.

He had expected her to live another two or three days, allowing him to dump the body on the northern stretch of his route, but she'd run dry early. That had thrown him off his schedule, forcing him to run short of blood and be without the prospect of a replacement for at least a few days.

It wasn't his favorite thing, to go without blood. There were hunger pangs, and his aged rotten fangs ached like sore teeth in need of fillings. Eventually his body would begin to tremble and he'd be forced to track down some wild animal in the forests lining the highway. Or, more his style these days would be to drive into some suburban neighborhood and take his sustenance from someone's pet dog or cat. The blood of domestics was a poor substitute for the blood of wild animals, or for the blood of humans, but it would be enough to keep him alive until he found another rider willing to climb up into his cab.

Like now . . .

Up ahead, at the end of the on-ramp that merged Highway 88 to the 400 just outside the town of Bradford, a young woman stood on the gravel shoulder with her thumb extended into the cool night air. Even though it was dark out, and the headlights from his Peterbilt still hadn't caught her in their beams, he could make her out perfectly in the darkness. A short raven-haired girl of about nineteen dressed in torn jeans, worn shoes, and an aged minor hockey jacket.

He couldn't be sure about the rest of it, but if she was anything like the others she wanted to get out of her small town and head for somewhere else, somewhere bigger, somewhere better, somewhere over the rainbow . . . What did it matter? She'd never get there anyway.

This one wanted a ride south.

Into Toronto.

The Big Smoke, they sometimes called it.

He'd be passing through the city on his way to the Tucana Northern yard in Mississauga, but he doubted very much if he'd be stopping to let her off.

He would stop at the rest station near Aurora, though. He'd get her a bite to eat and she'd be asleep all the way through Toronto and wouldn't wake up until they were back on the 400 heading north.

The more he thought about it, the more it seemed like a perfect setup.

He slowed the truck and pulled over onto the shoulder.

"Pretty," he said under his breath as she was caught by his headlights and he could make out her facial features more clearly.

He stopped the Peterbilt, shifted into neutral, and reached over to open the passenger-side door.

"Thanks for stopping," she said, still standing on the side of the road.

"Where are you headed?" Valeska asked, even though he already knew the answer.

"Toronto," she said. "We have a gig there Friday."

We, he thought.

Just then a long-haired young man appeared at the woman's side carrying a guitar case. He'd obviously been hiding in the bushes waiting for someone to stop to give his girlfriend a ride. Once the vehicle was stopped it was just a simple matter of convincing the driver to take both of them instead of just the one.

Sorry, thought Valeska. *Not possible.*

"Dude, thanks for the lift."

The girl climbed up a step and was ready to get into the

truck when she stopped and sniffed at the air. "What's
that stink?"

"Fuck off!" Valeska shouted. They weren't his favorite
words. And in fact, the words came out as two distinct
words instead of the single-word staccato gunshot of an
expletive it was when it rolled off the tongue of Canadi-
ans. Nevertheless, he knew that the words would be
something these two people would understand.

"Relax, pal," said the man. "We don't care if your truck
stinks like shit. We need the ride."

"I said, Fuck off!" he repeated, this time pushing the
girl out of the cab.

She vanished from the inside of the truck, falling onto
the shoulder and taking her boyfriend with her. The two
hit the ground hard, tumbling backward several times before coming to a stop.

Valeska slammed the door closed and angrily threw the
truck into gear.

"Stupid humans," he shouted. "I am not a bus driver."

As he pulled back onto the highway, his stomach
grumbled, reminding him of his true identity, and of his
need.

"I'm a vampire," he whispered under his breath, as a
bloody tear leaked from the corner of his eye.

— 3 —

When Ron reached Amanda's room, there were a few
nurses milling about in the hallway just outside the door.
They looked to be keeping a couple of print reporters at
bay, barring them from entering the room.

One of them glanced at the flowers in his hand and
said, "Who are you?"

"I'm her . . ." He hesitated a moment. He really wasn't

anything to her more than a friend. They weren't married, or even engaged, and they'd barely made plans about doing things together more than a few days in advance. He wanted to say, "I'm her husband," and would even settle for "fiancé," but those words required a commitment he hadn't been willing to make in the past. That might change in the future, but for now he was little more than a friend.

"I'm her *boyfriend*," he said, the word sounding all wrong. "Ron Stinson."

"Oh, Constable Sharpe said you might be coming by. And the doctor wanted me to tell you something before you saw her."

The nurse's voice had trailed off to a whisper, and Ron instinctively moved closer to hear her.

"She's been through a terrible ordeal. She might say things that might seem incredible, but it's better not to confront her about them, or suggest she's making anything up. She needs support right now, not another fight."

Ron nodded. "Sure, okay."

"Good," the nurse said, stepping aside to allow Ron past.

Ron walked down the hall and stepped through the doorway, surprised to find that Amanda had the room to herself.

She was lying on her back on the bed farthest from the door. There were bags hanging by her bedside and tubes running into her right arm. The left arm was in a cast. Her face was clean and her hair had been combed, but she looked like hell. There was hardly any color to her skin and her eyes were sunk way back into her skull. She'd only been missing a couple of days, but she looked as if she'd had the crap beat out of her for months.

Ron took a few tentative steps into the room and stopped.

Several seconds passed and Amanda still hadn't noticed him.

"Hey, Mandy!" he said at last.

She turned her head and when she saw him her eyes went wide for a moment before slowly closing in a critical sort of squint.

"About time you got here," she said.

"Sorry about that," Ron said. "But I only heard they'd found you after I'd finished work."

"You? Working?"

"Yeah, you remember Bobby Bloxam?"

She shook her head.

"Well, he coached me in minor hockey and he gave me a job with his landscaping company. I started the day you went missing."

"You've been working all this time?"

She sounded skeptical, but Ron wasn't worried. All he had to do was tell the truth this time, and it wouldn't matter if she believed him or not because, well, it was the truth. And to be honest, it was a much better feeling than when he'd had to lie to her about where he'd been and what he'd been doing. She'd believed most of his lies and over time he'd gotten really good at making them sound like the truth. This was something new for both of them and he didn't blame her for being doubtful.

"Every day on the job . . . most nights I was looking for you."

"Were you the one who reported me missing?"

"Yeah, after you didn't come back that first night."

Amanda was silent for a long time. Outside, the clouds drifted by, changing the ambience of the light in the room. It might have been a trick of the lighting, or it might not, but somehow the angry hard-edged exterior she'd shown when he first entered the room had melted away. She looked sad now, scared and vulnerable. He couldn't be sure at this distance, but she seemed to be shaking too.

"Who are those for?" she said at last, gesturing to the flowers held tightly in Ron's right fist.

He looked down at them, and realized he'd just about forgotten they were there. "Well, they're not for me."

"Yeah? Whose room did you steal them out of?"

Ron was glad to see that there was still a bit of Amanda's fighting spirit left.

"I didn't," he said, feeling a bit of pride over not having to lie about where he'd gotten them. "I bought them in the gift shop downstairs." He paused a moment, then said, "I was short a couple of bucks and the woman in the shop let me have them cheap. . . . I guess she thought I had an honest face, or something."

Amanda smiled at that, and then slowly, as if by degrees, her smile waned and she began to cry.

Ron wasn't sure why she was crying. It might have been because she was happy to see him, but more likely it was an emotional release of the pent-up anger, frustration, or fear that had built up over the course of her ordeal.

Ron still didn't know what had happened to her, but that was unimportant now.

Right now, she just needed somebody to hold her.

And that's just what Ron wanted to do at that moment, too.

He tossed the flowers onto the empty bed to his right and rushed to Amanda's side, wrapping his arms around her and letting her sob against his shoulder for as long as she needed.

When she was finally done, he asked, "What happened?"

* * *

Ron knew she'd been through an ordeal, but he had no idea it would have such a psychological affect on her. According to what she'd said, Amanda expected him to believe that she'd been kidnapped by a—he had trouble even thinking the word—a vampire . . . who held her captive for a few days while he drank her blood out of a needle in her arm.

Incredible.

Absolutely in-*fucking*-credible.

As he watched her rest, Ron tried to imagine the kind of horror she'd experienced. She was obviously trying to suppress the memory of her ordeal by making up a story about a vampire.

And what a story it was.

Ron had seen a few vampire movies before, but none of them had ever been anything as wild as this. This was, well . . . stranger than fiction.

The thought reminded Ron of the adage *truth is stranger than fiction*.

And that's when he first began to consider the possibility that maybe, just maybe, Amanda wasn't making up any story about a vampire. After all, she really didn't have a wild enough imagination to think up a story like that.

Maybe she was telling the truth.

Amanda opened her eyes and looked over at Ron. "What are you thinking?" she asked, her voice soft but somehow still quite strong.

"Uh, I'm wondering when they might let you out of here," Ron lied.

"The doctor said maybe tomorrow, maybe the next day. It all depends on how well my hemoglobin recovers."

"And then a couple of weeks' rest at home, right?"

She shook her head.

"You want to start working again?"

She shook her head a second time.

"Then, what?"

She was silent a moment, pausing as if she were unsure whether or not to speak. But then she drew in a breath and said, "I'm going to sharpen some pieces of wood."

"What?"

"And buy some garlic . . ."

"Oh, shit!" Ron said under his breath.

"And I need to get some crosses . . ."

"Mandy," he said.

She ignored him and kept on talking.

"Crucifixes, they call them."

"Amanda!"

"And maybe a rosary, too."

"Amanda, stop it!"

She looked at him then with a startled look on her face, almost as if seeing him next to the bed reminded her that he was in the room with her.

"I know you must have gone through hell, but you got away and you're going to be all right." The look on her face had slowly changed to one of disappointment, but Ron couldn't stop now. He just couldn't let her hurt herself like this. "You don't have to torture yourself. The police know who they're looking for . . . and eventually they're going to catch him."

"No, they won't."

Ron was going to say something else, but anything he said right now would probably lead to an argument.

"The cop investigating the last murder doesn't believe the guy's a vampire," she said.

Ron held his tongue, but he couldn't do anything about the expression on his face, which he was sure was giving away his true feelings on the matter.

Amanda's eyes narrowed as she stared at him. "You don't believe me either, do you?"

What's the right answer? Ron thought. If he said he didn't believe her he could kiss good-bye any hope of getting back together. And if he said he believed her, then he'd be lying. And not a little white lie either, but a big fat purple one. Right now, all he was willing to believe was that there was a possibility that what Amanda was saying was true. That was a long way from believing her 100 percent.

What to do? Ron himself didn't believe in vampires, but he had no problem accepting that Amanda absolutely believed what she was saying. Furthermore, it was easy to think that whoever had held her captive was a monster. And if she wanted to label that monster a vampire, then it was a vampire. Looking at it that way, it was easier for Ron to accept Amanda's story as truth. And besides all that, if the guy who'd held her captive was a vampire, it explained all of the weird shit that had happened to her, like her loss of blood, and the needle marks, and the blood she was covered with when they found her.

And finally, he loved her. He'd never told her that and he'd never really felt it before, but over the past few days he'd come to the realization that his life was empty without her. He wanted to make her proud of him, wanted to bring her close to him, and he wanted her to love him again . . . the way she did when they'd first met. And how could she love him if he didn't believe her?

"Do you?" she repeated, appearing to grow angry over his slow response.

"I believe you," he said.

She nodded, as if this were merely the way things should be. "And you'll help me, right?"

"I'll do everything I can."

"Like keep your job?"

Ron had been working hard the last few days and he had every intention of sticking with it. Judging by the way she'd said, "Like keep your job?" it sounded as if she didn't hold out much hope that he would keep working. It bothered him that she had such a low opinion of him, but he realized that he hadn't given her much reason to think highly of him in the last few months. But this was where it would all start to change. Instead of getting into a fight, he would just agree with her, and then he would *show* her he'd changed by hanging on to the job for as long as he had to.

"Sure, no problem," he said. "I'll keep working."

If she was surprised by his response, she didn't let on. "Good," she said, matter-of-factly. "Because we're going to need some money for what I have in mind."

~ 4 ~

"Jimmy!"

"Whaddya want?"

"Jimmy!" the voice called again.

Jimmy Paul was working deep within the stacks, far from the loading dock and whoever wanted his time. "Whaddya want?" he said again, this time louder.

"I'm here for a load," said the voice, closer now.

"Just a minute."

Nobody came by for hours, and then the moment he ventured back into the warehouse things would get busy. It never failed and Jimmy often thought that truckers purposely waited just outside the loading dock until he was nowhere to be seen, and that's when they decided to come looking for him.

He put his clipboard on top of the skid he was checking, then started walking down the aisle. He turned left, then right, and had a clear view of the aisle all the way to the bright lights of the loading dock. Jimmy always thought of those lights as the light at the end of the tunnel, or perhaps maybe at least the corridor. The goods he stored in the warehouse were like children in the womb. After they made the trip out to the light, they experienced birth and would go out into the world to fulfill their purpose in life.

It was corny, he knew, maybe even ridiculous, but hey . . . it helped to pass the time.

But as he neared the light at the end, a large dark figure appeared in front of it—a clearly defined black outline in the middle of the glow from the bright white lights shining from behind.

"Shit!" Jimmy said.

The short wide silhouette could only belong to one person, one of Jimmy's least-favorite truckers in the whole wide world.

"Konrad Valeska," he said, making it sound as if they were friends who hadn't seen each other in ages.

"I want my load," he said, his voice sharp and curt.

"All right, all right, I'd like to spend the night with Jennifer Love Hewitt but you don't hear me whining about it."

"I'm in a hurry," Valeska said. "I want to get back on the road."

Jimmy looked around at the skids and boxes surrounding him. "Yeah, well, I'm a busy guy if you haven't noticed."

"There's no one here."

"That doesn't mean I'm not busy."

And that's when Valeska grabbed him by the shoulders and stared directly into Jimmy's eyes.

"Hey, what the—"

Jimmy's eyes felt as if they'd been stabbed with a pair of Roundedge pencils. His brain had somehow been frozen and his soul temporarily shackled by wide iron bands. He was a prisoner to the man's gaze and couldn't do a damn thing about it.

"You will load my truck now," Valeska said. "Immediately."

As much as Jimmy wanted to tell him, "Fuck you!" all he could manage was, "Yes, sir."

Valeska let go of his shoulders and Jimmy was allowed to look away, but the power of the man's gaze was still inside him, compelling him to load the man's truck as quickly as he could.

Jimmy found Valeska's bill of lading, hopped on a forklift and went off in search of the load. He found it at the west end of the warehouse, an LTL load of twelve skids, destined for three different delivery points between Toronto and Winnipeg, as well as a three-skid delivery to Timmins.

Timmins . . .

The city name jogged something at the back of Jimmy's mind.

Timmins . . .

He thought about the city while he loaded Valeska's truck. The longer he was away from Valeska, the clearer he was able to think.

Someone had been asking about Timmins. It had been the cop, what was his name again? Thorpe, or Tarp, maybe. No, Sharpe, yeah, that was it. Constable Sharpe of the OPP. He'd wanted me to call him when Valeska came looking for a load.

One of the skids was stuck.

Jimmy climbed off the forklift and took a look at the problem. The edge of one skid was resting on top of the one he wanted to move. It was just barely touching and a good push on the offending skid would surely free the other. And so he planted his feet and gave the skid a push. It moved slightly, then fell three inches to the floor.

As it fell, a piece of steel strapping came loose from the top of the skid, whipped around the boxes, and caught Jimmy on the arm.

"Ow," he said, pulling his arm back as if it had been bitten by a snake.

He took a look at his arm and wondered why he'd rolled up the sleeves of his coveralls. There was a big red welt between the elbow and wrist, and a tiny scratch along the forearm. It hurt worse than it looked, but only because the steel had stung him. The discomfort would by gone in a minute, and then he could tend to the welt and scratch properly. After he'd dealt with Valeska. The guy gave Jimmy the creeps and he wouldn't be too broken up to see the man taken away in cuffs. He didn't know exactly what Valeska had done, but he guessed it was some pretty serious shit.

He flexed his arm a bit to make sure it was okay, then hopped back on the forklift and got back to work. Just a few minutes later, he'd finished loading Valeska's truck. But now that that was done he needed to stall Valeska somehow, then call the cop while the man was waiting. But Jimmy was by himself and there was little chance of him getting away from Valeska long enough to make a phone call.

"Want a coffee?" Jimmy said.

"No, I don't."

"Cigarette, maybe?"

Valeska didn't answer. He was staring at the scratch on Jimmy's arm.

"You want a cigarette?"

"I don't smoke."

"You won't mind if I have one, will you?"

"Are you finished loading?"

"Yeah, I just have to make a call to one of the customers to check on something. I won't be a minute."

Valeska said nothing, his eyes still locked on Jimmy's arm.

Jimmy turned and headed for the office.

The cop had given him a card with his number on it. If he couldn't get hold of the cop, then he'd just explain the situation to whoever answered the phone. If that didn't work, then he'd call 911 and let the cops sort it all out.

He sat down at his desk and began looking in the drawers. He had a couple of porn magazines in the bottom drawer on the right, a flask of Canadian Club in the bottom drawer on the left. Of course, the card wasn't in either of those drawers, he was just checking. He tried the top right drawer, then the one directly in front of him. No card. Finally, he pulled the top left drawer open.

The card was there, lying on a pile of scattered office supplies, candies, and empty cigarette packages.

He was about to reach for the card, when he felt a presence in the office with him . . .

"I'll be right with you," he said.

. . . a cold presence.

"I said—"

He turned to look behind him and felt a cold, cold hand on his head, holding it firm as another hand grabbed his wrist and pulled his arm away from his body.

And then cold lips and a point of hot, searing pain on his arm where he'd scratched himself.

"What the fuck are you doing?" he said, struggling against the hand on his head, but unable to move.

It was as if he were being held in place by ten men, maybe more.

"Let me go, asshole," he screamed, but already the strength was ebbing from his body.

He could feel something being pulled out of his arm, sucked out, as if by great force.

It hurt like hell, but slowly the pain subsided.

He felt light-headed.

Dizzy.

Eventually the hand came away from his head, and the guy's mouth—his goddamn mouth—came away from his arm.

The bruise was huge, and what had once been a scratch was now a long open rent in his flesh. But there was no blood coming out of it. He should have been bleeding profusely, but instead there was nothing.

Jimmy sat there in his chair for a moment, trying to hold his body up, but eventually losing the fight.

He toppled over, slamming the top left drawer shut on his way down to the floor.

The last thing he heard was the sound of a truck starting up out at the loading dock. It was a loud, angry sound at first, but then it slowly faded away into the distance.

Into the night.

Chapter 19

The days passed.

Amanda was released from Huronia District Hospital and placed under the care of her family physician. Since she and Ron didn't really have a family doctor, Amanda figured she could always visit a walk-in clinic if she really needed any further medical attention.

But after just a day at home, Amanda became restless enough to walk over to the Big Wheel and arrange to start work the next morning. They needed the money and she felt that waiting on tables would help keep her mind occupied during her waking hours—especially since she was at the mercy of her nightmares whenever she tried to get any sleep.

Murray, the owner of the diner, was happy to see her again and said she could start working whenever she felt she was ready. All of the regulars at the Big Wheel were glad to see her too, but Cookie was by far the one who gave her the most heartfelt greeting. There were big wet tears in his eyes, and when he gave her a hug, she could feel his whole body shaking. She was touched by Cookie's sincerity and didn't mind hanging around an extra half hour drinking coffee and eating the pie he insisted he buy for her as a sort of "welcome home."

She had a bite of the pie but the scarlet cherry filling reminded her too much of blood for her to have any more of it.

Cookie was more than happy to finish it for her.

Ron continued working his landscaping job, arriving on time, working late, and doing all that was asked of him with nary a grumble or complaint. His body was getting hard and every day the work got that much easier. He had aches all over, but they were the good sort of aches that came when a body was being reawakened from a months-long drunken stupor. It wasn't much of a job, raking leaves, cutting grass, digging holes, but if nothing else, he took a measure of pride in doing an honest day's work. Mandy was proud of him too and that was the thing that felt so good to Ron. He sensed that she'd regained some respect for him because of the effort he was making to turn his life around. If he did nothing else with his life other than prove he could hold on to a job for more than a few weeks, she'd be happy.

She would be happy, but he wouldn't.

Recent events, especially his new job and Mandy's abduction—whether it came at the hands of a vampire or not—had jogged Ron's mind and shaken up his entire being.

Being alone without a dollar in your pocket might be all right for a twenty-year-old, but it wasn't all right for a forty-year-old. He could continue moving from job to job and getting by day by day, but how long could he count on Mandy sticking with him?

She'd already left him once.

He couldn't allow the same thing to happen twice.

So on his way home from work, Ron stopped off at the

Northland Market and bought himself a ten-dollar Bell Quick Change phone card.

When he left the store, he walked over to the phone booth at the corner of the parking lot near the street and slid the card into the slot above the keypad. When the tiny blue screen at the top of the phone informed Ron he had ten dollars' worth of credit, he pulled out a creased and rabbit-eared slip of paper from his right pants pocket.

He pressed 1, then dialed the number as he read it off the slip of paper in his hand.

After several rings, a man's voice said, "Hello?"

"Hi," Ron said, "Is this Mr. Rutledge?"

"Yeah, who's this?" The voice was gruff and sounded annoyed over the call.

Ron took a breath. "This is Ron . . . Ron Stinson. I don't know if you remember me."

"Of course I remember you, how ya doin'?" The voice of the man at the other end of the line, Mr. Rutledge, had done a one-eighty and he now seemed genuinely pleased to be hearing from Ron.

"All right . . . I guess," said Ron.

"Why, what's going on?"

Ron took a deep breath, sighed, and started talking.

When he finally got off the phone, there was fifteen cents left on the card.

— 2 —

The nights passed, too.

Each night after work, Ron would drop by the Big Wheel and have a bite to eat while he waited for Amanda to finish her shift. Since it was dark by six o'clock, they would go straight from the diner out to the highway and one of the rest stops that dotted the north- and south-bound lanes of Highway 69.

And there they would wait.

Amanda was convinced that the vampire was still driving the route between Toronto and Winnipeg and was sure to cross their path if they watched the highway each night between sundown and sunrise.

Ron wasn't so sure. Why would the vampire—he still had trouble using that term, even in his thoughts—still be driving the highway when the OPP was out looking for him from Barrie to Kenora? But what did it matter? Amanda wanted to do this and he wanted to be with Amanda, so spending a few nights in the car watching the highway in search of a phantom was a small price to pay for her love.

Ron returned to the car after a bathroom break with a coffee for himself and a tea for Amanda.

"Anything?" he asked.

"No."

Ron marveled at the matter-of-fact way she always answered his question. No matter how many times he asked, she said no as if it were the first time, as if the answer could go either way. That sort of steadfast determination had placed a knot of self-doubt at the back of Ron's mind to the point where he often wondered, *What if she's right?*

"Brought you a tea."

She took the cup from him and smiled. "Thanks."

Ron slid into the driver's seat and cracked the plastic lid of his coffee cup and folded back the tab. He slurped loudly when he took a sip, reminding him how quiet the inside of the car was.

"It's cold tonight," he said.

"Yeah, it is."

There was another moment of silence between them where the only noise was the distant sound of cars and trucks rolling across the highway.

He'd made plenty of attempts at small talk as they'd sat in the car, each of them as successful as this most recent failure. It frustrated Ron that Amanda had so little to say these days, because there was plenty *he* wanted to get off his chest . . . if she only gave him the chance.

When the silence went on too long, he turned his head and watched her. As usual, her eyes were open wide and her gaze was locked on the highway as she studied each and every truck that passed them by. It was a difficult thing to do, recognizing trucks in the dead of night, but there was just enough light bleeding out from the rest station parking lot to make most of the company names legible.

Ron didn't want to disturb her concentration, but he had something to say and it seemed there would never be a *right* time to say it, so now was as good a time as any.

"Mandy?"

"Yeah." She continued to stare out at the highway.

"There's a couple of things I want to . . . no, that I *need* to tell you."

After a long silence, she said, "What?"

Ron cleared his throat with a cough, then swallowed. "I know I've said stuff like this before, but . . . well, I'm sorry that I hit you that night you left."

"I know."

"No, I really mean it, though." He took another deep breath to help draw up some courage. "I *know* I'm truly sorry because I've never felt so damn ashamed in my entire life. I mean, I've told you I was sorry a hundred times before, but this time I really *feel* it."

At last she turned to look at him. "I know."

He was happy to hear it, but it seemed so out of character for Amanda. "How do you know?"

"You're different now, a bit more grown up, a bit more responsible. It's a change for the better."

Ron nodded, breathing easier and feeling as if some

huge weight had been lifted from his shoulders. It was a great feeling, but there was still one more thing he needed to say.

"The other thing is I want you to know that I won't ever do it again . . . Ever."

She gave him a little smile. "I know you won't."

He smiled back at her, relieved to know she was willing to give him another chance. It was amazing. "You sound so sure of yourself," he said.

She shrugged. "It's just something I feel deep inside me. . . ."

He reached over and placed his hand on hers.

". . . besides," she continued, "if you ever hit me again, I won't run away. I'll stick around and kill you."

Ron laughed, fully expecting Amanda to as well, but her stoic face remained unchanged as she turned her attention back onto the highway.

Ron felt a chill run down the length of his spine.

He was tempted to remove his hand from hers, but decided against it. Instead, he left his hand where it was, hoping to share in some of Amanda's newfound inner strength.

It was just after midnight when Amanda saw it.

"Oh, my God," she said, her heart starting to pound in anticipation.

"What is it?"

"That truck that just pulled in."

Ron took a look over his left shoulder.

The long black semitrailer came to a stop well back from the rest station in the farthest corner of the lot. When its lights were shut off, the entire thing seemed to disappear into the darkness.

"Is that the one?" asked Ron.

Amanda couldn't be sure. It was black, and she was sure she'd read the words TUCANA NORTHERN on the side of the trailer. It was a close fit, but was this *the* truck? Amanda didn't want to sit on the fence on this, but she wasn't about to tell Ron it was Valeska's truck unless she was 100 percent sure of it. That was because although Ron had been incredibly supportive of her, Amanda suspected that he didn't fully believe she'd been kidnapped by a vampire. If she told him this was the truck and it turned out it wasn't, he probably wouldn't believe another word she said about anything. So she really had no choice but to be honest.

"I don't know," she said. "It looks like the truck and it's got the right name on it, but I can't be certain."

"Well, there's only one way to find out," Ron said, starting up the car. "Let's go check it out."

He backed the car out of its parking spot, then drove around the rest station to the back of the parking lot without ever switching on the headlights.

Closer now, Amanda was a little more sure that this was the right truck. The trailer was right and the tractor was dark, just like Valeska's had been, although she'd never really paid enough attention to the outside of the truck to know what make or model it was. All she knew was that Valeska's tractor had been dark, like the trailer, and this one was dark too, just like the trailer it pulled.

Right or wrong, it was worth checking out.

Ron parked the car about fifty feet from the truck and the two of them got out, closing the car doors carefully behind them so as not to make a sound.

Together, they crept across the parking lot in a half crouch, as if that might prevent them from being seen.

"Well?" Ron asked, when they were standing next to the trailer, well back from the tractor.

Amanda shook her head ever so slightly. These trucks

all looked the same to her. Valeska's had had shiny exhaust pipes, and so did this one. Valeska's truck had chrome wheels . . . ditto for this one.

She began to sniff at the air.

"What are you doing?" whispered Ron.

"The inside of his truck smelled a lot like shit, but I don't know if you can smell it from the outside."

Ron raised his head and sniffed.

They looked at each other. . . . The air smelled of grease and diesel fuel, not like shit at all.

"What are we going to do?" Amanda said.

Ron was silent a moment, then said, "You stay here. I'll go check it out."

"I'm not staying anywhere," she said. "If you go anywhere, I'm going with you."

Ron looked as if he was trying to come up with a reason why she should stay back. But there were no good reasons, of course. She'd had contact with the vampire and knew what could hurt him. And besides, Ron had to be thinking that if there really was a vampire inside this truck, he would need all the help he could get.

"All right," he said at last. "Just be careful!"

Amanda nodded, and they moved up the side of the trailer.

As they got closer to the tractor, they could hear muffled sounds coming from inside, as if someone were struggling in there.

Amanda's heart began pounding and she could see Ron's chest rising and falling as he began breathing harder in anticipation of fight or flight.

He pulled the garlic chain that was around his neck out from under his sweater and took the squirt gun filled with holy water from his pocket and held it by his side like some television cop about to round some dangerous corner. Following Ron's lead, Amanda pulled her garlic chain over top of her clothes and took out her own water pistol. They were also armed with a couple of wooden stakes and hammers to drive them with, but those things were for killing vampires in the daytime, not for defending themselves against them in the night.

"Ready?" Ron said, silently mouthing out the word.

Amanda nodded.

Ron reached up and tried the door handle. Amazingly, it was unlocked. It clicked as he pulled on it, but judging by the sounds escaping from the now open door, no one in there had heard a thing.

"On three," he said.

"One . . ."

Amanda felt her body trembling.

"Two . . ."

She'd never felt like killing anything before in her life, but she wanted to kill now.

"Three!"

Ron yanked the door fully open.

The sounds coming from inside suddenly grew even louder.

Someone was screaming.

Ron climbed up inside the truck, his water-filled gun leading the way.

Amanda followed him in.

"Holy shit!" someone screamed. A man's voice.

"Don't shoot!" said a second voice. This one a woman's. "Please."

And then there was silence.

Awkward, awkward silence.

Amanda moved from side to side in an attempt to see past Ron and find out what was going on, but she stopped the moment she realized that they were in the wrong truck. Nothing inside the cab was even remotely familiar. And the smell inside was actually quite pleasant, like perfume and incense and maybe a scented candle or two.

"What the fuck is wrong with you?" said the man's voice. He was angry now, and understandably so.

"Sorry . . ." Ron said.

"Guy can't even make love to his wife without some perverted asshole breaking in trying to get a piece of the action."

"I thought you were someone else. Sorry."

"Get the fuck out of here, buddy, before I get *my* gun."

Amanda backed out of the truck.

Ron jumped down to the pavement a moment later, closing the door quickly behind him.

"I'm guessing that wasn't him, right?" Ron asked.

Amanda couldn't help but smile. "No, it wasn't."

— **3** —

Several days had passed and Constable Sharpe still hadn't heard from the dispatcher at Tucana Northern. He tried to remember the man's name, but couldn't do it without the aid of his notes.

Jimmy Paul.

The phone number for Jimmy was there in his notes as well, so Sharpe picked up the phone and dialed the Tucana Northern number.

"Evening. Tucana Northern," said a voice.

Sharpe couldn't be sure, but it didn't sound much like the voice he remembered.

"This is Constable Sharpe of the OPP calling. I'd like to speak to Jimmy Paul. Is he working tonight?"

The line was silent for several seconds, then the man said, "Who are you again?"

"Constable Sharpe, OPP."

Another pause. "And you're calling for Jimmy?"

"Is he in?"

"Jimmy died three days ago, man."

Now it was Sharpe's turn to be lost for words. Finally, he said, "How did it happen?"

"They're not sure if it was an accident, or if he was murdered. There was a cut on his arm, but they couldn't find any blood anywhere."

"Did this happen at night?"

" 'Course it happened at night. That's the only time Jimmy worked." The man sighed. "The police went over this place for two days, asked everyone here a million questions. . . . Don't you guys talk to each other?"

Sometimes, thought Sharpe, *not as well as we should.* But he wasn't about to admit that to this guy.

"Thanks for your help."

"Yeah, sure."

Sharpe hung up the phone, looked up the main number for the Peel Regional Police, and started dialing.

— 4 —

Days at work and nights on the lookout were taking their toll on Amanda and Ron. With darkness falling around six in the evening and the sun rising at six in the morning, it was almost impossible to find the time to rest. With twelve hours of darkness each night, and an eight-hour day at work, that only left four short hours to do everything else in their lives.

Something had to give.

Tonight it was their bodies that gave in to the overwhelming urge to close their eyes and go to sleep. They had been taking turns on watch, first one, then the other, but it couldn't last. Amanda had taken the first watch from midnight till two, alternating between watching the highway and reading one of the books she'd picked up at the library. The one in her hand was called *The Vampire in Legend, Fact and Art*. She'd read halfway through the book, and now she'd snuggled against Ron's body, her head against his chest, her breathing deep, and her body at rest.

Ron blinked his eyes several times, trying to squeeze the sleepiness out of them, but it was a constant losing battle. As he watched the wide empty highway waiting for the next truck to creep by, his thoughts drifted to the sound of Amanda's breathing.

It was so deep, so peaceful, and so rhythmic.

Like the sound of ocean waves lapping at the shore.

It reminded Ron of a time . . .

When he'd been asleep.

And dreaming.

— 5 —

The scenery on either side of Highway 17 east of Thunder Bay was barren and bleak. This far into November, the trees had lost all their leaves and looked like rows of dead men lining each side of the road. Elsewhere, wisps of snow slithered and snaked along the highway's shoulders, blown by an icy wind in search of a place to gather into snowbanks and help get winter started.

And it was dark.

The farther north he went, the longer the nights became, up to twelve hours or more. If it were not for the cold, it would be paradise. The cold didn't bother Valeska, and indeed he wore the same clothing twelve months out of the year, but it was more difficult to find hitchhikers out on the road between November and March than it was during the other months of the year. There were still plenty of runaways and travelers, but they tended to stay close to the rest stations where it was warm. By picking them up in such places Valeska risked being seen with the missing person and it was generally a bad idea.

But he still had to feed.

Out here, so close to nature, he could sate his hunger with the blood of animals. A young buck, a beaver perhaps, and he'd be good for another day or two, but there was no substitution for fine human blood.

He needed it regularly and if he went without, then his blood lust became a beast too powerful to keep under control. And the result was an episode like the one at the Tucana Northern yard.

Jimmy Paul.

He'd never intended to kill the man. In fact, he hadn't even wanted to feed upon him, but he'd scratched himself and the blood . . . the blood was bubbling up from the wound on his flesh. How could he possibly control himself in such a situation?

He was vampire after all.

And he'd never really liked Jimmy Paul much. A vile little human looking down his nose at Valeska all the time as if he were the superior being. Him! A shipper in a truck yard superior to Konrad Valeska, former Count of Krosno, onetime Lord and terror of the lands north of the Carpathians, and a third cousin of the late great Vlad Tepes.

Feh!

Former.

Onetime.

Past.

Late.

Valeska clenched his rotten teeth together so hard they ached under the pressure.

All of his honors and distinctions were former glories from the golden age of his kind when the killing was easy and fear was an effective tool in keeping the masses bowed to his will. But today, a lowly dispatcher of trucks held a higher wrung on the social ladder.

Perhaps, but only in life.

In death, it was Konrad Valeska who lorded over the teeming masses of human vermin.

He decided who lived and who died.

And it had been Jimmy Paul's time to die.

Just as it would soon be time to die for the young man walking by the side of the road farther up the highway.

Valeska first saw the reflective patches on the man's backpack, but once he'd identified those two flashes of light, it took no time at all for him to realize that his next meal was only a few hours away.

He began slowing down even before the man turned around to face the oncoming truck. And by the time he stuck out his arm to ask for a ride, Valeska was already slowing to a halt on the side of the highway.

Valeska judged the man to be in his early twenties. Forty years ago he might have called him a hippie, but in the twenty-first century his long curly locks, patch-covered denim jacket, and backpack sporting both the Canadian flag and a peace sign, Valeska just thought him a freak.

He brought the truck to a stop and opened the passenger-side door.

The young man popped his head into the space left by the open door, but he didn't climb up into the truck. Instead, he just hung there by the side of the truck, like an animal inspecting someplace dark and unknown.

Valeska needed to entice him into the truck.

"Cold night out, eh?" He'd never used the expression before while hunting in Canada, but it didn't hurt to say "Eh?" every once in a while to make the humans feel at ease, and to make them think he was one of them.

"You got that right," he said, still not venturing farther into the truck.

"Got a Thermos full of coffee if you're cold."

"Sounds good."

Valeska had been prepared to welcome the man into the truck, but he still wasn't moving. Instead, he continued to stand there, examining the truck closely, looking up at the sun visor, down at the rubber boot at the base of the shifter, and then back behind Valeska at—

The curtain leading into the sleeper was open, Valeska realized.

The man's eyes were squinted halfway shut as he peered through his tiny granny-style black-framed glasses. The glasses were already beginning to fog up from contact with the warmer air inside the cab, but the man could still easily make out the table with the restraint straps, and the boxes of needles, tubes, and vials sitting off to one side.

"What the hell is back there?" he said, making just the slightest move backward away from the truck.

Valeska saw his meal, his very sustenance, backing off and walking away.

He couldn't allow that to happen.

"It looks like some kind of torture cham—"

In a single, fluid motion, Valeska moved to his right, grabbed a handful of the young man's long curly hair, and pulled him straight into the truck.

The man screamed at the top of his voice, perhaps in pain, perhaps in fear, but the sound was short-lived.

Valeska slammed the man's head against the truck's

dashboard—putting a slight dent into the smooth unbroken surface and silencing the man's screams.

Less than ten minutes later, Valeska's hunger was sated, and he was back on the road headed for his next delivery.

Chapter 20

Light shone against Ron's eyes. There had been dark-ness and blackness there for the longest time, but now everything seemed to glow a bright, bright red.

He could even feel the warmth of the sun against his jacket. It was hot in places and reminded him of Saturday mornings in bed with Amanda with the whole day in front of them with nothing else to do but sleep in each other's arms.

He opened his eyes and took a look around.

Amanda was beside him, but he wasn't in bed. He was in the car and they were in a rest station parking lot a long way from home.

Ron glanced at his watch.

"Shit!"

It was almost seven-thirty. Ron had to be at work by eight—eight-thirty at the latest—and there would be barely be enough time for him to drive straight to the yard. There was no time to eat anything, or even go to the bathroom.

He started up the car and put it in gear.

"Did you see it?" Amanda said, her eyes fluttering open. "Was that the truck?"

"No, there's no truck," Ron said, pulling out onto the

highway and merging with the light morning traffic heading south toward Parry Sound.

"What happened, then?"

Ron thought about telling her some story, but he knew that whatever story he made up would be found out eventually. Besides, he knew from past experience that he was sometimes a terrible liar. "I fell asleep," he said as plainly as he could.

"For how long?"

"I don't know. Four hours, maybe."

"And you think the truck went by while we were asleep?"

Ron was about to say something sharp and biting, but he caught himself before the words escaped his lips. "No, it's not that. I mean, I don't know if the truck went by or not. It's after seven and I start work at eight." He pushed a little harder on the gas pedal, bringing the Buick's speed up to 120 kilometers per hour. "If I miss a day or I'm late, I'm finished there. And if I can't keep this job for more than a few weeks you can be sure no one else in town is going to hire me for anything else."

Amanda was silent for the longest time, just looking at him as if . . . well, Ron couldn't be sure just what she was thinking. All he knew was that her eyes were moving over him as if she were sizing him up and preparing to dis him big time.

"It's been tough, hasn't it?" she said at last.

"What has?"

"Working days and coming out with me at night."

Ron wasn't sure where this was going. He'd expected her to be upset that he'd fallen asleep, but that didn't seem to be such a big deal to her. He wanted to tell her he couldn't handle the pace anymore, but he wasn't about to let her down. So this time, instead of the truth, he tried a little white lie. "No, it's been okay. I just got a little tired is all. We'll be back out here tonight and if he's on the road we'll find him."

Amanda began shaking her head.

"What?"

"The OPP and every other police organization in the province, maybe even in Canada, is looking for him and they haven't been able to find him yet, so why should we?"

That's a good question, Ron thought, hoping that she might be about to give up on this goose chase and return both their lives to something resembling normal. "I don't know," he said.

"I wouldn't be surprised if he's got some kind of ability that makes him hard to notice, especially in a crowd . . . like out on the highway, or in a rest station. He's supposed to have the ability to change his shape, you know. Like into a bat or wolf. That would make him almost impossible to catch."

"Maybe it's just dumb luck," Ron offered. "I mean, he's driving a truck, for crying out loud!"

There had been plenty of serial killers who'd been able to evade intensive searches and manhunts before, not because of any great skill or cunning on their part, but simply because of dumb luck and happenstance. For example, the "Beltway Sniper" killed and wounded almost a dozen people in the Washington, D.C., area late in 2002 and had been able to elude one of the largest police manhunts ever mounted for several weeks. After one of the killings, instead of driving away in a car and risking meeting up with police, the sniper simply walked back to his hotel room a few hundred yards from the scene of the crime and stayed there while police set up roadblocks and searched individual cars for miles around.

"Yeah, maybe," Amanda concurred. "But we'd be relying on the same dumb luck to find him the way we've been looking . . . and that can't be a good plan of action."

That was probably true, thought Ron. Waiting for the truck to pass them by on the highway was like looking for the proverbial needle in a haystack. "But how else are we going to find him?"

"Do you have any money?"

"Money?"

"Yeah, do you have any?"

"A few bucks. I've only been working for a little while—"

"No, I mean real money. In-the-bank money. Savings money. Money-for-a-rainy-day money?"

Ron had a few Canada Savings Bonds worth about one thousand dollars stashed away in a safety deposit box in the Parry Sound CIBC. It was all he had to show for his stint in pro hockey and it was basically all he had to his name. He'd put it away as soon as he'd gotten it and had all but forgotten about it since then. Since he'd bumbled and stumbled his way through life, leaving the money in the bank was a way to prevent himself from ever really hitting rock bottom. He'd always felt bad for not telling Amanda about the bonds, but he'd wanted to hang on to them for the day he figured out what he was going to do with his life. He wanted to spend the rest of his life with Amanda—he was sure of that now—so there didn't seem to be any reason to keep the money a secret from her anymore.

What's yours is mine, and what's mine is yours.

"I've got some bonds in the bank," he said.

"What are they worth?"

"Face value of them is one-thousand, but there's some accumulated interest. . . ."

He'd expected her to be upset that he'd been holding out on her, but the opposite was true. She seemed ecstatic. "That might not be enough, but it's a good start. There's probably a few things we could sell off, you know . . . like in a garage sale."

"Why? What do you need the money for?"

"I don't know if we'll need the money or not to catch Valeska, but even if we don't, it'll be good to have on hand, depending on what happens."

Ron didn't like the sound of that, but he liked the way Amanda talked about them as a team. She kept on saying *we* as if they'd be together for a long, long time, no matter what the hell happened in the next little while.

"Have you got some kind of plan?"

"Yeah." She nodded. "I haven't got it all worked out yet, but I do have a plan."

— 2 —

Days had passed without a single tip, lead, or new development in the case. Constable Sharpe had been tempted several times to give the killer a name like the "Roadside Ravager" or the "Northern Ontario Nutcase," but as usual, the media had beaten him to the punch, dubbing the killer the "Trans-Canada Killer" since the bodies had, for the most part, been discovered on the side of the Trans-Canada Highway. It was as good a name as any, especially since it made no mention of the word *vampire,* or referred in any other way to the killer's penchant for blood.

Thank God for small favors.

Sharpe was in the lunchroom, preparing himself a cup of coffee and checking the notices placed up on the board. There were a couple of minor hockey teams in town looking for coaches, and there was a 20-percent-off sale at the Eddie Bauer Outlet Centre where EMS work-

ers and members of police organizations could get an
extra 20 percent off and shop two hours before the store
opened to the public. It was a good deal, but Sharpe had
more than enough parkas and hiking boots to see him to
his grave.

He took a sip of his coffee and decided it needed a
bit more milk. Although the lunchroom was stocked
with Tim Hortons coffee and he'd just made himself a
fresh pot, it didn't taste the same as the coffee you got
over the counter at Timmies. *It* has *to be the cream,* he
thought. *Either that, or there's just something about
coffee from a donut shop that makes your body think
"good coffee."*

"Hey, Sharpie," someone called from the doorway.
"Fax for you."

With a full mug of hot coffee in his hand, it took
Sharpe a moment to turn around and by the time he did
there was no one at the door to the lunchroom. Hopefully
the fax would be in his mailbox when he got back to it.

And it was.

The document was a report from Peel Regional Police's Forensic Identification Service on the scene of
Jimmy Paul's murder in the Tucana Northern office in
Brampton. Much of it was routine, describing the
weather conditions outside, lighting, temperature, and
general state of the room the body was found in, as well
as the orientation and condition of the body when it was
found, and in particular, the state of the wound on the
man's arm. As Constable Sharpe had suspected, the report noted that the body appeared to have been drained
of blood (a fact also confirmed in the coroner's report).
Another curiousity was the fact that there were virtually
no blood spatters on, near, or around the body, or even
anywhere else in the warehouse save for a few drops
found deep in the stacks. It was concluded that the vic-

tim injured himself in the stacks, but there was no trail of blood from the stacks to the office that would account for such a significant loss of blood.

And then there was a line in the report that had Sharpe's own blood running cold.

"Several drops were found on the floor of the office with the use of Luminol, but their faintness and the residue surrounding the spots suggests they were either wiped away by a cloth dampened with saliva, or lapped up by a tongue."

Lapped up by a tongue, Sharpe thought, feeling a shiver run through his body.

Am I looking for a man or a dog . . . or maybe a wolf?

The thought of a wolf jogged Sharpe's memory.

There had been wolves ravaging the fifth victim when she was found. And vampires, weren't they supposed to be able to transform themselves into wolves as well as bats, or at least be able to summon and command wolves at will? But while that might be true, there were no wolves roaming around the industrial areas of Mississauga. At least Sharpe didn't think there were.

Maybe it was Valeska, a *vampire,* crouching down on all fours and licking every last drop of Jimmy Paul's blood off the floor.

Sharpe tried to picture the scene in his mind, and the image made his body go numb.

Still immersed in thought, he reached for his mug of coffee and tried to take a sip, but only managed to spill most of it down the front of his shirt.

— 3 —

That night Constable Sharpe was parked in his cruiser on the east side of Highway 69 just north of Parry Sound.

It was a good place to watch the traffic go by, and to catch up on his notes from calls he'd made earlier in the night.

With his notes all in order and up to the minute, he tossed the notebook onto the dashboard of the cruiser and looked out over the river of vehicles flowing past him. There were all kinds of trucks heading north, all makes and models in all the colors of the rainbow, but none of them were the truck he was looking for. At least he didn't think they were. In the middle of the night, it was difficult to make out the sides of the trucks as they passed. Without the aid of lights, the side of a black trailer would be almost invisible in the darkness. Sharpe had parked his cruiser so his lights would shine out onto the highway, but even then he had just a few seconds to make out each truck as it passed.

It was no easy task.

"Where are you?" he said in a whisper, drawing the words out like a song.

The Highway 400/69 combination was one of the busiest roadways in the entire country, moving thousands, if not hundreds of thousands, of vehicles north and south through the province each day. And on any given day there might be a dozen or so hitchhikers thumbing rides along the highway. But while Sharpe hadn't seen any hitchhikers around Parry Sound in the past few months, the suspect, Konrad Valeska, hadn't seemed to have had any trouble finding people along the side of the highway looking for a ride.

And he'd had no trouble killing them either, five so far, with just one lucky girl getting out alive.

It was uncanny how a man in a truck the size of a house could virtually disappear from sight the moment thousands of police officers were on the lookout for him. Of course it was entirely possible that Valeska had already left the province and was now cruising another highway in some other part of the country, or maybe even somewhere in the United States. That would be the logical next step for him, especially if he'd been reading the papers and had clued into the fact that his last victim had survived. Of course, all that made sense, but the thing about this case was that not a lot about it had made much sense at all, and Sharpe had a feeling that this guy was just a bit too arrogant to run when the situation got hot for him. He seemed more like the type that would probably hang around in defiance of authorities, almost daring police to catch him. Then, when the end was truly near, he'd skip town and start all over again somewhere else.

That made the most sense, *if* the guy was a vampire.

If the guy was a vampire—which Sharpe was now willing to consider, but not quite accept as fact—maybe he had a bunch of extraordinary powers. Say he could change his shape; that would sure help him elude capture. And if he could command wolves, that would explain why the bodies of his victims were always torn apart, especially in areas that don't have large wolf populations. The man must have *something* going for him or else he wouldn't have been able to get a driver's license issued in Ontario with a Clifton Hill address and a picture of Brad Pitt on it. That was an official government document and he would have had to break into a licensing office to make the false registration, or else convince an employee to do it for him. Sharpe supposed people could be bribed, but if the guy was a vampire he could have just hypnotized someone—or whatever it is they're supposed to be able to do with their eyes—into doing his bidding. In *Dracula*, wasn't Renfield controlled by Count Dracula, doing his master's bidding in exchange for a vague promise of eternal life?

Sharpe thought about that a moment. If he was going to be doing such wild speculation, he should probably pick up a copy of *Dracula* and read it from cover to cover. Who knows, maybe he'd find some parallels that might help him with the case.

Sharpe suddenly laughed out loud and shook his head. "What the hell am I thinking?" he said. "And maybe I should call in Lieutenant Columbo to help out on the case while I'm at it. And why not Ben Matlock or even Perry Mason to defend him . . . with Judge Judy presiding over the whole damn thing . . ."

His laugh trailed off and he let out a long sigh.

He only had a couple of years to go until retirement and he'd be damned if he was going to spend them all looking for this asshole. From his experience, Sharpe knew that criminals were either dumb or cocky, or both, and the possibility of being caught never really entered their mind until they were already behind bars. They all made a mistake eventually, so why would this guy be any different?

Just then a call came over the radio.

It was a message for all units to be on the lookout for a dark, late-model Ford sedan that had been seen fleeing the scene of a convenience store holdup in Huntsville. When the dispatcher reported she had a license plate, Sharpe reached for his notebook and opened it up to take down the information. . . .

Konrad Valeska was heading north on Highway 69, approaching Parry Sound.

It was a nice part of the country, even in the dead of night, and it held a special place in Valeska's heart since it had been the place of his last abduction. A pretty, pretty girl whose blood was some of the sweetest he'd ever tasted. Too bad she hadn't lasted longer. But, as the humans have so often said, *All good things must come to an end*.

He had another human in the back of his truck, but this one wasn't nearly as good-tasting as the young woman had been. His blood was strong enough, but he screamed all the time, and when he wasn't screaming he was crying like some newborn child. A shining example of the race's finest he was not.

At that moment, Valeska felt a bit of unease. He couldn't be sure what the problem was, but there was something to be wary of up ahead.

He squinted his eyes slightly and peered into the darkness before him.

There on the left, a police car.

One man inside . . . looking for him.

Or perhaps not.

Something told Valeska the man was being distracted, preoccupied for the moment with some mundane task that required all of his attention.

Valeska eased his foot off the accelerator pedal and checked that his speed was a respectable 110 kilometers per hour. The posted speed limit was 90 and speeds of up to 120 were generally overlooked, so 110 was a good inconspicuous speed, even for a tractor-trailer.

There were a few critical moments when the truck and the cruiser were separated by a distance of less than fifty yards, but then that moment was gone . . .

And Valeska was out of sight.

The note taking had taken all of twenty seconds. When he was done, Sharpe tossed the notebook back onto the dashboard and resumed his search of the highway. The only difference was that now he was looking for a dark, late-model Ford, as well as a long black semi-trailer with the words TUCANA NORTHERN written on the side.

— 4 —

It was a cold day, even for November, but at least it wasn't raining. Conventional wisdom said that yard sales in the Parry Sound area should be held during the months of July and August, preferably on a long week-end when the area was overrun with campers and cottagers. The summer population of the town was 35,000, but by late November the summer crowd had been gone for two months and the 3,500 who lived there year-round were all getting ready to brave the long, dark months of winter.

But Ron and Amanda couldn't wait for July to sell off their things because they needed money now. Be-sides, they didn't really have many possessions that would interest the tony vacationers who came into the area from Toronto. However, the items they had on sale were definitely valued by their fellow trailer park res-idents and as a result, business was brisk.

"How much for these skates?" someone asked.

Ron turned around and saw Cookie standing behind him with a pair of Tacks in his hand.

"I didn't know you could skate, Cookie."

"Can't. How much?"

"Then what do you want them for?" Ron didn't re-ally care what the old-timer wanted the skates for, but Cookie's answer might help him decide how much to charge for them. They were worth two hundred dollars easy, but there was no way Cookie had more than twenty on him. The price would have to be somewhere between the two amounts.

"Call 'em an investment," Cookie said.

"Investment? How do you figure that?"

"You played junior in these skates, right?"

"Yeah, but—"

"So, I'm gonna keep 'em till you become a big star, and then I'm going to sell 'em back to the city for the display they're gonna build in the new arena."

"What new arena?"

"The one they'll be building in fifteen years or so."

"Complete with a display case, right?"

"That's right."

Ron was flattered, but he couldn't be sure if Cookie was crazy or drunk, or both. "Hate to tell you this, Cookie, but I haven't done shit in hockey since junior. And I have to actually be playing somewhere before I can become a big star."

Cookie shrugged. "It'll happen. You play again somewhere . . . You're too good not to make it eventually."

Ron smiled in an attempt to hide the lump in his throat. After all he'd done, or perhaps a better way of putting it was, even though he'd done so little, people around here still believed in him. Ron believed a bit in himself too these days, but he still had his doubts. He'd been too much of a failure to want to try again and fail, but if someone like Cookie still thought he had a chance, then hell, maybe he did.

"So how much?" Cookie prodded.

Ron would feel like a criminal taking the man's money now. For a moment he considered the possibility that Cookie had just said what he did to get a deal on the skates . . . but it had sounded too sincere to be anything but the truth. Besides, Cookie just wasn't that sharp a guy. "Twenty bucks," Ron said.

"Bullshit. Here's forty, and I'm still walking away with a steal."

Ron laughed.

"Just don't waste what you got, okay, boy?"

Ron stopped laughing, pressed his lips together, and nodded as if he'd just been put in charge of some sacred trust.

At that moment Amanda appeared by his side. "You sold your skates?" she said, gesturing in Cookie's direction.

"Yeah, but I've got a better pair in with my equipment."

"How much did you get for those?"

Ron was still feeling warm all over from his encounter with Cookie. What did it matter how much money he'd gotten for the skates? You couldn't put a dollar value on the newfound pride and confidence that was swelling inside his chest. "More than I ever thought I would."

"And how much is that?"

"You mean in dollars?"

"Yeah, in dollars?"

"Forty bucks."

Amanda looked at Ron strangely, as if she was expecting some sort of explanation.

Ron just smiled back at her, saying nothing.

By early afternoon most of the stuff that was worth anything had been sold. The rest of it, old clothes and broken appliances, was hardly worth carrying back into the trailer.

"So," said Amanda's friend, Lisa Amato, as she

strolled up to the trailer through the tracks of unsold junk, "how'd you guys make out?"

Amanda shrugged. "A few hundred dollars. It would have been more if *someone* hadn't practically given most of his stuff away."

"Hey, I asked for what I thought was fair," he said.

"Why are you guys getting rid of this stuff anyway?" She picked up a clothes iron. "Won't you be needing a lot of it to, like, live?"

"We need to raise some cash," Amanda said.

Lisa's eyes went wide. "Are you pregnant?"

"No."

"Ron's in trouble with the police, then."

Ron shook his head. "Not me."

"Are you moving?"

Amanda smiled. "Not planning on it."

"Then what is it?" There was a bit of frustration in Lisa's voice, as if she were playing a game that was just a bit too hard to be any fun. But there was also a touch of worry in her voice that Amanda found touching.

"There's just something we have to do," she said.

Ron nodded. "And we need your help, actually."

Lisa looked at them, first one, then the other, as if she was trying to decide if they were serious or just having some fun with her. She must have figured it was the former because she said, "Okay, what is it?"

Ron pulled a sealed envelope from inside his jacket.

"If you don't see us around here by, say, the end of the week, I want you to give this envelope to the police, preferably an OPP constable named Sharpe."

Lisa took the envelope from Ron and turned it over in her hand. At last she looked up at the two of them and said, "This is some deeply serious shit, isn't it?"

Amanda nodded.

Ron put his arm around Amanda and said, "The deepest."

— 5 —

That night, Ron and Amanda went to bed early.

The sex they had was slow and loving and unlike the hurried and frenzied sessions they'd had in the past. They were savoring each other, making the moment last for as long as they could.

And when it was over, they lay awake in each other's arms, neither one wanting to do anything to spoil one of the rare perfect moments in their relationship.

But the silence between them was eventually broken.

"When we do this thing," said Ron, "what do you hope to accomplish?"

It was a good question. Amanda wasn't quite sure what she hoped to achieve other than revenge for the humiliation and fear she'd felt in her three days of hell.

"I want to get Konrad Valeska for what he did to me."

"Yeah, I know that, but what *exactly* do you want to happen?"

"I want him to be punished for what he did."

"You want to punish him, or do you want him to be punished by the police and the courts?"

"Both, I guess."

"But I had those wooden stakes made."

"Yeah."

"Well, whether he's a vampire or not, putting one of those things through his chest will *kill* him."

"And?"

Ron let out a sigh. "Well, not to put too fine a point on it . . . but you're asking me to maybe help you kill somebody."

Amanda felt a jolt of reality rock her body. She'd never really thought about it in those terms. Yes, she had no doubt that if it came to it, she would kill Konrad Valeska without hesitation. But was it right to ask Ron to do the same? She knew why she'd be doing it, but Ron could be throwing away his life just to help her exact her revenge and that wasn't fair.

"If you don't want to see this through to the end, I'll understand," she said, trying to keep her voice even and unemotional. The last thing she wanted to do right now was coerce Ron into doing something he didn't want to do.

"It is a big step."

She tried to gauge what Ron was thinking from the way he said those five little words, but they'd been spoken without a hint of emotion.

"It is a big step, but I'll kill him if I have to." She swallowed to clear her throat. "This man . . . this *vampire* held me captive for three days. He put a needle in my arm and drank my blood. Then, when he was done with me he . . ." She paused a moment. She'd never told Ron about the sexual assault that ended the ordeal, but if he was going to make a decision he had a right to know everything that happened. "When he was done with me he raped me, first with his hand, then with his, his . . . thing." A shudder coursed through her body. "Then he sprayed his bloody seed all over me and tossed me out of his truck, onto the side of the road, like I was garbage." Another pause, this time to sniff. "So if I have to kill him, I will. And if I'm going to kill him, you can be sure I'm going to enjoy doing it."

She sniffed a couple more times, then lay still and quiet.

Ron said nothing for the longest time as he held her tight in his arms.

"I'd made up my mind a while ago to help you any way I can," he said. "But if you need to hear it . . . I'll hammer the stake into his chest for you if that's what it comes to."

She lifted her head and gave Ron a long, soulful kiss.

Then they made love one more time.

It was the best they'd ever had.

Chapter 21

Early Monday morning, before most people had begun their workday, Amanda called for directory assistance hoping to get the telephone number of the trucking company called Tucana Northern. She feared that the company might be located in some small Ontario town like Aurora or Newmarket and she'd end up playing a sort of Battleship-type game all day long, asking the operator to try town after town till she finally recorded a hit.

But, playing the odds, she began with Toronto and was pleased to learn that the company was listed in the Toronto book even though it had a 905 area code and was located outside the city in neighboring Mississauga.

After jotting down the number on a piece of paper, she looked over at Ron and said, "Here goes."

But before she could dial the number, he put a hand over hers and said, "You sure you want to do this?"

She nodded without hesitation, and he pulled his hand away.

Then she slid a fresh ten-dollar calling card into the slot and dialed the Tucana Northern number.

"Tucana Northern," said a man's voice.

"Hi there," Amanda said.

"Yup, what can I do for you?"

"Uh, I'd like to have something . . ." The word didn't immediately pop into Amanda's mind. "Shipped."

"Okay," the voice said. Then there was a long silence before he said, "Do I have to guess the details or are you going to tell them to me?"

"I've got two pallets of, uh . . . coffin nails that need to go from Parry Sound to Toronto."

"Coffin nails?"

"Yeah, they're used to make coffins?" She looked over at Ron and rolled her eyes. "Can you send a truck?"

"Cost you extra for less than a load."

"That's okay, I'm not worried about the cost."

"You ever ship with us before?"

"No."

"Okay then, give me your company name so I can do a credit check. If everything comes back all right, I'll dispatch a truck for you."

"No, never mind that," Amanda said. "I don't want to set up an account or anything."

"But I can't send a truck unless I know your credit's good. Don't worry, it only takes a few minutes to do the check."

"No, that's okay," Amanda said, stopping herself to refresh her voice. She had felt herself beginning to sound a little too desperate. "I'd prefer to pay cash, since . . . since I don't know if I'll want to continue using you after you make this delivery." That was more like it—businesslike and professional.

"We don't take cash. Certified check or money order, paid in advance."

"That's fine. Who do I make the check out to and where do I send it?"

He gave her the information she needed and when that was done, he said, "Now, what's your company name and where do I send the driver?"

"Our company name is . . . Amandaron, but the name doesn't appear on the outside of our building."

"Okay, fine. Where's the pickup then?"

She gave him the address of the abandoned warehouse on Bowes Street in Parry Sound that she and Ron had checked out the day before.

"Okay, great."

"Uh, there's one last thing, though," Amanda said.

"Yeah, what?"

"I need the pickup to be made at three in the morning."

"Our guys are usually sleeping at that time of night," he said. "And so's the rest of the world, come to think of it."

"I realize that, but I work two jobs and three in the morning is the only time I can be sure I'll be there to see the pallets get loaded onto the truck properly."

"Pickup at off hours will cost you extra."

"I realize that," Amanda said. "And I'm willing to pay. As long as the load is picked up at three A.M." She was rocking gently back and forth with the phone cradled into the small of her neck. She'd done everything right, but she couldn't be sure it was going to give her the result she wanted.

"Wait a second," he said. "We've got a guy who works nothing but nights . . . actually prefers it. I didn't think of him at first because I've only been working nights for a week or so. . . . Anyway, this sounds like his sort of load, especially with all the extra money that goes with it."

Amanda looked over at Ron and mouthed the word, "Bingo!"

– 2 –

"Sergeant McSherry wants to see you," Constable Boneham said as Constable Sharpe arrived at the detachment a half hour before his shift began.

"Say what he wanted?"

"Can't be sure, but from the look on his face I think it's not to chat."

"Okay."

Sharpe dropped his bag off in the constable's room and continued on to the sergeant's office just off the main reception area. He rapped his knuckles against the doorjamb and said, "You wanted to see me?"

"Sit down."

Sharpe didn't like the tone of the sergeant's voice. He had a feeling the sergeant was about to come on like a freight train and there was nowhere he could go to get out of the way.

The sergeant was looking over a few papers on his desk, and then without warning looked up and said, "Another kid went missing on Sixty-nine. Eighteen-year-old boy from Toronto by the name of Jay Chlebo."

"Aw, shit!"

"Shit is right," the sergeant said. "And it's about this close"—he held his right thumb and index finger about an inch apart—"to it hitting the fan."

Sharpe didn't know exactly how to respond. It was true that he hadn't made an arrest yet, but neither had the CIB officers in the northern part of the province, and they'd been working on the case a lot longer than he had. "Is there something special about this victim?"

"Special?" the sergeant said, a touch of incredulity to his voice. "You mean other than going missing when we know the suspect's name and have been looking for him and his truck for almost a week?"

"Oh," said Sharpe, feeling his asshole begin to pucker. It was a conditioned response a lot of police officers experienced when they were being grilled or were otherwise on the hot seat. The sergeant was right.

They had Valeska's name and they knew what kind of truck he drove, so how hard could it be to find the man?

The sergeant let out a long sigh. "Look, I know you've been working hard on this case and are probably more frustrated about it than any of us, but the truth is that if we don't find this guy in the next little while the media is going to have a field day with us, wondering why we can't find one big black truck on a highway we're supposed to be patrolling provincewide."

Sharpe was about to say, "I've been wondering that very same thing," but decided it wasn't the time or place for it. Instead, he answered, "Yes, Sergeant."

"Now, there's already a bunch of jurisdictions involved in this case including ourselves, Toronto cops, and the Peel Regional Police. I've heard that the RCMP have been looking into similarities between our victims and a bunch of unsolved homicides in British Columbia and Alberta, and maybe Manitoba."

Sharpe knew what was coming and could feel the blood beginning to drain from his face.

"If you don't come up with, what's his name . . ."

"Valeska, Konrad Valeska."

"If you don't come up with this Konrad Valeska pretty soon, the RCMP will be coming on board and you might very well be asked to take up a supporting role."

Ask, my ass, thought Sharpe. *I'll be told and that will be the end of that.*

"So, whatever you've been doing up till now obviously isn't working."

Sharpe nodded. That much was true.

"Maybe it's time for a fresh approach. Another way of thinking. What do they call it . . . thinking outside . . ."

"Outside the box."

"That's right. Maybe you should be coming at this

case from a different direction, with a new perspective."

"I'll do my best."

"Fine," Sergeant McSherry said, his voice softer now, as if he was done exercising his authority and returning to the same level of the officers around him.

Sharpe left the sergeant's office and headed off to change into his work clothes with his mind filled with thoughts of the RCMP taking over his case. The RCMP was the equivalent of the American FBI and Sharpe couldn't get the idea out of his head that some Canadian version of Mulder and Scully would be arriving on the scene to proclaim that the murders were the work of some vampire trucker.

I already know that!

Sharpe stopped in his tracks.

Do I know that? he wondered.

Did he somewhere in the back of his mind or deep in his subconscious *know* that the killer was a vampire? Was that what his gut feeling—the thing television cops talk about all the time—had been telling him all along, only he was too unwilling to admit it? It was crazy, right?

A vampire truck driver, feh!

Yeah, but it was the only theory that connected with all the aspects of the case. As bizarre as the idea was, a truck driver who was also a bloodthirsty vampire was the only thing that made sense.

Sergeant McSherry had asked him to come at the case from a different direction, to think outside the box on it.

And maybe that was just what he should do . . . consider Konrad Valeska to be an honest-to-God bloodsucking freak of a vampire.

Sharpe was almost willing to believe, but before he

took that final leap into Mulder's world, he wanted to have one more talk with Amanda Peck, the only victim of . . .

Sharpe hesitated using the term, but then relented.

. . . the only victim of *the Vampire Valeska* to have lived.

— 3 —

Valeska felt the urge to feed.

It wasn't a full-blown blood thirst, but rather a tiny gnawing pang in the pit of his belly. It told him that he needed a little sip of blood to carry him through until morning. Then, with the pickup in Parry Sound completed and his work done for the night, he'd drink more fully at dawn, sating his hunger so he could rest easily during the day without the aches and agony that went along with an empty stomach.

He pulled over onto the side of the highway just west of Sudbury. He had plenty of time before he had to be in Parry Sound and much of that time could be spent savoring the last of the young boy's blood. He'd almost drunk the boy dry already, so anything more than a sip would probably empty the boy of his lifeblood. Valeska preferred to save most of what was left for just before dawn when he would ravage the boy's body and suck every last drop from his veins like marrow from a bone.

Just thinking about it made his decayed fangs ache with anticipation.

"Easy," he said aloud, knowing full well that saving the last of it for later would make the boy's blood taste twice as sweet.

Valeska's movement and words caused the boy to awaken.

"What?" he said in a groggy sort of haze. "What is it?"

"Snack time," Valeska answered, smiling down at the pale-skinned boy.

"No," he screamed. "No, not again. Please!"

Valeska shook his head. Four times he'd fed on the boy's blood and every time he had screamed like a child. Even now, even with his blood almost completely gone from his body, he was somehow still able to find the strength to cry out. Such a waste of energy. Too bad he couldn't have channeled it into something useful like inner strength or courage. The way the boy was acting represented everything Valeska despised about weak and cowardly humans. The girl before this one had been strong and Valeska had admired her fortitude.

"Shut up!" Valeska said, preparing the needle and tube.

"Please, don't hurt me anymore. I'll pay you to stop. My parents have money, they'll give it all to you in exchange for my life, I swear."

Valeska stopped what he was doing and put a hand on the boy's head. "If you don't keep quiet I'll use the iron on you."

There was a moment of silence inside the truck, and then the boy started screaming again. "Don't hurt me! Please, I'll do anything you want, just don't do it again."

Valeska reached below the table the boy was lying on and grabbed the tire iron he had stowed there.

"And if you let me go I promise I won't tell anybody about what you did to me. . . . It'll be our little secret, yours and mine. Nobody needs to know, especially not the po—"

Valeska brought the tire iron down on the boy's head, not hard enough to kill him, but more than hard enough to knock him out cold for a couple of hours.

"Stupid, noisy, human child!" Valeska spat.

He slid the needle into the boy's arm and watched as

the dark red liquid flowed up from the needle and along the clear plastic tube.

He raised the end of the tube to his lips and let the blood drip, drip, drip, into his mouth.

A smile broke over Valeska's face.

The boy's blood was tinged by the taste of fear.

It was delicious.

– 4 –

When Constable Sharpe pulled up in front of Amanda Peck and Ron Stinson's trailer he had to turn the steering wheel hard to the left to avoid a living room chair that was sitting out on the driveway. A closer look at the place revealed that a lot of household items had been left lying around, as if they'd had a fight and one of them had thrown the other out, along with all of their stuff.

He shut down the cruiser, got out, and approached the trailer hoping that the one who'd stayed might be at home. Actually he wanted to speak with Amanda again about Konrad Valeska. The more he thought about the man, the more he was inclined to believe her vampire theory. However, before he considered it the God's honest truth, there were a few more questions he wanted to ask her about Valeska's behavior and abilities.

He stepped over a bookcase to get to the front door, then knocked on it gently with his right hand.

No answer.

There were no lights on, and no sounds coming from inside either.

He knocked again.

"Anyone home?" he said.

A light came on in one of the trailers down the road.

He knocked again, a little harder this time.

"There's nobody in there."

Constable Sharpe turned to his left and saw what looked like a woman approaching. She was wrapped up in a blanket, wearing a pair of soft-soled pink slippers. Her legs were bare—and attractive—causing Sharpe to wonder about whether or not she had anything on beneath that blanket.

Probably not.

"Who are you?" he said, pulling his Scorpion flashlight from his utility belt and shining its beam at the woman.

"My name's Lisa Amato. I'm a friend of Mandy's."

Sharpe lowered his light until its white circle shone on the ground near the woman's feet so she could better see where she was stepping.

"Where is Amanda?"

"I don't know. Her and Ron go to work during the day, and at night . . . well, they're never around anymore."

"You have any idea where they might have gone?"

She shook her head. "They haven't been telling me anything lately. But they're up to something, I know that."

"What are they up to?"

She seemed to hesitate a moment, then shrugged. "I don't know, but they gave me this envelope and told me that if I didn't see them around here by the end of the week, that I should give it to an OPP constable by the name of Sharpe."

"I'm Constable Sharpe." He took out his badge to identify himself.

A white number-ten envelope suddenly appeared from beneath the blanket. "It's early still, but maybe I should give this to you now."

"Yes," said Sharpe. "I think you should."

She handed it to him and he ripped it open with an index finger. At first he tried to read it in available light, but couldn't make out half the words. He pulled out his Scorpion again and shone it directly onto the paper.

Dear Constable Sharpe,

Just a note to let you know that Ron and I did a crazy stupid thing.

You see, after spending a few nights trying to spot Konrad Valeska on Highway 69 it became obvious to us that we'd probably never catch him that way. So instead of just waiting for him to drive by, we decided to make him come to us by arranging for him to pick up a load at the old warehouse on the south side of Bowes Street at three o'clock Wednesday morning . . . where we would be waiting for him, of course.

Pretty ingenious, eh? Although, I suppose that if you're reading this, we're obviously not as clever as we thought we were.

Anyway, we gave it a try.

See, you and everyone else were treating Valeska as if he were an ordinary criminal, *but he's not. He's a* vampire. *I know it's true because I saw him drink my blood, I felt his power overcome me, and I felt his bloody seed spray all over my body.*

We went after him with holy water, crosses, garlic, and wooden stakes, but obviously it wasn't enough to take him down. If you come looking for us, or go after him, *I suggest you at least take the same precautions we did. If you do, you might stand half a chance against him. If you don't, you might as well not even bother trying because he'll just laugh at you, tear your body apart, and drink the blood from all the bloody holes.*

Yours truly,
Amanda Peck (and Ron Stinson)

Sharpe looked up from the letter and stared blankly into the darkness, thinking.

Either the girl's crazy, or this guy really is a vampire.

"What does it say?" Lisa asked.

"Nothing you need to know about."

"Are Amanda and Ron in trouble?"

Sharpe glanced at his watch. It was coming up to eleven, which meant there were still a few hours before Valeska was scheduled to show up at the warehouse.

"Not yet they're not."

"That's good to know."

Sharped looked at her a moment, then said, "You wouldn't happen to have any garlic in your trailer, would you?"

"I don't know," she said, adjusting the blanket to allow Sharpe a view of one of her breasts and its rather large nipple, which had stiffened impressively in the cold night air. "Why don't you come back with me and we'll see if I do?"

It was a tempting offer, but Sharpe had too much to do before three A.M. to spend time flirting with a woman less than half his age.

"Maybe another time," said Sharpe, turning on his heels and hurrying toward his cruiser.

Behind him he could hear the woman mutter, "Jesus, what does a girl have to do to get laid these days?"

Chapter 22

They were positioned outside the warehouse, crouching between a stack of old pallets and the building itself. The warehouse was an old industrial supply facility that had been abandoned about ten years ago. They said people lived inside the building, especially in the warm summer months, but Ron and Amanda had found no evidence of that other than a bunch of newspapers and magazines lying around that were all at least three months old.

The entrance to the warehouse was at the other end of the building on the other side of the two loading bays, one of which was locked, the other of which had been locked at one time but was locked no longer.

"Do you really think all this stuff will work?" asked Ron, searching through the contents of the bag that was slung over his shoulder.

Amanda looked at Ron a moment and decided she had to be honest with him. "I have no idea."

"Aw, jeez . . ."

"Hey, if everything goes right, we won't need to use any of it."

"Yeah, *if everything goes right*. But if it doesn't and we

have to use this stuff, it would be nice to know if it's gonna work or not."

"Listen," she said, staring him straight in the eye. "The only thing I know for sure is that Konrad Valeska is a vampire. He told me he's a vampire and he lived off nothing but my blood for three whole days. What I don't know is if this shit really works." She lifted the crucifix off her chest and pulled it tight against the chain around her neck. "It said in all the books that a vampire can't bear to look upon a cross or a crucifix, or even at anything that forms a cross or casts a shadow of a cross. And, if you touch the cross to the vampire's flesh, it's supposed to sear it and leave a permanent scar."

Ron lifted his own crucifix and took a look at it, pressing it against his palm and pulling it away . . . with no effect.

"Vampires can't stand the smell of garlic, which is supposed to work on them like poison gas. So that's why we've got garlic paste smeared all over our necks."

Ron sniffed and coughed. "It would keep me away from me."

"Believe me, you've smelled worse," Amanda said, hoping some humor might put Ron more at ease.

Ron smiled.

"And the ultraviolet lamps . . ." Amanda lifted her heavy portable lamp and shone the light in Ron's face. "They say even a single beam of sunlight falling upon a vampire's body will bring on absolute disintegration. It's a few hours till sunlight yet, so we have to carry our own sun."

"And the water pistols?"

"Holy water won't kill him, but it's supposed to hurt like hell. Best of all is that it gives us a weapon with some range, because if he gets too close to us, he'll easily be able to tear us apart with his bare hands."

Ron swallowed, and found his throat was unusually dry.

As Amanda rooted around in her bag, she pulled out a pair of knives she'd taken from the butcher's block in their kitchen, and put one of them into Ron's bag.

"What's the knife for?" he asked.

Amanda shrugged. "You never know."

Ron shook his head. "Tell me again why I'm doing this."

"Because you love me and because you want to help me do everything I can to make sure I don't live in fear for the rest of my life . . . which will be spent with *you*, by the way." She gave him a quick peck on the cheek.

"Oh, yeah?" he said.

"Yeah!"

They came together in an embrace and Amanda kissed Ron full on the mouth, holding him tight and pressing her lips against his as if it might be the last time they'd ever be so close.

Ron's hold on her was tight and strong, as if neither of them wanted to be the first to let the other go.

Eventually, Amanda pulled herself away.

"We can't stay out here all night," she said. "I'd hate for Valeska to find us here with our pants down."

"Ouch! That would be bad," Ron said.

"We better go inside and get things ready."

"After you."

Amanda headed for the entrance.

When she got there she found the door unlocked.

Broken actually.

She pushed it open and slipped inside the warehouse.

Ron followed.

And the door closed behind them.

— 2 —

The truck arrived just before three. They could hear the diesel engine rumbling on the other side of the loading bay doors, as the tractor backed up to the loading dock.

"That must be him," Ron said.

"Yeah, say what you want about him," Amanda said. "You can't call him a bad truck driver. He's even here early."

"Let's hope that's the only thing that doesn't go according to plan."

Amanda nodded, said, "Good luck," then gave Ron a quick hug and slipped out of the warehouse to take up her position outside and around the corner from the loading dock.

"Thanks," Ron said after she was gone. "I'm sure I'm going to need it."

Their plan was a simple one.

Ron would pose as a shipper and would be loading two pallets of boxes filled with rocks into the back of Valeska's trailer. After the first pallet was on the truck, Ron would exit the trailer to get the second one, leaving Valeska alone inside the trailer to secure the load. But instead of getting the second pallet, Ron would close the rear doors of the trailer, locking Valeska inside. After that, all they'd have to do is wait for the sun to come up and call the police, who would take a now powerless Valeska out of the trailer and off to jail.

Piece of cake.

Then why do I feel so unsettled? Ron wondered. *Because this guy* is *a vampire and if things go wrong here they're really going to go wrong.* Somehow, knowing that, and being able to admit it to himself, made things just a little bit easier for Ron to deal with.

"Right," he said under his breath as he rolled up the heavy loading bay door. "Let's do it!"

The long black Tucana Northern trailer was already backed up to the loading dock with its two barn doors swung open and secure against the sides of the trailer. The dock itself was outside, covered by a large metal awning that provided some protection against the elements. Ron and Amanda had thought about having both pallets waiting outside, but that wouldn't have allowed much time for Ron to close the trailer doors on Valeska.

"Evenin', buddy," Ron said, seeing the driver walking up alongside the trailer.

"You have two pallets for me?" Valeska answered, climbing up onto the loading dock.

The first thing that struck Ron was how un-vampire-like the man was. He was short, fat, and bald, and even ugly to look at. And he smelled bad, as if he'd been rolling around in the dirt *and* had just shit in his pants. If he'd done even half the things Amanda had said he'd done, then he deserved whatever he was going to get.

"I said, you have pallets?"

"What? Oh, yeah," Ron said, realizing he'd been staring. "They're right inside." He pointed into the warehouse. "I'll get the first one."

Ron went into the warehouse.

Most of the interior was dark, except for the west side, which was lit by the ambient light coming from a couple of fluorescent tubes that were still on inside the warehouse office.

They'd found the pallets inside the warehouse. The boxes on the pallets had been collected from the back of Northland Market and the rocks and bits of scrap metal inside the boxes had been picked up in and around the warehouse grounds. The warehouse had been an old industrial supply depot so there were plenty of bits of metal and rusty gadgets lying around, along with a lot of garbage. They'd stacked the boxes only four high, since a shipment of coffin nails would be heavy and they didn't want to overload the pallets and have Valeska have to handle any of the boxes to even out the load.

Ron took the Blue Giant they'd rented from Georgian Rentals on Queen Street and began moving the first pallet toward the truck. He'd worked as a shipper in a few warehouses in his time and knew how to move the Giant around to make it look as if he'd worked at the job all his life.

"Mean night, eh?" he said as he pushed the pallet over the steel ramp and into the back of the trailer.

"Just the way I like it," said Valeska, without a hint of expression on his pale, pale face.

"You like working nights, then?" Ron asked, steering the Giant first left, then right.

"Love it," Valeska answered. "Especially since I usually don't have to deal with chatty shippers all that much."

Ron got the message and moved the pallet the rest of the way onto the truck without another word.

Valeska guided the pallet onto the right side of the trailer in behind another load.

Ron dropped it there and said, "I'll be right back with the other one."

Valeska nodded.

And then, just as they'd hoped, Valeska remained inside the trailer, waiting for Ron to return.

Ron pulled the Giant into the warehouse and to the side of the loading bay door where Valeska couldn't see it. Then he slipped out of the warehouse through the entrance door.

As he approached the trailer, Ron saw Amanda on the ground, unlatching the trailer's barn doors and swinging them close to the loading dock so Ron could close them in a hurry.

"You want to hurry up!" Valeska said from inside the trailer. "I haven't got all night, you know."

That's when Ron swung the first door closed.

As the door slammed against the trailer, Valeska looked over at him, his eyes glowing strangely in the darkness of the trailer.

"What the fuck are you doing?" he shouted.

But before he'd even said the words, Amanda had pushed the second door closed. Ron caught it in mid-swing and slammed it shut against the trailer.

But how to lock it?

Ron had loaded a lot of trucks with overhead doors, but this one had big steel latches that hooked into a notch at both the bottom and top and squeezed the door shut. Ron managed to get the first door secured, but the second one was a little out of alignment and Ron couldn't get the bottom tooth to bite into its notch.

"You asshole, what do you think you're doing?" Valeska said, his accent making the word *asshole* sound more like *ice-hole*.

Ron struggled to get the door secured, but it wasn't going easily. Amanda was helping now, but two hands weren't having any more luck with it than one.

"You'll pay for this!" Valeska said.

And then he pushed against the door from the inside.

Luckily for Ron and Amanda, Valeska had chosen the right door first. That was the one that had already been locked. Valeska couldn't push it open, but he was able to bend the door noticeably.

"Holy shit!" Ron exclaimed at the sight of the door bowing outward, as if it were being pushed from inside by a forklift or backhoe.

"Keep working," Amanda said.

Ron turned his attention away from the malformed door and back onto the second latch.

It still wasn't catching.

But then Valeska moved from the right door to the left. He was pushing on it from the inside as Amanda and Ron were pushing it from the outside. Together, their efforts moved the tooth into exactly the right place and it caught.

Ron turned the latch out toward the side of the trailer, squeezing the door shut and locking Valeska inside.

Ron and Amanda stood up straight.

"You'll pay for this," Valeska said.

"Fuck you, Valeska!" Amanda said.

For a moment everything was quiet.

"Do you recognize me?" she said. "You recognize my voice?"

"You?" It was the only word he said, but somehow there was no doubt that he knew exactly who Amanda was.

"That's right, asshole, it's me. I survived. And now you're screwed." There was a bright, wide smile on Amanda's face. "Don't worry, we'll let you out . . . when the sun comes up. Then we'll see how powerful you are, you son of a bitch!"

Ron put a hand on Amanda's shoulder.

They'd done it. They'd actually gone and captured the vampire without anyone getting hurt.

Just then Valeska let out a loud, shrill scream that sounded as if he were trying to shake the rivets loose on the trailer. Ron had never heard anything like it before. It was like, well, like a wild animal in agony. And not just any wild animal, but some huge ferocious animal like a lion, or maybe even a bear.

He looked over at Amanda, and the look on her face told Ron that she was every bit as scared as he was.

Wham!

Both Ron and Amanda jumped back.

Valeska had pounded against the door with such force that it had buckled. There were creases and dents in the steel and a few of the bolts securing the latch to the door had popped loose.

Wham!

He hit the door again. The sound was like a full-size car hitting the door at highway speed.

Ron inspected the door. More of it was broken now and it wouldn't take more than a few more blows like the last one to have it hanging off its hinges.

"What should we do?" Ron asked.

Wham!

A bolt popped off the door and hit Ron in the chest.

"Maybe we should run," offered Amanda.

"No, he'll catch us easy over open ground."

Wham!

There was a slight opening between the doors now, and Valeska's arm was reaching out of the hole trying to tear the door open with his bare hands.

"We have to go inside the warehouse where we can hide, and hope all our weapons work the way they're supposed to."

"But—"

Wham!

The door was almost open now. One more blow and the hole would be big enough for Valeska to crawl through.

"Let's go!"

Ron took Amanda's hand and led her into the warehouse.

Wham!

The left trailer door exploded open, the top hinge snapping off and the door left hanging at an angle from just the lower hinge.

A moment later, Konrad Valeska stepped from the

back of the trailer, his shredded hands covered in blood. His eyes were red too, filled by the same bloody rage that had brought his old and decrepit fangs to the fore.

There could be no doubt.

He was out for blood, and wouldn't rest until he had it . . .

All.

Chapter 23

— 1 —

Ron had taken up a position toward the back of the warehouse behind a stack of old and broken pallets. The wood probably wouldn't provide him with all that much protection, but it was the best he could manage on such short notice.

In fact, there wasn't all that much in the warehouse to hide behind, period. There were piles of scrap metal pieces against the wall farthest from the loading bays, stacks of pallets in the middle of the warehouse, and large metal racks—most of them empty—closest to the loading bay doors. At the west end of the warehouse was the office with a few lights still on, and at the east end was a line of old and discarded machinery, presses mostly, which hadn't turned out a widget in years.

Not exactly the best place to kill a vampire.

And they would have to kill him, that much was obvious now. If he'd been able to break out of a trailer— smash his way out with his bare hands—then there was no way they were going to be able to capture him and hold him. And there was no way the guy was going away. He was pissed off big time now and he'd be out to kill them for what they'd done and what they knew. So, it was a simple matter of *him* or *us,* and Ron had no qualms about doing everything he could to make sure it ended up being *him*.

"You can't hide from me," Valeska screamed.

The sound of his voice scared the shit out of Ron. It wasn't a human voice at all. It was deep and throaty, as if he were speaking through some huge cavern and made Ron think of some dank sucking pit that was warm and wet and smelled really, really bad.

"You can try and hide all you want," he said, "but I can smell the both of you, especially you, girl. I've tasted your blood and I'll be able to find you anywhere in the world."

Ron took a moment to consider what Valeska had said. He'd come to believe Amanda's story about the vampire, but there had always been a sliver of doubt in the back of his mind that maybe, just maybe, none of it had actually happened. Perhaps he'd kept hoping that because the truth had been too horrible to accept. But here Valeska was *admitting* that he'd fed off of her body, that he'd drunk her blood. And now he was telling her that he would stalk her for the rest of her days, to the very ends of the earth if need be.

Ron couldn't allow that.

"Over here, asshole!" he called out.

Ron crouched down behind the pallets, listening for the approach of footsteps.

But he heard none.

In fact, the first thing he heard was a tiny laugh behind him. It was a subtle thing, like a chuckle under someone's breath, and worst of all it wasn't the sort of laugh he'd ever heard from Amanda.

"You look like you're in pretty good shape," Valeska said.

Ron slowly turned around.

"I could do with some really healthy blood," he said.

"Because I think I'm going to need my strength over the next couple of weeks."

This is it, Ron realized.

There was no way he could run from the vampire. After two steps Valeska would be on Ron's back and digging a hole into his neck the size of a hockey puck. His best chance . . . his only chance, was to stand up to Valeska and fight him with every trick he had in his arsenal.

He turned to face Valeska.

"The garlic's good," the vampire said, "but it just makes it easier for me to find you."

Ron stood firm. "Then why don't you just take me?"

Valeska smiled, exposing more of his fangs to the dim light. "I'm a hunter. I like to savor the kill. . . ."

"Over my dead body," Ron said, switching on his ultraviolet lamp and shining it at Valeska's face.

Valeska put up his hands, as if to shield himself, much like anyone would do when a bright light was shone into their eyes.

"You think you can overpower me with tricks?"

"No," Ron answered. "But it's worth a try."

Just then a light came on behind Valeska.

Amanda.

They had trapped the vampire between them and he was obviously being affected by the power of the artificial sunlight.

Ron lifted the cross from his chest and held it in front of the light so that Valeska could see it clearly.

Valeska hissed and turned away, bringing his hands in closer to shield his eyes.

It's working, Ron thought. *It's actually working!*

"Amanda," he said, "get the water."

Ron reached into his own bag for his water pistol.

Valeska closed his eyes and lowered his hands.

Ron raised the pistol and took aim at the vampire . . .

And Valeska jumped straight up.

One moment he was there.

The next he was gone.

"Where'd he go?" Ron said.

The question was answered by Amanda.

In the form of a scream.

~ 2 ~

A moment later there was a *crash* and Amanda's ultra-violet lamp winked out.

Ron swept the darkness with the beam from his light and found Amanda about twenty feet away.

She was lying stomach-down on the floor with her hands splayed out at her sides. Valeska's right boot was on her neck, pressing it firmly against the concrete. He held her left leg in the air and had rolled up her pant leg to expose her calf.

"You did not put the garlic oil over all your body, did you?" he said.

Ron raised his lamp and caught Valeska in its beam.

Valeska closed his eyes and turned his head, but he didn't release his grip on Amanda's leg.

"Let her go!" Ron said.

Valeska just laughed. "Why should I?"

Ron drew his pistol. "I've got holy water in here."

"Which would hurt me about as much as a tiny stream of boiling water might hurt you. It will sting, but it will not make me drop this bitch."

Ron tried the pistol, sending a stream of holy water in Valeska's direction. The water hit him in the shoulder and there was a slight hissing sound, but true to his word the vampire did not ease his hold on Amanda.

"You'd need a bucketful of it to hurt me, you fool!"

Ron dropped the pistol and raised the cross around his neck.

Again Valeska turned his head, but still held Amanda firmly in his gasp.

"That won't save her," he said. "Nothing will save her now."

"Get out of here, Ron!" Amanda screamed. "Run, get away—"

The vampire applied more pressure onto Amanda's neck and the words were choked off in her throat. Still, she somehow managed to get one last message out.

"I love you. . . ."

Ron felt a little bit of himself die inside. Valeska was going to kill Amanda whether he did something to try and stop him or not. And after he killed Amanda, Valeska would kill him, too.

Guaranteed.

So no matter what Ron did, he was going to die. And if he was going to die, he might as well do something to try and save Amanda's life.

He slung the lamp over his shoulder. Then he reached in his bag and pulled out the kitchen knife.

"Let her go!" he said, pulling back his sleeve and placing the blade against the underside of his arm.

Valeska didn't move.

"You want blood?" Ron said, drawing the knife across his flesh. "Then come and get it."

The first pass of the knife barely broke the skin, so Ron drew the knife back and forth, feeling as if fire were biting into his flesh.

Finally blood began to bubble up to the surface.

Valeska's grip on Amanda eased slightly.

His eyes were locked on Ron's arm and the fresh pool of blood forming on the floor beneath it.

"Athletic blood," he said, flicking the knife at Valeska, sending droplets of blood flying. "It'll invigorate you. Make you strong . . ."

The vampire sniffed at the spatters of blood on his jacket, then lapped the spots off the shiny leather surface.

"It's good, isn't it?"

Ron felt a little weak, but he wasn't about to let up. Not while Amanda was still in danger. He snapped his arm in Valeska's direction, sending a line of blood arcing through the air.

Valeska let go of Amanda's leg, stepped over her body, and slowly began moving toward Ron.

"Run!" Amanda cried.

But Ron resisted his body's natural impulse to run. He knew full well that he wouldn't get very far, especially after the vampire had tasted his blood and wanted more.

Instead, he fell to his knees and hoped that his death would be quick and painless.

Valeska lunged.

Ron closed his eyes, held his breath.

Valeska hit Ron with all the force of a Mack truck, knocking him flat on his back and slamming the back of his head down hard onto the concrete floor.

And then Ron could feel his arm being pulled, and a moment later, heat on his skin.

Valeska was beginning to suck Ron's blood, suck his life, directly out of the wound on his arm.

Ron felt himself getting weak, and the world getting smaller around him.

And from somewhere behind him . . .

A gunshot.

Ron heard the bullet *zip* past his right ear.

Then he heard Valeska cry out in pain.

He opened his eyes in time to see Valeska fall.

The vampire hit the floor hard, a hand over his left shoulder.

Obviously he'd been hurt, but by whom?

Ron turned his head and saw Constable Sharpe moving forward with his gun drawn. As he passed Ron, he squeezed the trigger of his side arm four more times, putting each round into Valeska's body.

The air was filled with the smell of cordite . . .

And Konrad Valeska's agonized screams.

— 3 —

"Constable Sharpe!" Amanda said.

Ron, a little groggy from loss of blood, but recovering quickly, looked up and saw the constable standing over the writhing body of Valeska. "What the hell did you shoot him with?"

"Garlic paste," he said. "In the tips of my hollow-points."

Both Ron and Amanda looked at Sharpe strangely.

"You said he's a vampire, right?" said Sharpe. "And a while back you suggested I do that to my ammunition if I wanted to catch him."

"And you believed me?" Amanda said.

"It took me a while, but I came around."

At that moment Valeska groaned.

"Speaking of coming around," Ron said, rolling onto his side and reaching into his bag with his good right arm. "I think he's not going to die until we put this into his chest." There was a hammer, and a thick wooden stake shaped like a giant pencil, in his hand.

"Wait!" said Constable Sharpe. "Don't use that."

"Why not?"

"People will ask where you got the stake from. When

you tell them you had it with you in your bag, there'll be a strong case for premeditated murder."

Sharpe walked over to a pile of broken pallets and tore away a long, spike-shaped piece of wood from one of them. "Use this," he said, handing it to Amanda. "It'll be a lot easier to explain in my report."

Amanda nodded and placed the spike against Valeska's chest.

Ron, on his knees now, raised the hammer . . .

And brought it down with all the force he could manage.

The spike broke the skin and pierced Valeska's chest, sliding in five or more inches before coming to a stop.

Valeska's body heaved and he let out a cry that started out strong, but slowly faded away until it eventually died in his throat with a wet sort of gurgle. His body collapsed onto the concrete floor and a long whisper of air slowly escaped his lips.

Until at last all was silent.

And Valeska's body was motionless and . . .

Dead.

— 4 —

Amanda quickly slipped out of her jacket, pulled her T-shirt over her head, and began tearing it into strips.

"You're bleeding," said Constable Sharpe as if he'd only noticed Ron's wound now.

"I'll live," Ron said, turning his arm to examine the wound. There was a three-inch-long cut across the underside of his arm, and two holes on either side of it, each looking as if they had been made by a hard jab of a ballpoint pen. And then all of a sudden, it hit him. *I've been bitten by a vampire*. "But maybe I'll be turning into a vampire now too."

Amanda shook her head and began tying off his arm, bandaging up the wound as best she could. "It doesn't work that way. Vampires *can* make other vampires, but for that to happen, you would have had to drink *his* blood."

"Oh," Ron said, breathing easier.

"If anything, you're more at risk for diseases like hepatitis B or HIV."

"Oh," he said again, this time feeling sick to his stomach.

"But there's probably no reason to worry," she said without looking up from the work she was doing on his arm. "I'm sure Valeska stayed away from people with diseases like that."

Ron smiled uneasily.

When she was done and the flow of blood from the wound had been stanched, she looked at Ron and said, "You saved my life."

Ron shrugged. "I did what I could."

Amanda turned to face the constable. "You should have seen him."

Amanda's pride in him was obvious. It was a wonderful feeling, and had a rejuvenating effect, making Ron feel stronger than ever before in his life, like he could do . . . well, just about anything he wanted.

"Yeah, I wish I had seen it," said Constable Sharpe.

"He was strong," Ron said, flexing his arm to test out the bandage. It held firm. "I didn't think he would be so powerful."

Amanda put her jacket back on and said, "He must have just fed before he got here."

Both Ron and the constable looked at her for a moment, then turned and headed for Valeska's truck.

The doors were locked, so Sharpe used the butt of his side arm to smash the window on the driver's side.

"What a stink!" he said, using the gun to clear away the leftover shards of glass.

He opened the door.

"Holy shit!"

"What is it?" Ron asked, coming up behind the constable.

A young man was lying in the truck's sleeper. He was held down by half a dozen straps and there was a needle stuck into his left arm. He looked pale and weak . . . like he was dying.

"He doesn't look so good," Ron said.

"Might not be time for an ambulance," Sharpe said. He looked over his shoulder at Ron. "Help me get him into my cruiser."

Together they unstrapped the young man and gently lowered him out of the truck and into the back of the constable's car.

"I'll be right back," Sharpe said.

"Don't you want us to come with you?" asked Ron.

"No. You two stay here and watch over Valeska's body until I get back."

"Don't worry," Amanda said. "He's not going anywhere."

"Maybe," Sharpe said, sliding into his cruiser. "But he's a vampire . . . a supernatural being. He may still have a few tricks up his sleeve yet."

Ron felt a chill run the length of his spine.

Judging by the look on Amanda's face, she'd just experienced the very same thing.

Without another word, they turned and hurried back toward the warehouse without even waiting for Sharpe to drive away.

Chapter 24

Valeska's body was just where they had left it.

The wooden spike was still sticking out of his chest, but the bullet holes had stopped bleeding.

Ron sat down on a stack of pallets while Amanda made a seat out of an old plastic milk box. For several minutes they just stared at Valeska, saying and doing nothing.

Finally, Amanda spoke up. "You know, it's not fair."

"What's not fair?" asked Ron.

"After what he did to me, and to that guy Sharpe's taking to the hospital, and the ones he killed . . . it's not fair that he just gets to die like this." She shook her head. "It's not enough."

"He's dead. What more do you want from him?"

"I want him to suffer. I want him to hurt, to be in pain, and agony. I wanted him to die slowly . . . wishing for his life to be over because it would mean an end to his suffering."

"Too late for that now," Ron said. "He's already dead."

"You think so?"

"Look at him!"

"Sure he looks dead, but he's a vampire. His normal state is already *un*-dead, neither living nor dead. Who knows? He might just be sleeping or in some comalike state. . . . Even the constable thought he still might be able to do something."

"So what do you suggest we do?"

Amanda looked over at the open loading bay door. It was lighter outside now and the sun would be rising soon.

"All the books I read said that no vampire can survive the purifying qualities of daylight, and prolonged exposure brings about complete annihilation of a vampire's body."

"Complete annihilation," repeated Ron. "That sounds good. Why don't we do that, then?"

And so together, Amanda and Ron dragged Valeska's body out onto the loading dock.

The sun was minutes from rising in the eastern sky.

"You want to just leave him here like this?" Ron asked.

Amanda shook her head. "No, we can do better." She paced back and forth a few times and then stopped on a dime.

"I've got it!"

— 2 —

Amanda had wanted to tie Valeska onto the hood of his truck so that his body would be flat and directly under the sun all day long. However, in reality Konrad Valeska was a big man and there was no way Ron and Amanda were going to be able to lift him onto the hood of his Peterbilt, almost six feet off the ground.

They came up with a compromise.

Instead of putting Valeska on top of the hood, they tied him to the front of it.

First they moved the body into position and while Amanda held it upright, Ron climbed up onto the hood and secured a rope around Valeska's neck and tied it to the chrome bull's head in the center of the radiator grill.

Then with the body stable, it was a simple matter of tying Valeska's arms to the headlight supports on each side of the grill.

Ron pulled the rope as tight as he could, Valeska's black leather jacket preventing the rope from sliding along the arms while he secured the other end of the rope to the truck.

"His legs, too," Amanda said.

"Right."

Ron lashed Valeska's legs to the Peterbilt's huge chrome bumper, wrapping each leg several times with the nylon cord before tying it off on the bumper.

When Ron was done, Valeska looked like a grotesque hood ornament on a truck that was probably going straight to hell.

"What now?" asked Ron.

"We watch the sunrise," Amanda said, slipping her arm around Ron's waist.

It felt good there.

Like they were a team.

— 3 —

The first thing they noticed was the sound.

The sun had been up and shining on Valeska's body for several minutes with seemingly no effect, but then Amanda said, "Listen!"

It was a faint sound, like a pot of water on a stove that was just beginning to grow warm.

They moved in closer, listening.

"What's happening?" asked Ron.

"His flesh is burning," Amanda said with obvious delight in her voice.

"So that's it for him, then?"

"Basically, yeah."

Ron let out a long sigh. "I'm glad."

— 4 —

As the minutes passed, the sounds coming from Valeska's body got louder and louder until there could be no doubt that his skin was sizzling under the light of the sun.

Burning, too.

It was a foul smell, but one that Amanda seemed to enjoy.

"I wonder when Constable Sharpe is coming back?" asked Ron.

She looked at Valeska's body, smoking now under the rays of morning sunlight. "Not too soon, I hope."

They were silent for a few moments, listening to Valeska's body blister and hiss, like bacon in a pan.

Then Amanda said, "What do you think we should do now?"

"What do you mean?"

"I mean, now that this is over."

"I guess we'll wait for Sharpe to come back, and then maybe go home and sleep for a—"

"No, not that. With our lives?"

Ron studied Amanda closely, wondering where she was going with this. Finally, he said, "I don't know, what do you think we should do?"

"I think we should go."

Ron looked at her curiously. "Go where?"

Amanda gave a slight shrug of her shoulders and said, "Somewhere else."

"What? You mean just up and leave?"

"That's right. We've got a car and some money. . . ."

"What about your job? And mine?"

Amanda's head tilted slightly to the right. "I can get a job waiting on tables anywhere. And you're not a land-scaper, you're a hockey player. A good one, too."

Ron was silent for a while, thinking. Then he took a deep breath and said, "There's this guy I know from ju-nior hockey. He's been in Dundas a few years now coaching a senior team there called the Real McCoys."

"Dundas? You mean, Dundas, Ontario?"

"Yeah." Ron nodded. "They have a team in the OHA Senior A League." Ron paused to give Amanda the chance to say something, but she was patiently, perhaps even eagerly, waiting for him to continue. "Anyway, he always used to say how much he'd like to have me on his team . . . so I called him up a few days ago, you know, just to say hello and to ask him if he could use a left winger."

"What'd he say?"

"He said if I could get down there, and if I was sober, he'd give me a tryout."

"Really?"

"Yeah, but even if they sign me up, it would only be something like a ten-day contract."

"That's great!"

"And there wouldn't be a lot of money. Hardly any, ac-tually . . . and if you came with me we probably wouldn't do any better than a fleabag motel or a trailer even smaller than the one we're living in now."

"So what?"

Ron smiled. "You'd want to come with me, then?"

"It's semi-pro hockey, isn't it?"

"Sort of. I don't think they pay, but they might help me get a decent job in town if I make the team."

Amanda shook her head. "It doesn't even matter. It would be something new, something different, someplace else. . . . It could be the place where we start over again, building our lives together."

He pulled her close, and wrapped his arms around her in a tight, warm hug.

Ron didn't know exactly why, but he was sure that this was the start of a whole new life for him. This time he wasn't going to blow it, because even if he faltered, Amanda would be there to make sure he would not fail.

Together, they were going to make it.

── 5 ──

Valeska's body continued to smolder, burning without fire beneath the sun of a glorious new day.

Epilogue

Ron had been playing for the Real McCoys for just three weeks, but he'd already established himself as the team's top player and one of the best in the entire league. He'd scored fourteen points in just six games and the word was that a half dozen NHL scouts would be taking in the first game of this weekend's home-and-home series with the Brantford Blast.

Actually the number of scouts was probably closer to a full dozen, with ten of them introducing themselves to Ron outside the Dundas dressing room before the game. Ron was happy that his play had attracted such attention, but he wasn't about to get ahead of himself. While his goal was to work his way back into the NHL, it wasn't going to happen overnight. Amanda had suggested he play out the season in Dundas and then see who was around at the end of the year with a contract in hand. With close to a full season under his belt, maybe a scoring championship to go with it, and (most importantly) months of incident-free sobriety, Ron would be in a much better bargaining position than he was now.

Besides, Ron was happy where he was.

He and Amanda had a small apartment above a pharmacy in the center of town. They lived there practically rent-free while Ron worked for the pharmacist (one of the team's biggest boosters), doing odd jobs around the store and delivering prescriptions to elderly customers each afternoon. Meanwhile, Amanda had gotten a job at the local Tim Hortons and together they were starting to build a life for themselves.

Best of all, things kept getting better all the time.

Like tonight for example.

Ron had scored twice in the first period and the Real McCoys looked to be on pace to notch their fourth straight win, and earn a share of first place in the league standings.

But then a strange thing happened.

Ron was parked out in front of the Blast net after a shot came in from the point. He was digging under the goalie's pads looking for the loose puck when he was brought down by both Blast defenseman, one taking out his skates from behind him with a stick, the other giving him a hard shove to the chest.

Ron struggled to stay on his feet, but couldn't keep himself upright. He fell backward, his skates flying wildly through the air before landing flat on his back and striking his head hard against the ice.

But the fall wasn't the worst of it.

One of Ron's stainless steel skate blades had caught the Blast goaltender in the neck, cutting the flesh wide open and severing the man's carotid artery.

Blood spurt like a fountain from the rent in the goalie's neck, splashing onto Ron's face and jersey.

Ron knew he should have been horrified by what he saw, but he wasn't.

Not at all.

Instead, he was enthralled by the sight of all that blood. *It was so red . . .*

Ron's teeth ached and the wound on his arm where Valeska had bitten him began to throb.

. . . hot . . .

He licked a bit of blood from the corner of his mouth with a flick of his tongue.

... *delicious* ...

And he wanted more.

ABOUT THE AUTHOR

Bram Stoker and Aurora Award winner Edo van Belkom is the author of two hundred stories of horror, science fiction, fantasy, and mystery, which have appeared in such magazines and anthologies as *Storyteller*, *RPM for Truckers*, *Year's Best Horror Stories,* and the Mammoth Book of *On the Road*. He is also the author of "Mark Dalton: Owner/Operator," an ongoing adventure serial about a private investigator turned trucker that has been published continuously in the monthly trade magazine *Truck News* since June of 1999. His more than twenty books to date include the novels *Scream Queen*, *Martyrs,* and *Teeth* and the short story collections *Death Drives a Semi* and *Six-Inch Spikes*. Born in Toronto in 1962, Edo worked as a daily newspaper sports and police reporter for five years before becoming a full-time freelance writer in 1992. He lives in Brampton, Ontario, with his wife, Roberta, and son, Luke. His Web page is located at www.vanbelkom.com.